Twice Shy

Books by Suzie O'Connell

NORTHSTAR
First Instinct
Mountain Angel
Summer Angel
Twice Shy
Once Burned
Mistletoe Kisses
Starlight Magic
Wild Angel
Forgotten Angel
Last Surrender

TWO-LANE WYOMING
The Road to Garrett

SEA GLASS COVE
The Abalone Shell
The Driftwood Promise

www.suzieoconnell.com

Twice Shy

A Northstar Novel

SUZIE O'CONNELL

SUNSET

Rose

BOOKS

ISBN-13: 978-1-950813-03-2

In loving memory of my step-dad.

Charlie, this one's for you.

One

"DO YOU REALIZE this is the first time we've gone anywhere together without Jessie?" Aaron Hammond asked, twining his fingers with his wife's as they strolled across the street to their favorite restaurant. It was early yet for dinner—a little after four—and with the temperature hovering just a few degrees above zero, few people were out and about.

"Thank you, Aaron, for reminding me. I've been trying very hard to *not* think about that."

He gave her hand a reassuring squeeze, spun her deftly to him in the middle of the street, and planted an adoring kiss on her lips. He was rewarded with one of his favorite smiles, the one that ignited her entire face with love. The brisk January air coaxed a rosy glow from her cheeks, which in turn brought out the green flecks in her hazel eyes.

"Happy second anniversary, my love," he whispered. He kissed her again, lingering a little longer.

"Right back at ya, babe, but we should probably get out of the middle of the street. There's a car coming."

With a laugh, he pulled her toward the sidewalk. Tires screeched, and the car slid to a stop. Aaron instinctively stepped in front of Erica to shield her, all at once feeling entirely naked without his sidearm. He wasn't on duty, and there shouldn't be a need for it, but he couldn't ignore how the back of his neck tingled. When the driver—a vaguely familiar man in his mid-twenties—lurched out of the car with a nine-millimeter in hand, Aaron's unease exploded into terror.

"You!" the man spat. "You're the son of a bitch who put Jerry away."

The drug bust. Back in May, Aaron had pulled this man's younger brother over for a faulty brake light and blown the lid off the largest drug ring in the county's history.

"Look, Joseph, I'm sorry, but—"

"Yeah, yeah. You were just doing your job. Jerry wasn't hardly involved! He won't make it on the inside."

"If he keeps his nose out of trouble, he'll be paroled in two years."

Joseph shook his head. "You don't get it. Zach'll kill him for ratting him out."

"No one's going to let that happen."

"You don't know Zach. His old man taught him well—he's got connections everywhere. You gotta get Jerry out of there."

"You know I can't."

"You have to find a way. If Jerry dies… I'm coming after your family. Starting with her. We'll see how you like losing someone you love."

"Put the gun down, Joseph. You're not going to solve anything with it."

"Jerry's never really been in trouble before, and he helped you and that damned Sheriff Rogers and the county attorney take down Zach's entire operation." The man pointed the gun in Aaron and Erica's general direction, but his hand shook. "That plea bargain was a piece of shit deal. He shoulda gotten a slap on the wrist."

Aaron's heart pounded, threatening to break out of his chest. From the corner of his vision, he saw a man shove a woman back inside the restaurant and thought he heard someone shout for the police to be called. The street was otherwise deserted, but Aaron sensed people watching from the safety of the buildings, and he prayed they had the smarts to stay there. He wished desperately that he could send Erica running to join them. Behind him, she let out a small, terrified noise and dug her fingers into the meat of his shoulder. He was only a sheriff's deputy from a rural county. What the hell did he know about defusing a situation like this?

A momentary flash of anger shoved the words out of his mouth before he could stop them.

"Yeah, Rogers is an asshole, and yeah, he and the county attorney had a hard on for this case. It was a shining example of the good ol' boys system at work, but the fact of the matter is that Jerry's in prison because he screwed up. He made the choice to get involved with your dickhead cousin. If he hadn't, I'd've had absolutely no reason to arrest him." Reigning in his temper, Aaron said carefully, "You might want to consider what you're doing right now because threatening me is only going to make it worse for your brother. And for you."

The man hesitated, and Aaron wondered how much of his threat was nervous bravado. His hand trembled worse now, and he swallowed repeatedly. Would he really pull that trigger? Aaron took a step forward, drawing the man's attention and aim.

"You just stay right there, pig."

"You're not going to shoot anyone."

"Jerry's just a damned kid! You don't get it. Zach's going to kill him. You don't do something, Jerry'll be dead by this time next week. He's just a stupid kid who made a dumb mistake."

Aaron glanced over his shoulder at Erica and inclined his head toward the restaurant, silently begging her to sneak toward it. She shook her head, unwilling to leave him.

Please go, he mouthed, willing her to understand that he needed her safe.

With one last, fleeting glance at Joseph, she inched away. Aaron returned his attention fully to the man who still had a gun aimed shakily at his chest and prayed Joseph wouldn't notice Erica slipping away. He held the other man's gaze and listened as the elder Mackey brother blamed himself for not raising Jerry better in place of their parents and for failing to keep him out of their cousin's greedy trap.

Even with adrenaline surging and heightening every sense, it was hard to ignore the pang of pity for the brothers. Aaron had watched his boss—the same man who, while working for the Devyn Police department before running for sheriff, had arrested Aaron's entirely upstanding older brother on a false assault charge—make an example out of a scared, skinny, and unlucky kid with the same hopeless sense of unfairness Joseph now railed against. He'd even felt guilty for arresting Jerry Mackey, but right now, it was only terror that seized him as Jerry's older brother jerked the gun around with each point he made. Even if he lacked the conviction to intentionally shoot someone—

The boom reverberated off the buildings behind them, loud but not so deafening that Aaron missed the unmistakable *thwump* of a bullet boring into flesh or the soft gasp of surprise. He jerked around just in time to see Erica falter and lunged to catch her before she fell. Her eyes widened with shock and pain before a frown deeply furrowed her brows. She'd made it just a few steps toward the restaurant.

Agony ripped through his soul when she coughed and a foam of vibrant blood splattered her chin. A strangled scream burned his throat. He sank to the ground with her cradled in his arms, certain even through the deluge of confusion and denial that he couldn't save her. Even if the paramedics arrived right then, she was beyond help. The resignation in her eyes cut him with the precision of a scalpel; she knew she was dying and she had already let go. She met his gaze, and inexplicably, her lips lifted in a smile that softened the agony in her eyes. Without a word, she said everything he ever needed to know. She loved him.

Then she was gone.

"No. No, no, no. Don't go. Please don't go. I love you."

Vaguely aware that people were screaming and

crying, he curled himself protectively around her, clutching her to him as if he could keep her spirit with him a little longer if he just held on tight enough.

A second shot cracked in the bitter afternoon, and Aaron waited to feel the bite of the bullet, not caring if he died with his wife. No, *wanting* to die with her.

That pain didn't come, and when he realized it wasn't going to, he dared to look up for a moment. Joseph lay sprawled in the street a few feet away with his pistol gripped tightly in his hand and a pool of blood spreading quickly beneath his head. In a remote, detached corner of his mind, Aaron wondered if he should feel relieved or gratified, but he didn't. There was only more heartache for the waste of another life.

After what felt like hours but was probably only a few minutes, someone rested a hand on his shoulder and looked up to see Sheriff Rogers, the police chief, and a pair of paramedics standing over him. His boss's mouth moved, but Aaron couldn't make sense of what Rogers said. Finally, the sheriff pointed to the ambulance, and Aaron reluctantly released Erica's body into the care of the paramedics. Blood stained the front and the back of her, and when he glanced down, he saw that his Carhartt coat was destroyed.

"Ah, Jesus Christ, Aaron," the sheriff said, squatting beside him. "Jesus. Are you hit?"

He shook his head, unable to form even a simple *no*.

"Are you sure?"

He nodded. "It's all…." Swallowing, he tried again. "It's all Erica's. She's dead. Oh, God. My wife is dead."

He lay back on the pavement, covered his face with his hands to block out the sight of the ambulance crew and the police crawling over the street trying to piece together what had happened, and gave in to the grief.

* * *

Four and a half years after Erica's death, the memory was still agonizingly sharp. So was the memory of later that night, when he'd faced her parents, Jim and Jessie Robinson. The chief of police had already informed them of what had happened, but Aaron had needed to give them the exact details. He had prepared himself to be turned out of their family, but they had embraced him with shared grief and had cried with him for hours. It had taken him a while to realize he wanted to see condemnation in their faces, but instead, he'd seen the same love that had outshone the pain in his wife's eyes. How could they still love him when she had died because he'd failed her? Though his self-loathing had gradually turned into gratitude, he hadn't yet answered that question and didn't know if he ever would.

He hadn't found a way to get past the fact that Joseph had essentially died for nothing, either. Contrary to Joseph's fear, his scumbag cousin and cohorts had not once tried to hurt Jerry in any way, and not only because they were kept apart in prison for the very reason Joseph feared. Zachariah Neely had, like Jerry, been a model prisoner thus far, no doubt with the same intent as his cousin—to get that early, good-behavior parole.

"Did you hear me, Aaron, honey?"

The dispatcher's voice jarred him out of the memories. Pearl, who had been at her job as long as he'd been alive, regarded him with a worried frown, and he didn't doubt that she knew exactly what had distracted him from their conversation.

"Yeah," he replied. "Jerry's getting out. I hope he stays out of trouble this time."

It had been a little over two years since he'd last seen Jerry Mackey. Aaron had been following up on a fistfight he'd broken up the previous night at the Big Sky Truck Stop south of Devyn, and Jerry had waltzed into the restaurant and without a word of warning punched him in the back. It hadn't taken Aaron long to subdue the kid, who couldn't weigh more than about a hundred and forty pounds and had the musculature of a twig, and within twenty minutes, Jerry was on his way back to jail with a parole violation guaranteeing he finished out his five-year sentence.

"More to the point," Pearl remarked, "I hope he's had time to realize you did everything you could to help him."

He shifted his weight. "When's he getting out?"

"A week from Friday."

"That soon? Damn."

She reached across the counter and patted his hand. "Go home, Aaron, enjoy your four days off, and don't worry about Jerry Mackey. I won't be there to enforce it, but I fully expect you to ask a pretty girl to dance at Vince and Evie's wedding on Saturday."

"I'm not making any promises, Pearl, but I'll do my best to enjoy my time off."

"I guess that will have to do. Go on, get out of here."

Aaron strolled out into the hot August afternoon before he decided to find an excuse to work a little longer.

The cab of his truck was sweltering, but instead of cranking the AC, he rolled the windows down, craving fresh air. The sun blazed in a smoke-hazed blue sky, further bleaching the summer-baked grasses of the sprawling ranching valley and the sage-blanketed foothills of the surrounding mountains. As Aaron drove up the highway toward home, he glanced back at the tapestry of golden wheat fields and green hay and alfalfa fields. It was all as familiar as his own heartbeat, and normally, the sight comforted him, but today even the scorching sun couldn't burn away the chill that was nearly as sharp as if he were again kneeling on that winter-grayed street.

He was pulling up in front of the Robinsons' wood-sided ranch house before he knew it. His daughter waited for him on the wrap-around porch, sipping what looked like lemonade with her grandmother and namesake. Jim was likely out working somewhere on the ranch.

"Daddy!" Jessie squealed and raced out to greet him.

He picked her up and hugged her tightly before carrying her back to the porch. "Hi, pumpkin."

"How was work, honey?" his mother-in-law asked. "And before you answer, I already know by the frown on your face that it wasn't so good. So you just go ahead and get it out."

"Jerry Mackey will be paroled a week from Friday."

She took a moment to digest the information and then, with all the grace and strength her life on the ranch had given her, nodded once and pushed it aside. "Don't you worry about telling Jim. I'll do that."

He let out a sigh of relief. With his free arm, he hugged her. "Thanks, Jessie."

"You know I'd love for you to stay and chat, but Tracie called a few minutes ago to say she needs you and Nick to get that front door fixed on the rental cabin. Evie's friend from Washington will be here soon if she isn't here already."

"All right. I'll see you at the wedding if not before."

* * *

"Maybe, if you were more sexual, I wouldn't have to go elsewhere for pleasure."

The memory blindsided Skye as she crested the last hill before the turn to Northstar and forced her to pull over at the turnout. She stared out the windshield at the wall of mountains but couldn't make out much detail through the wavering sheen of tears and wasn't sure if she wanted to cry or throw up as the memory unfolded.

She had stopped by her house for only a moment on a break between on-site photo shoots to grab the tripod she'd taken out to Olympic National Park the previous weekend. Hearing strange noises coming from her bedroom, she had padded down the hallway with adrenaline pumping through her veins and a dozen scenarios running through her head. Anyone else might have jumped to the conclusion that it was an intruder, but she hadn't. Well, not an intruder of the criminal kind. Instead, she'd discovered a marital intruder in her bed with long, artificially tanned legs wrapped around her husband's waist and cherry-red nails digging into his back.

Shock had rooted her in the doorway, and she'd listening as their moans escalated into cries of ecstasy. The woman——*Leslie*——had at least had the decency to scream in startlement when she'd at last spotted Skye. Darren had only flopped onto his back, regarded his wife with unveiled satisfaction, tucked his hands beneath his head, and proceeded to blame his cheating on Skye.

She'd filed for divorce the next day, but that wasn't enough, a fact that had been proven beyond a doubt only a few days ago. Though it wasn't technically required, she foolishly wanted him to sign the divorce papers to bring closure to their relationship. She wanted him to admit that their marriage was over. When she'd asked him to sign again a few days ago, he'd adamantly refused. Again.

"I'm not going to sign the damned papers because I still love you and I'm giving you the chance come back," he'd said, then finished with a thinly veiled, stinging insult. "I don't want you to spend the rest of your life alone." As if he truly believed she'd never find anyone else to love her.

That alone should have made her walk away and never look back, but instead, she'd taken the bait like always and asked, "And what about the cheating, Darren? Am I supposed to just ignore that?"

"Well, it's not like you enjoy sex, so if I get it else-where, you're off the hook. What's the big deal?"

Even now, his response still made her jaw drop, and it was that disbelief that had snapped the spell—with a start, she'd realized that she was seriously considering going back to him. Abruptly, she'd stalked away. Then she'd made plans to extend her stay in Northstar, knowing she needed to be very far away from Darren for a while. She could not and would not go back to him… even if that meant being alone.

Skye frantically wiped the tears away as they spilled over. Anger, grief, and self-loathing quivered through her, and she cursed her philandering soon-to-be ex-husband and his too-apologetic, voluptuous, blonde mistress. She studied the landscape and let the wild, semi-arid beauty of it—so different from the perpetually damp, thickly forested hills of Western Washington—distract her. Finally, she was calm enough to get back on the road, and she drove the rest of the way to the cabin she'd rented steadfastly refusing to think about Darren or Leslie or her divorce or anything other than her best friend's wedding and all the pictures she planned to take during her stay.

When she pulled up in front of the two-story log cabin, her best friend was standing on the front deck, beaming.

"Skye!" Evie squealed, racing down the steps and throwing her arms around her friend's neck as soon as Skye stepped out of her SUV. "It's so good to see you!"

"Likewise. I hope you haven't been waiting long."

"Not at all. I got the keys for you from the Hammonds. Tracie wanted to be here to show you around, but there was some kind of emergency on the ranch. She said she'd try to stop by a bit later to introduce herself, and Nick and Aaron will be here in a couple hours to fix the door."

Evie handed her the keys. As soon as she stepped through the damaged door, Skye inhaled sharply in appreciation. With an open layout and a vaulted ceiling over the living and dining rooms, it was beautiful. Big, south-facing front windows wonderfully let in a lot of light, illuminating the golden tones of the hand-peeled logs. The cabin was furnished with log furniture, and the hunter green accents nicely complimented the natural wood tones. This was exactly what she needed.

"So, was I right or was I right?" Evie asked.

"You were right," Skye replied. "It's gorgeous."

"If you think the cabin's gorgeous, you should meet

your landlords' son Aaron. He's the widower I told you about. I'm sure if you're in the mood for a romp—or is it roll?—in the hay to help you get over Darren.... Well, I imagine he wouldn't be too *hard* to convince." She paused only long enough to giggle at the cringe-worthy pun. "Let me tell you, Skye, he's a tried-and-true, blond-and-blue, genuine cowboy, and he has the most adorable little girl. He is the whole shebang, honey. Sexy as hell and a family man. Can't go wrong with that rare combination."

Skye waited patiently for her best friend to finish before she responded. "Darren is still refusing to sign the divorce papers."

Evie's mouth fell open, and she swiveled to face Skye. "What?!"

"You heard me."

"Yes, I did, but jeez, Skye." She gave a disgusted sneer. "As if walking in on him screwing some bimbo wasn't bad enough. Why can't he just make this easy?"

With a pinched and humorless smile, Skye carried her bags up the stairs to the loft and set them beside the dresser. She didn't understand why Darren refused to let her go. It wasn't like he truly cared about her. More likely, his refusal to amicably dissolve their marriage was just one more way to demean and torture her. It had taken years for her to see the truth about him, but at last she had, and now she couldn't un-see it. In the moment when she had walked in on him rutting with *Leslie*—undeniable confirmation of what she'd long suspected—she had realized *exactly* what breed of asshole he was. She had also realized that she didn't deserve any of those little stingers he constantly used against her, that how he made her feel wasn't a reflection of who she was.

Of course, she wasn't even sure who she was any-more. Surely, if she had known what she did now, she never would have married Darren. It was easy to blame youthful ignorance—after all, they'd married right out of high school—but the truth was she should have known. Her biggest clue should have been when he'd quit their high school football team and tried to talk her into quitting as manager and photographer for the team instead of supporting her decision to stay on.

Well, she had plenty of time now to figure out who she was. She only hoped she'd gotten out before it was too late to salvage herself.

Thank goodness for Evie's invitation, she thought for the thousandth time since the elegant envelope postmarked from Northstar had been delivered to her mailbox.

She pressed the heels of her hands to her travel-weary eyes, dragged her hands over her face, and decided it was best to keep her thoughts on the matter to herself. With her wedding only days away, Evie didn't need any more to worry about, but it was nice to know that her friend would be only a phone call and a short ride away for the next six weeks. Lindsay would be here, too, in a couple days to spend a week and a half in Northstar with them. It'd be like old times, the three of them together, and her two best friends would talk her out of going back to Darren if the impulse again crossed her mind.

"You're still coming out to dinner with us at the Ramshorn in an hour, aren't you?" Evie called from down-stairs.

"Of course."

Skye joined her in the living room, gazing out the front windows at the sweep of the narrow ranching valley. A wall of granite peaks rose steeply to her left, and another, lower wall of thickly forested mountains stood to her right. In a place like this, she might actually be able to put more than physical distance between her and Darren. She'd be too busy with her camera to have time to devote to thoughts of him, especially if the stand of aspen behind the cabin turned gold before she left.

"Remind me, when do the leaves change here?"

"Usually the last week of September. Do you want a hand with your camera gear?" Evie asked with a knowing grin.

"No, I can get it. I'm sure you have places to be and things to do."

"I do, but I can stay a little while longer to help you get settled."

"Go, Evie. I probably won't be doing much settling just yet."

"All right. After dinner, I'll show you my dress. It's gorgeous."

"I can't wait."

After Evie left, Skye finished dragging her last three bags out of her compact SUV. A nap sounded absolutely marvelous, but the sight of her camera bag sitting atop her luggage changed her mind. The brilliant afternoon sunlight was not ideal, but she didn't care. She wasn't on an assignment; she was getting familiar with her temporary home. With her camera slung over her shoulder, she stepped out the kitchen door and strolled down the metal grate ramp.

The shade of the aspen grove drew her, and beneath

its glowing green canopy, she discovered a lush, spring-watered carpet of grass. The soft breeze made the leaves shiver, and the dappling shifted in the most magical, entrancing way. She lifted her camera, chose what looked like a wild iris as a focal point for her shot, and pressed the shutter button. The familiar and intense concentration brushed away her resentment over Darren's infidelity and wrapped her in a soothing embrace of creativity and fulfillment.

"Hello there!"

She straightened at the sound of the feminine voice and glanced over her shoulder to see a woman in her late fifties with silvering blonde hair striding toward her. For a moment, Skye worried she had left the cabin's property and trespassed on someone else's land, but then the woman smiled. She was slender and spry, Skye mused, and her knees were slightly bowed as if she'd spent a fair amount of her life in a saddle.

"I'm Tracie Hammond," the older woman said, extending a hand.

"Skye Hathaway. It's a pleasure to meet you in person."

"Hathaway? I thought you said it was Fitzhugh."

"It was. Well, it *is*, but it won't be for much longer."

Genuine concern flickered over the woman's face, telling Skye that her companion had noticed the trace of bitterness in her voice. "Are congratulations in order? Or condolences?"

"Both, I suppose," she replied. "It is certainly for the best, Mrs. Hammond."

"Please, call me Tracie. So, Hathaway is…."

"My maiden name and the name I use for my

photography. Am I all right to be taking pictures here?"

"Absolutely. The cabin sits on ten acres, and there is a fence surrounding the property, so you'll know when you get to the edge."

"How are folks around here about letting people on their property?" Skye inquired. "Just so I don't accidentally wander onto someone's land and get shot at."

Tracie laughed. "You needn't worry about that. As long as you're respectful of our land, we're all pretty friendly people. You are, of course, always welcome on the Lazy H, and I imagine Nick or Aaron would be happy to show you around, maybe take you riding, if you want. As would Ty Evans, whose family owns the Bar E Ranch behind you. And you probably know most of the Carlyles already. As for the rest, just ask—and remember to close gates—and you'll likely have the whole of the valley at your disposal."

"That's very kind. I appreciate that... and your invitation. Truly."

"I had another purpose for coming back here other than to introduce myself. I wanted to let you know my sons Nick and Aaron will be here shortly to replace that front door. I also wanted to invite you to dinner down at the ranch house, if you don't have already plans."

"I do, actually. Evie and Vince are taking me out to the Ramshorn."

"I figured as much, but I wanted to make sure you got something decent to eat after your long drive."

"Thank you," Skye replied, touched by her landlady's generous and friendly offer.

"I'll let you get back to your pictures. Remember, if you need anything at all, just give us a call."

"I will. Thank you again."

Skye watched the rancher's wife walk away. If Tracie Hammond was a good representation of the inhabitants of this tiny Montana community—Evie's descriptions of Northstar led her to believe she was—the next six weeks were going to do wonders for her.

Glancing at her watch, she wasn't entirely surprised to see that she'd already used up three quarters of an hour. With a sigh, she headed back to the cabin to clean herself up a little before heading to the Ramshorn Hot Springs and Lodge for dinner with Evie and Vince. Tracie's sons had not yet arrived, and after Evie's suggestion that she should use the widower Aaron to distract her, Skye hoped she would be able to sneak out of the cabin before they showed up.

When she stepped through the kitchen door, she immediately noticed a red light flashing on the answering machine. She leaned over to look at its tiny screen and saw a number two displayed. Hesitantly, she pressed play and let out a sigh of relief when her parents' voices greeted her with a request that she call them to let them know she'd made it to Northstar in one piece. Smiling but feeling a tingle of guilt for not calling them before she'd gone out to take pictures, she picked up the cordless handset. Then the second message started playing, and her blood chilled.

"Please come home, Skye," Darren said. "You're being silly and impulsive, and that isn't like you. You know I love you. I'm sorry about Leslie. I'm a weak man, but I promise it won't happen again."

At the mention of the woman's name, Skye sneered, unable to prevent the memory from barreling into her mind's eye for the second time in as many hours with the finesse of a rampaging bull. She sank to the floor beside the counter and cursed the tears that again stung her eyes. If Leslie had been the first, Skye might have believed she would be the last, but there was at least one other woman she was certain Darren had slept with—his own mother had ratted him out about that one after Skye had caught him with Leslie—and she suspected there were at least three others.

"Please, baby, I don't want a divorce," her husband's recorded voice pleaded. "I can't live without you. Those other women… it was just physical. I didn't love them. I know you don't understand, but I need to touch and be touched, and you never gave me that. Please come home, baby. We can work this out."

Lies, she reminded herself. *Nothing but lies, and you don't deserve any of them.*

"You need me, too. You're too delicate to be alone, and you've never had to take care of yourself. You've always had someone—your parents or me."

Two stingers in one message, first when he again implied that she was at fault for his affair—*affairs*, she corrected—then following it up with an insinuation that she wasn't strong enough to make it on her own. He certainly hadn't lost his touch. His tone was all sugar and honey, and for too many years, she had allowed herself to be sweet-talked, but no more. Now that she knew the real meaning beneath the saccharine coating, she couldn't return to ignorance. She wouldn't, she promised herself. Without a moment's hesitation, she erased the message, picked up the phone, and dialed her old home number.

Darren answered on the fifth ring. "Hello?"

"How in the hell did you get this number?"

"Skye," he breathed with relief. "Baby, please. This is foolish, and—"

"Don't call me again."

She poked the end-call button hard enough to elicit a complaint from her finger. Not fifteen seconds later, the phone in her hand rang, and the caller ID showed Darren's number. She accepted the call and spat, "Stop calling me. It's over."

Again, she hung up on him. This time, however, she didn't wait for him to call back and quickly set the phone back on the base, then strode toward the front door. She settled her camera back in its bag on her way by the dining room table.

She yanked the door open only to find a very attractive man in his mid thirties standing on the other side with his fist lifted to knock. She smiled and held her hand over her heart as if that would slow the erratic beating.

"Sorry I startled you, Mrs. Fitzhugh," the man said.

"Hathaway," she corrected quietly.

"Excuse me?"

"I'm Skye Hathaway," she said more loudly, extending her left hand in greeting since he clutched a bucket of tools in his right. "It won't be Fitzhugh much longer. Better yet, call me Skye."

"My apologies, Skye," he replied, shaking her hand.

When she caught the glint of a plain gold band on his ring finger, she wondered if this was Nick or if Aaron still wore his wedding ring. A moment later, he answered her unspoken question.

"I'm Nick Hammond. Call me Nick."

Another man of nearly identical build, stature, and coloring—and no wedding ring—crested the steps with a stack of what appeared to be one-by-fours balanced on his shoulder. Aaron, she decided. Like his older brother, he had dark blond hair just long enough for a woman to bury her fingers in and kind blue eyes that smiled at her from a handsome face. Her brows lifted in appreciation as her gaze drifted over the rest of him. He wore a plain black T-shirt that fit well enough to accentuate broad shoulders, toned chest, and flat stomach and jeans that hugged his narrow hips and long legs. The muscles in his arms flexed mesmerizingly as he lowered the stack of lumber to the deck and extended his hand in greeting. Feminine interest set her heart to fluttering.

"I'm Aaron," he said.

"Skye."

She shook his hand, acutely aware of the warmth and strength in his grip. "It's very nice to meet you," she said a little more breathlessly than a first introduction warranted. Evie's comments rippled through her mind. *Tried-and-true, blond-and-blue, and sexy as hell indeed. And the last thing you need right now. Down, girl.*

With her pulse jumping too quickly, she decided it would be best if she didn't linger to chat with the Hammond brothers. "I hate to be rude, but I'm supposed to meet Vince and Evie at the Ramshorn in a few minutes. If you'll excuse me…?"

"Certainly," Nick replied. "We should be done and out of your hair by the time you get home."

"Thanks."

Skye smiled politely and strode across the deck with an unsettling combination of desire and nerves weakening her knees. Pausing at the top of the steps to collect herself, she turned her face toward the sun, hoping it would warm away this odd, unbalancing sensation. After a couple deep breaths—and stubbornly resisting the urge to glance over her shoulder at the Hammond brothers—she headed to her SUV.

Following the directions Evie had given her, Skye turned right from the cabin's driveway onto the packed dirt and gravel of Elkhorn Road. Once she was headed north on the main road through the valley, she rolled her windows down and allowed the pine-scented air to cleanse away the rest of her anger at Darren. It didn't take long. On this stunning, blue-skied summer day, she had much to celebrate. Her best friend was getting married in just three short days, she was surrounded by beauty and wide-open skies, and she was free to be her own person for the first time in her life.

Darren was right about one thing. She *had* always had someone to take care of her, but now she was independent. And that felt wonderful. Giddy abandon bubbled up inside her, and she laughed. If she wanted to stay up until the wee hours of the morning to finish a project, there wouldn't be anyone to chastise her for staying up half the night. If she wanted to spend all afternoon with Evie gossiping about the handsome men of Northstar with the same giggling amusement as they'd had talking about boys back in high school, there was no one to make her feel guilty. When her brief meeting with Aaron Hammond danced into her mind, she laughed. If she wanted to have a wild fling with a willing cowboy, well hell, she could do that, too.

Maybe giving in to the promise of adventure that lay before her was rebellious and childish, but she didn't care. Playing it safe and obedient had only helped Darren beat her down, and she was done with that.

* * *

Aaron watched over his shoulder as the striking brunette stopped before descending the stairs. There was something about the way she tilted her face to the sun that spoke of a woman in need of some peace and quiet. The tone in her voice—a trembling anger with a touch of sadness—when she'd told Nick that her last name wouldn't be Fitzhugh much longer was a pretty clear indicator that the name change was due to divorce, and Aaron couldn't help but wonder why her marriage hadn't worked out. Less than two minutes and only a handful of words were hardly enough to form an accurate opinion, but it was plenty for a basic assessment.

Dark, wavy hair cascaded over proud shoulders, reaching halfway down her back, and her trim waist, gracefully swaying hips, firm backside, and shapely legs begged to be caressed. She walked with a subtle, natural confidence rather than a practiced poise, but there was something much deeper than her outward beauty that instantly snagged his attention and invited his gaze to linger. Though she'd glanced over him with obvious appreciation, there had been a shyness about her appraisal that contradicted the almost defiant way she'd distanced herself from her married name. She was wounded but strong. Stronger, he thought, than she probably realized.

She was the kind of woman a man could get lost in, not just for a night or two but for a lifetime. What kind of idiot let a woman like that go?

With a shake of his head and a low whistle, Aaron turned toward the cabin and the work to be done. "How long's she staying?" he asked his brother casually.

Nick regarded him with brows lifted and amusement thick in his eyes. "Through the end of September, so about six weeks."

"Well, I guess we'd better get this door fixed, eh?"

Knowing it was stupid in the extreme to entertain any ideas about their parents' tenant, he pushed the lingering image of her out of his head and focused on the task at hand.

The last tenants, who had vacated the two-bedroom log cabin only a few days ago, had somehow managed to skew the hinges and break the doorframe. The door itself, which Nick was now beginning to remove, bore what looked distinctly like claw and teeth marks on the inside. Aaron didn't want to think about what the rest of the house had looked like before Nick and their parents had cleaned it and replaced rugs and carpet.

"What the hell did they do?" he asked, trailing his fingertips over the gouges in the once-silky pine panel. "They were only here for two weeks."

"Left their monster of a dog inside while they went digging for crystals at Crystal Park. The dog freaked."

"Obviously. Do me a favor, Nick. If I ever get it in my head to buy a vacation rental, slap me, would you?"

"Only if you promise to do the same for me."

"So, why'd Ms. Hathaway suddenly decide to rent the cabin for so much longer? I thought she was only supposed to be here until Labor Day."

Nick shrugged and handed him a hammer, and he again pushed the beautiful new tenant from his mind. If she'd decided to extend her stay because she needed space from her ex-husband or because she just wanted to take some time to enjoy Montana, it was none of his business. He had enough of his own issues to worry about without taking on a total stranger's, he reminded himself, hoping the kid he'd sent to jail not once but twice would keep his nose out of trouble this time.

As much as he would rather spend his evening with his daughter, Aaron was glad for the work. Prying the boards of the old doorframe from the logs allowed him an outlet for his pent-up emotions about Jerry Mackey's parole, and Nick's quiet, steadfast companionship was a soothing balm. He and his older brother had always been close, and they worked well together.

"Mom said Pearl called after you left Devyn," Nick said gently. He screwed down the top hinge while Aaron held the new door steady. "You all right with that Mackey kid getting out?"

"I guess I'll have to be."

"He didn't kill Erica, you know, and his brother didn't mean to, either."

"I know, but sometimes it's not so easy to remember that."

"I know it isn't, but you're man enough to understand it."

Aaron frowned at his brother. "What makes you say that?"

"When he came after you at the truck stop, you did your job instead of giving in to the urge to beat the hell out of him. And you can try to deny it, but I know you wanted to."

"I *did* give him a black eye," he replied with a brief smile, then sobered again. "Maybe I should hate him, but I don't. He's just a dumb, skinny kid who got bullied by his cousin into doing something stupid. I just hope he's over blaming me for his brother's suicide."

"If not… maybe you should thump him a little more thoroughly next time." Nick winked.

To his surprise, Aaron laughed. After Nick tightened the last screw and backed out of the way, he swung the door closed. "Smooth and quiet. We're done here, so let's get down to the main house."

"Mom *did* say she was going to feed us for this, right?" Aaron asked.

"Yes, she did. And she's had baby back ribs smoking all afternoon."

Still smiling, Aaron helped Nick pile the tools and scraps in the back of his brother's pickup, then climbed in the passenger side. He'd be all right, he decided, regardless of Jerry Mackey's release. He was beginning to doubt that he'd ever marry again, but he would be all right.

Two

"ABOUT TIME YOU SHOWED UP!" Aaron called to his twin brother, who was finally striding across the broad, freshly mowed front yard of the C-Diamond Ranch's main house. He and Pat O'Neil hefted a picnic table off the flatbed trailer and maneuvered it into place a few feet away from the last they'd unloaded.

"Sorry I'm late," Henry remarked. "Livia waylaid me and had me setting out the chairs for the ceremony. Man, she is really cracking the whip today."

Aaron chuckled. "When is she not?"

"Good point. How many more tables are coming?"

"Nick, Ben, and Luke should be back shortly with the last load," Pat replied. "Now that you're here, Henry, I'm going to go back to work on the dance floor before my wife decides to skin me."

A few yards away, Aelissm lifted her head from her task and grinned at the lot of them before returning her attention to the dance floor she was constructing.

"I should've jumped at the chance to claim her," Henry remarked. "I'd probably be a happily married man right now."

"What makes you think you ever had a chance with her?" Aaron shot back.

"I saw the looks she gave me back in college."

"You mean those looks of boredom?"

"You're one to talk. You actually *dated* June, but you let her slip away, and now she's a happily married woman, too. I guess if you snooze, you lose."

Aaron didn't respond to that one. Although Henry was teasing, he was right, and Aaron refused to let himself think about it. He was not one to covet another man's wife, and anyhow, if he and June had been meant for each other, it would have happened. Or so he kept telling himself.

Almost as if the turn of his thoughts had summoned them, Nick returned with June's husband and son sitting in the bed of the pickup. Luke barely waited for Nick to bring the truck to a full stop before he leapt out of the back.

"Well, look who it is!" Henry called. "Northstar's very own football star. Luke, kid, how've you been?"

"Good," the young man replied and shook Henry's offered hand. "You?"

"Can't complain." Henry leaned back to inspect the young man with a bemused shake of his head. "I still can't get over how much you've changed in these last few years. You've got to be as tall as Pat now, so please tell me you're finally done growing."

"Yeah, I am, and I really hope I'm done. Six-four is plenty tall enough, thank you. Speaking of football, you *are* coming to the game with everyone on Saturday, right?"

"You bet. Wouldn't miss the opportunity to see you start in your first-ever college game. I've been waiting a year for it. Hell, I was more annoyed that they red-shirted you last year than you were."

"Why would I be annoyed?" Luke asked, helping Ben unload a table. "Grant was a great quarterback. Besides, it extended my scholarship, which means I'll have time to get an extra teaching endorsement."

Henry chuckled. "You *would* look at it like that, you bookworm."

"Pardon the interruption," said a feminine voice.

Everyone looked over to see two young women striding toward them. Aaron immediately recognized Skye Hathaway, again clad in jeans but this time with a black tank top. Her hair was pulled back in a cute, tomboyish ponytail. His pulse quickened in recognition like it hadn't since he and June had called it quits. Her redheaded companion was dressed in a vibrant yellow, flirty summer dress. He guessed she was Lindsay Miller, Evie's other friend from Washington. Despite himself, Aaron's brows lifted and a faint smile of appreciation curved his lips as he glanced between the friends. They were both attractive women, but he found his gaze drawn to Skye like iron to a magnet.

To their credit, the married men in his company seemed entirely unaffected by the svelte redhead or the graceful brunette. Not that Aaron could blame them. If Erica were still alive, he probably wouldn't have paid either woman more than a fleeting glance, and he almost scolded himself for allowing his gaze to linger, but four years was a long time.

"What can we do you for?" Henry inquired brightly.

Aaron turned away to hide his amusement. His twin had long perfected his ability to turn an innocent phrase into an innuendo without giving his listener a hint of his underlying meaning.

"Mrs. Carlyle wants to know when she should start sending out table runners and centerpieces," the redhead replied.

At first, Aaron thought she had missed Henry's come-on, but then he saw her gaze flick over him with something hotter than amusement. *Oh, Henry, you may be in trouble.*

"This is the last load," Henry answered.

"Tell Livia she can start sending the decorations out," Ben added.

When Aaron met Skye's gaze, she blushed prettily and smiled. He hadn't really noticed yesterday, but her eyes were the breathtaking color of sun-struck amber.

After several moments, she turned those incredible eyes to Luke. "Evie described my assistant as the tallest and youngest of the blonds, so I'm guessing you're Luke Conner."

"You must be Skye," Luke replied. "When do you need me?"

"Right now, if you can be spared. The families want some pictures of everyone getting ready, and since I'm in the need-to-get-ready camp...."

Luke glanced between his father and Aaron and his brothers, silently asking if they could spare him.

"We can handle things here," Nick said.

As Aaron watched Luke stride off with the photographer, he felt a very unusual pang of envy. Right then, he would very much like the excuse to spend a few hours with the lovely Skye Hathaway. Instead, he tore his gaze away, though that didn't clear the image of her enchanting golden eyes from his mind.

"Hen, let's get this one off first." He walked around to the table at the back end of the trailer. And waited. When his brother didn't appear, he glanced over his shoulder to see Henry still talking to the redhead. Irritation flared. "Henry!"

His twin glanced at him, excused himself from Lindsay, and joined Aaron at the trailer. The woman hurried after Luke and Skye.

With a half-cocked grin, Henry said, "Hot damn."

"Would you quit thinking with your dick long enough for us to finish this?" Aaron snapped more harshly than he intended.

Surprise briefly widened Henry's eyes before his brows dipped in a scowl. "Maybe you oughta *start* thinking with yours again so you wouldn't be such an uptight ass all the damned time," he retorted and stalked away a few paces.

"Henry!" Nick growled. "Would you give him a break?"

"Why? It's been almost five years, Nick. I miss Erica, too—we all do—but she's gone, and he needs to get that through his head."

"Jerry Mackey's getting out on Friday," Nick explained, "but you'd know that if you actually bothered to talk to him, instead of heading straight for the bar at the

Bedspread as soon as you rolled into the valley last night."

"We've all got problems, Nick."

Aaron stared at his twin with his mouth hanging half open. Normally, Henry would have brushed off Aaron's remark, or even laughed at it, but there was no trace of amusement on his usually carefree face. There had been a time when the two of them were inseparable, but now…. Aaron had assumed his twin had broken their tradition to have a beer together at the Bedspread—something they did every first night of Henry's visits—because he'd been exhausted by his drive from Denver to Northstar.

"You were at the Bedspread last night?" Aaron asked.

"Yeah, I was. Pat had to drive me home." Henry looked up at Pat with a humorless smile. "Thanks, by the way, in case I didn't say it last night."

"You did," was Pat's reply. He offered to help Ben unload to give the brothers a chance to talk.

"It's been a long time since someone's had to drive you home," Aaron remarked, suddenly concerned. "What's going on, Hen?"

"Don't ask like you give a rat's ass any more than anyone else in this family."

"You're my brother, Henry. Of course I care."

"Bullshit. Since Erica died, you've been too lost in your own sorrow to care." He glanced at Ben, then added, "For a little while, when you were dating June, I thought you might be starting to come back, but then you gave up and slunk away with your tail between your legs."

"Oh, come on, Henry, I haven't been that bad."

"Maybe I'm exaggerating, but you sure haven't been the same Aaron who used to party with me back in high school and college, the Aaron who was up for anything, any time."

"I have a daughter."

"Yeah, you do."

The tone of his voice told Aaron that that was his point, and when he sat heavily on the bench of the nearest unloaded picnic table, Aaron thought he knew the source of his brother's animosity, or at least, the general direction it came from. He sat beside his twin, and Nick sat on Henry's other side.

"You and Melanie on the outs again?" Aaron asked.

"That's one way to put it. You remember me telling you that everyone always says Dylan looks nothing like me?"

"I do. I've thought the same myself."

"Well, that's because he's not my son."

"Ah, hell. You're sure?"

"Yep. She isn't sure who his father is, but the paternity test confirmed that it's not me." Henry's voice faltered. "He's a year old, and she's had me thinking all this time that he's my kid."

"I am so sorry, Hen."

"I am, too. I love the little stinker."

"That means you're over for good, right?" Nick asked.

"Yeah." A moment later, a broad grin sliced through the sadness. "Have either of you met the new tenant in Mom and Dad's rental yet?"

"We met her briefly last night," Nick replied. "And you met her just a few minutes ago—she's the brunette. I get the feeling she's going through a divorce right now, so go easy on her, all right, Henry?"

"Hey, I'm always easy."

Aaron and Nick both laughed.

"I *so* want to make a smartass remark right now about you and Melanie, but I won't, because I can see it's still a tender subject." Aaron gave his twin a good-natured pat on the back. "Contrary to your earlier accusations, I *do* care."

"I know you do," Henry replied. Then he chuckled. "Thanks for *sort of* not being a smartass."

Aaron pushed to his feet and went back to work. As he strode away from his brothers, he heard Henry say to Nick, "Actually, I wasn't asking about the tenant for me. I was asking about her for Aaron, because the man seriously needs to get laid. Besides, I'm a little partial to that redhead in the yellow dress."

Nick grinned but said, "Let's just leave things well enough alone for now and get back to work."

* * *

The wedding ceremony was held out behind the Carlyle ranch house with the mountains as a stunning backdrop. Evie was absolutely beautiful, and Vince had cleaned up nicely, too. The matching smiles on both their faces outshown the sun, and Aaron felt the familiar pang of grief mixed with his happiness for the couple.

If Evie was beautiful, Skye was simply gorgeous. Dressed to perfection in a dark red, floor-length gown, she was entirely elegant with her graceful neck, shoulders, and back on display. The smoky eye makeup she wore made her luminous, burnished-gold eyes stand out even from where Aaron sat several rows back. He couldn't keep his eyes off her. After years of focusing solely on being a father and subverting his own needs with only the brief few weeks he'd dated June for contrast, it was strange to suddenly feel desire dancing through him again.

With a grunt, Aaron forced his attention back to the ceremony, only to regret it moments later when the minister asked Vince and Evie to recite the vow "until death do us part." Aaron prayed death would wait far longer to part the bride and groom than it had to take Erica from him. He spent the few remaining minutes of the ceremony attempting to keep the heartache at bay. It was a pity that he had come to hate weddings.

Finally, after the minister announced the couple to their friends and family for the first time as Mr. and Mrs. Vincent Carlyle, Aaron took his daughter and hastily escaped to the refreshments tent around the front of the house. He was just pouring Jessie a cup of lemonade when he sensed someone behind them.

"Are you all right, Aaron?"

His heart lurched at the sound of June's kind voice, and he forced a smile when he turned around. Seven months pregnant with her first biological child, June Conner was as beautiful as ever in her soft turquoise dress. Maybe even more so.

"Tracie told us about Jerry Mackey getting out."

"Word spreads fast around here."

"It always has. But you didn't answer my question."

"I'm okay. Thinking about Erica too much, but that's nothing new." He shrugged.

June wrapped her arms around his neck and hugged him, pressing her belly against him. Through the thin material of his shirt and her dress, he felt a nudge. It was a punch to the gut, reminding him that he and Erica had not intended Jessie to be their only child, but even the agony of that thought wasn't enough to dim his amazement at the miracle of a new life.

"Someone's busy," he said. "Was that his foot?"

"I think it was an elbow," she replied, beaming.

"Are you having a boy?" Jessie asked.

"We're pretty sure, yes."

"I want a little brother. Or a little sister, but only if she likes horses and not dolls. I don't like dolls."

Another punch to the gut, Aaron thought. When he'd recovered from his daughter's innocent remark, he asked June, "So, who's more excited, Ben or Luke?"

"That's hard to say. They're both ecstatic."

"Were you excited before I was born, Daddy?" Jessie asked.

"I was over the moon about you," Aaron replied and picked his daughter up to kiss her cheek. "And for now, maybe June will let you treat her sons like honorary brothers."

"Luke already said he'd be my big brother," she said proudly. "I asked."

"Wow, June," Henry announced, striding over. "You are looking absolutely stunning these days."

"You're such a natural liar, Henry, that I actually believe you," she teased.

"I never lie."

Moments later, Ben strolled over to claim a picnic table. June, Henry, Aaron, and Jessie joined him, sitting with their backs to the table to watch the goings-on. Shortly thereafter, Aeli—who was only a week or two behind June in her third pregnancy—and Pat and their two young children gathered with them at the table, followed by Nick and his wife Beth and their son Will.

"Ms. Hathaway sure is easy on the eyes, ain't she, Aaron?" Henry inquired lightly.

"Mmm," Aaron replied distractedly. The woman in question was currently taking over the photography from Luke. "Yes, she is. Beautiful."

"Fascinating."

Aaron regarded his twin with narrowed eyes. "Mind your own damned business, Henry."

"Can't, bro. Sorry. Because I have an idea. You and I should take her and that sexy redhead out on a double date in Devyn or maybe Butte. Better yet, we can take them to Luke's game on Saturday. A little birdie told me that Lindsay—she's the redhead—and Skye both like football. *Really* like it, as in they were managers for their high school team. C'mon, Aaron, how can we go wrong with that? We'd better make our move fast, though, because the groomsmen are interested, and they already have a foot in the door, being part of the wedding party, and all."

Aaron rolled his eyes, but he didn't say anything, not even to dissuade his brother from the idea of a double date. He'd probably regret allowing the possibility to germinate, but he couldn't bring himself to form the words to tell Henry no. Instead, he changed the subject.

"So, how did Luke get roped into helping with the photography?" he asked, watching June and Ben's son as he chatted with Evie's friend, pointing occasionally to the screen of her camera and—Aaron guessed—asking questions. It was good to see him smiling so openly and easily again.

"Evie asked him to help," June replied. "She wanted Skye to be in the wedding, so she needed someone to take pictures of the ceremony. He's quite enjoying it."

"He seems like he's doing a lot better these days," Henry observed. "He doesn't look so… tormented."

"He *is* doing better," June agreed. "It's been good for him to get away from Devyn for a while."

"Please don't tell me people still blame him for what happened to Mike and Carol."

"Not openly, but some do, and even those who don't are still curious. We all got pretty tired of the sentiments of sympathy that were nothing but bald-faced probes. The blame and the constant reminders took a toll on him—prevented him from dealing with the real effects of what JP did. For a while, I wasn't sure he'd ever…." She took a deep, calming breath and leaned into her husband. Ben tucked a reassuring arm around her and kissed her cheek, which brought a genuine smile to her face. "Away from all that, he's finally been able to analyze everything that happened and to focus on accepting it and moving forward. It's been a relief this past year to watch him come back."

"At last," Aaron murmured. "We're all very glad to see it, too, June."

"Daddy, can we go play?" Jessie asked.

"Sure. Just stay out of the way of the photographer and the wedding party, okay?"

She raced off with her cousin and the O'Neil kids in tow. The conversation shifted to more pleasant topics, and Aaron again found himself watching Evie's photographer friend. It fascinated him how passionate she was about her craft and that she seemed excited to give Luke some pointers. He continued to watch, trying—and probably failing—to make it look like he wasn't staring. Evie and Lindsay flanked the photographer, and they all chatted with Luke for a few minutes before Becky Epperson stole him away and dragged him over to join June and Ben. Aaron mumbled a distracted greeting to the two young people, still unable to tear his gaze away from Evie Carlyle's enchanting maid of honor.

"Yo, Aaron! Are you asleep, or what?"

He blinked at Henry and frowned. "No. Why? Did I miss something?"

"Your daughter seems to have taken a sudden interest in photography," Nick responded, inclining his head.

In his fixation with the woman, Aaron hadn't noticed his daughter slyly inching her way closer. By the time he returned his gaze to her, Evie and Lindsay had departed, and the woman was listening to the little girl with an indulgent smile. Jessie pointed to her father, and Aaron felt a jolt when he locked gazes with Skye Hathaway again. She smiled—damn, she was beautiful—and said something to his daughter that made the little girl beam.

"Oh, hell. What is she doing?" he muttered.

"Looks to me like she might be playing matchmaker," Henry remarked. "Atta girl, Jessie."

"Keep it up, smartass," he replied and jogged away from his companions to rescue the photographer from his daughter.

* * *

"Well, we did it, Skye. We got our Evie married off."

Skye spared Lindsay Miller a glance and a brief smile

before returning her attention to the bride and groom. Evie made a beautiful picture in her full-skirted, strapless white gown with its vines of delicate red roses. Her mother had pinned some of her long, thick brown hair back in an elegant, knotted bun, leaving much of it flowing free in natural waves down her back. Her groom, Vince Carlyle—who wasn't necessarily tall at five-ten—towered over his bride in his tailored black tux and deep red vest. With the mountain setting, perfect weather, and more than two hundred people in attendance, Evie's wedding completely put Skye's small ceremony to shame. Skye knew in her heart that Evie and Vince's marriage would put her eight years with Darren to shame, too, and was amazed that she could still believe real love existed.

Another quick glance at her other best friend showed her that Lindsay, though undoubtedly happy for Evie, was also feeling the pangs of a failed relationship. Skye gave her hand a squeeze, and was rewarded by a weary smile.

"It'll happen for us, too," Lindsey murmured. "Someday we'll find the *right* men."

"I hope so. In the meantime, I'm glad Evie had found her right man."

The woman in question excused herself from her guests to join her friends. "I'm a little surprised at you, Skye. I was sure you would've taken your camera back by now."

"I'm a little shocked myself," Lindsay agreed. "You're always so particular about your photography and your camera that I'm honestly surprised you seem to trust Luke so effortlessly."

The familiar, delicious pulse of anticipation licked through Skye, and she was excited to delve into her craft to force her bitterness from her mind, but instead, she watched her assistant take more pictures, comforted that he didn't go for the straight-on, eye-level photos. He dropped to one knee or tilted the camera, looking for the more artistic angles, and took time to set up his shots. As long as he was using the right settings, the photographs of Evie's wedding ceremony would be beautiful.

Skye cocked her head to the side to study *him* for a moment, rather than his occupation. With that golden hair, blue eyes that she could only describe as insightful, and boyish good looks, she imagined he was quite the heartbreaker, though she had seen no trace of the arrogance she expected from one. In fact, he was quite humble.

Very polite and quite the cutie, she thought. To her friends she said, "He certainly seems to know his way around a camera. How old is he?"

"Almost nineteen and a sophomore at Montana State University. He's legal, if that's what you're thinking," Evie said with a suggestive wiggle of her eyebrows.

"That's not at all what I was thinking." Coming from anyone else, Skye might've been appalled by the implication, but since it was Evie, she couldn't help but laugh. "Good lord, Evie. I was just curious."

"That's probably a good thing because I don't think he's on the market, anyhow," Lindsay said. "Or so I've been hearing from the young ladies present."

"Girlfriend?" Skye asked.

"No, still getting over one," Evie explained. "She was murdered a couple years ago, right here in Northstar. Right up by his family's cabin, actually. It was a bad, bad deal."

Skye cringed. *Way to put your foot in it.* "Poor kid."

"You look amazing, Emily Victoria Carlyle," Lindsay said, abruptly changing the subject. "So amazing that I won't even complain about being a redhead in a red dress and looking like a tomato."

They hugged Evie, laughing, and Skye heard the unmistakable and familiar sound of her camera's shutter. It was a perfect moment, and one Skye was glad Luke had captured, though she was a little startled that she hadn't noticed his approach.

With an amused smile, he handed her the camera. "You probably want this back."

"I do, but please don't take that as an insult, because it's not. There are too many photo opportunities, and the photographer in me is itching to make use of them."

"I completely understand, and no offense taken. Do you want to take a look?"

"Sure."

It was too bright out to really admire his shots, even shielding the camera's screen with her hand, but it was quite clear that he had taken some great pictures. Lindsay and Evie leaned in close to see with their arms tucked around her and their chins nearly resting on her shoulders.

"So, boss, did I do all right?"

"You did fantastic," Skye replied, slowing her perusal to better critique the shots. "You're hired. Seriously, Luke, these are great. You have a very good eye."

"Thanks."

They discussed techniques for several minutes while Lindsay and Evie fawned over the images. Despite their bubbly praise, Luke retained his polite demeanor, and Skye was all the more impressed.

"Luke!" someone called.

A teenaged girl with dark hair and lively gray eyes, maybe a year or two younger than Luke, trotted over and threw her arms around him. He hugged her tightly in return. *No girlfriend, huh?* Skye mused.

"Hey, it's about time I get to see you!"

"Sorry, Becky. I would've swung by the ranch, but I didn't get in until late last night. Practice ran long."

"Eh. No worries," the girl replied. She turned her smile on Skye and Lindsay, extending her hand first to the redhead, then to Skye. "Hi, I'm Becky Epperson."

"Lindsay Miller."

"Skye Hathaway." When she glanced at Luke, a question popped unexpectedly out of her mouth despite the fact that the answer wasn't any of her business. "Your girlfriend?"

A shadow passed briefly over his face, but it was gone in a heartbeat, and he gave a soft chuckle. "No. She's my cousin and best friend."

"I'm sorry. That was rude of me. I don't know why I even asked."

They both shrugged, grinning.

"That's Northstar for you," Becky said. "Do you mind if I steal your apprentice?"

"Not at all. I need to get back to work in a moment, anyhow."

Skye watched the pair wander off toward a crowded table. It didn't take a master's degree to figure out that the group they joined were a combination of family and close friends. She immediately recognized the Hammond brothers, and though the twins looked quite a bit alike, they clearly weren't identical. They were, all three, attractive men. So were the two other men in the group—one with dark auburn hair who looked to be about Luke's height, and another with rich, nearly black hair. Like Nick, they were quite obviously married, and with little ones on the way, Skye noted. The wife of the dark-haired man looked familiar, and after a moment, Skye realized she'd met the woman at the Ramshorn Lodge on her first day in Northstar, though she couldn't for the life of her remember her name.

"Mmm, mmm, mmm," Lindsay purred. "Quite a good looking group over there, eh, Skye?"

"Mmm-hmm." Skye's heart fluttered when her gaze sidetracked to Aaron. She'd caught him watching her during the wedding ceremony, and the fact that such a handsome man found her so alluring was a powerful salve on the still-bleeding wound of Darren's infidelity.

"Before the drool starts dripping, allow me to quickly explain who's off limits," Evie said.

"I'd say it's pretty obvious," Skye replied with a smile.

"I will enlighten you anyhow, because you'll probably run into them frequently while you're here. The man with the dark red hair is Pat O'Neil, and that's his wife Aelissm beside him, and their two kids, Ant and Iris. The O'Neils own and operate the Bedspread Inn and its restaurant. You've met Nick and Beth and Will, right, Skye? And you said you briefly met Aaron the other night. Anyhow, that's the third Hammond brother, Henry, next to Aaron, and I'm hearing rumors that he has recently rejoined the dating pool, too."

"That's what he said when I talked to him last night," Lindsay remarked with a gleam in her eye.

"You met him last night?"

Lindsay nodded.

"You didn't want a solitary drink," Evie surmised, "when you said you needed some time alone to get over being pissed at Max."

"No."

"What about the rest of them?" Skye inquired before Evie could continue in her current vein of conversation. "Who are they?"

"The dark-haired man next to the O'Neils is Ben Conner, and that gorgeous blonde and also pregnant woman he has his arm around is his wife, June."

"Wait. I met June the other day, remember? When we went out to dinner at the Ramshorn."

"Ah, that's right. She and Ben are Luke's parents, in case you didn't already put two and two together with the last name. Hey, speaking of Luke, he'll be starting in his first college football game next Saturday. A bunch of us are going to Bozeman to watch, so you should both come with us."

Skye stole a glance at the kid, and wasn't at all surprised to learn he played football. He was tall and fit, and moved with grace and a natural athleticism. "Is that why you and Vince aren't leaving on your honeymoon until next Sunday?" She turned to Evie, amused. "Really? A college football game?"

"Yep."

"But you can't know him that well. You haven't lived here long enough. I mean, it's your honeymoon, Evie."

"It'll wait, and I imagine that it won't be long before you understand why. Trust me, Skye. Northstar is like a great big family. That's part of why I thought it would be a good idea for you to spend a little time out here. You could use that kind of love to help rebuild your ego and make you realize you're worth so much more than what your jackass of an ex-husband thinks."

Skye jerked back and stared at Evie. Her perpetually cheerful friend rarely spoke so bluntly.

"So, are you coming?"

"I am," Lindsay replied. "Henry asked me this morning to go with him."

"Are you serious?" Skye demanded of the redhead.

Lindsay shrugged. "Maybe Evie's right that I need to go on a date while I'm here."

Skye stared with a brow lifted.

"Oh, c'mon, Skye. Football games are our thing, and you said yourself that the Hammond brothers are handsome men. What's the harm in going to the game with the twins?"

"I'll think about it."

She caught Lindsay's exaggerated eye-roll and grinned, then turned her gaze on the Conners. Skye thought they looked far too young to have a son Luke's age, but since she'd already stuffed her foot in her mouth twice concerning the young man, she kept the comment to herself. "Back to our earlier conversation, why will I be seeing a lot of the Conners?"

"Well, they work at the Ramshorn and are in the process of purchasing it. They're good people, the lot of them."

"An interesting bunch, to be sure," Skye said. The group as a whole fascinated her, as did the palpable bond of friendship between them, but it was Aaron Hammond who drew her gaze again and again. She couldn't, however, say whether it was a physical attraction she felt or something else. Whatever it was, it was potent. More so than anything she'd felt in a long time.

"All right, ladies, I should go rescue my husband," Evie asserted. "Don't have *too* much fun with those boys. I'll see you in a few minutes, Skye. Lindsay, Livia said something about wanting your help getting everyone settled."

"I'll be right there," Lindsay replied.

They watched as their newly married friend sauntered away and was immediately folded into a crowd of wedding guests.

"Do you get the feeling she's trying to set us up with the Hammond twins?" Lindsay asked her.

"Oh, yeah. You know, I think happiness enjoys company even more than misery. I mean, just look at Evie. She's in bliss… and she's downright obnoxious."

"Is that such a bad thing?"

"Absolutely not. Maybe we should listen to her because you and I apparently don't have a clue about real love."

"In that case… I have dibs on Henry," Lindsay whispered in her ear. More loudly as she slipped away, she said, "See you in a bit."

Before Skye could question the suggestive wiggle of Lindsay's brows or her sudden departure, she heard a young voice ask, "Excuse me?"

She looked down to see the adorable little Hammond girl with shining blonde hair and wide, innocent hazel eyes standing beside her.

"Hi, sweetheart," Skye replied brightly. "How can I

help you?"

"I think my daddy wants to talk to you, but he's too shy," the girl replied. "He thinks you're pretty."

"Does he?"

"Uh-huh. I think you're pretty, too."

"Well, thank you, sweetheart, but I'd say the prettiest one here is you."

Bitterness again crept into her thoughts as a pang of maternal longing speared her. She had planned to be a mother by now, but Darren had never given her the sense of security she needed to start a family—something she'd come to realize consciously only in the past few months.

"Will you come sit with us? Please?" the little girl asked.

Skye hesitated before she answered. She was supposed to sit with the wedding party, and with the ache of denied motherhood settling into the pit of her stomach like a block of ice, it was probably a very bad idea to spend too much time with the girl's father, but the little girl and Skye's own insatiable curiosity were impossible to resist. "I have some work to do, and I'm supposed to sit with the bride, but I suppose I could go say hi first."

Before she could take a step toward the large group, Aaron rose and jogged toward them with a look of mild exasperation on his face.

"Jessie, honey, I asked you not to bother the photographer," he said when he reached them. "I'm so sorry, Ms. Hathaway."

"Please, call me Skye, and don't worry. She's not bothering me at all."

"Are you sure?"

"Positive. Your daughter is a beautiful and charming little girl," Skye said and gently tugged on a golden strand of the little girl's hair.

"Can she come sit with us?" Jessie asked her father. "I like her."

He smiled fondly at his daughter with a flicker of sadness in his eyes. "That's fine by me, but only if she wants to, Jessie. We don't want to be pushy."

Aaron's daughter curled her arm around her father's leg and beamed at Skye. Jessie was positively adorable, and it was clear that she had inherited at least some of her cuteness from her daddy, Skye thought, quickly taking in his kind blue eyes, dark blond hair, and broad-shouldered, lean build. He had a quiet confidence she found appealing but also a melancholy that tugged at her heartstrings. She had the feeling there wouldn't be a quick roll in the hay with him—as Evie had suggested—because there was nothing quick about him. Which meant she should probably ignore the enjoyable fluttering of her heart and stay well away from him. A fling was one thing, but with her divorce not quite finalized, the last thing she needed right now was to get seriously involved with another man.

Raising his gaze again, he asked, "What do you say? After you've finished taking your pictures and fulfilled your duties as the maid of honor, of course."

"I'd like that," she replied before she could stop herself. *So much for staying away from him.*

"All right, then. We'll see you in a bit."

She watched him walk back to his family with his daughter in tow, then headed off to set up her photo shoot, wondering with each step she took what she was starting by accepting his invitation.

Three

A FEW HOURS LATER, when dusk colored the sky, the voice telling Skye that she should stay away from Aaron Hammond was silent. In the centerpieces on the picnic tables and in the Mason jar lanterns strung around the Carlyles' front yard, vanilla candles burned brightly, their merry flames dancing in a soft breeze. Laughter and music flowed through and around Skye, and she felt more relaxed than she had in… years. Tonight, she was at peace with herself and her decision to end her marriage. Maybe it was the glass of champagne she'd been sipping for the last hour, but she doubted it. The evening was nothing short of magical, and her companions were delightful.

She had eaten with the wedding party, made her toast, and taken hundreds of pictures during the shoot, then promptly taken Aaron and Jessie up on the offer to sit with their group. With only a few interruptions to take more pictures—mostly candid shots of the merry reception—she had been with them since. The Hammonds, O'Neils, and Conners had folded her into their circle as if she were an old friend instead of a new acquaintance.

At the moment, Jessie was perched on her knee, jabbering on about her cat and the dog her daddy had rescued from the shelter last month. Skye listened intently, forming an enticing impression of a man devoted to his daughter.

Leaning toward her, Aaron asked too quietly for his daughter to hear, "Are you sure you don't mind? I know she can be a little demanding at times, especially of women. I think she may be starved for feminine attention."

Six hours ago, she might have thought his statement was a blatant pick-up line, but she knew enough about him now—through the comments of his friends and family and from her own observations—to understand that his explanation was just that. An explanation.

"Really, I think she's quite charming and beautiful, Aaron." Skye stroked the girl's silky blonde hair and met Aaron's concerned gaze. "And I doubt she's *that* starved for attention. I've spent several hours watching your friends and neighbors spoil her."

He looked down but not before she saw the shadow of guilt in his eyes. "It's not the same thing. Don't get me wrong because I am beyond grateful for every bit of help we've been given, but most of the time, it's just her and me, and there's so much I can't do for her."

"I'd say you're doing just fine."

He glanced at June Conner, and sighed. "Maybe I should've tried a little harder to move on, for Jessie's sake.

I want her to have a normal family, to have a mom to braid her hair…."

Startlingly drawn by his vulnerability and afraid to allow that attraction to take root, Skye jokingly asked, "You realize that we're at a wedding, right? And that weddings are supposed to be happy things?"

He chuckled and shook his head. "Sorry. I didn't mean to unload on you like that."

"Actually, I rather like your openness. It's refreshing."

"Thanks."

"All right, everyone!" the DJ announced over the speakers. "Now that the sun's gone down and the air is cooling off, it's time to heat things up. Yeah, you know what I'm talking about! Vince and Evie Carlyle, show us all how it's done in your first dance as husband and wife!"

A cheer rose from the crowd as the newlyweds ventured onto the dance floor Aelissm and Pat O'Neil had finished only that morning, then hushed as the couple danced to a slow, romantic melody. Skye watched, sitting with her back against the table, and couldn't help but smile at the love that glowed on both Evie's and Vince's faces.

When the song ended, the DJ selected an upbeat country tune that elicited another cheer from the wedding guests. "All right, Northstar. Let's help this lovely couple celebrate. I want to see you move your bodies!"

Skye felt more than saw Aaron rise to his feet.

"Would you care to dance?" he asked.

Dance? Skye gaped at him, utterly baffled by the invitation. She had only once managed to drag Darren into dancing with her at their wedding and had spent most of their high school dances either standing by the wall with him or dancing with her friends.

"Um, yes, of course," she sputtered. She smiled to cover her graceless answer. "Sorry, it's just been a long time since anyone's asked me to dance."

"That's a shame."

She tilted her head and studied him, then smiled faintly. "It really is."

"Jessie, I know I promised you a dance, but is it all right if I dance with Skye for a little while?"

His daughter bounced to her feet, nodded emphatically, and zipped around the table. Skye didn't see where she went; Aaron captured her attention when he offered his hand, and her smile widened as she settled her hand in his and let him pull her to her feet. Other members of their group joined them, but within moments of stepping onto the dance floor, she forgot about everyone but Aaron. He handled her with breathtaking poise, more than compensating for her lack of practice.

"Where did you learn to dance like this?" she asked, amazed.

"My parents. Mom still occasionally teaches ballroom dancing, and she and Dad used to compete back in the day."

"Well, I'm impressed."

"Sorry to interrupt," Luke Conner said, stepping close with Jessie clinging to his hand, "but I think it's proper to ask a girl's father for permission before I ask her to dance. Or, in this case, before I accept her invitation."

Aaron chuckled. "You go right ahead, Luke."

The little girl grinned, and Luke winked as she dragged him a few paces away.

"He seems like a very good kid," Skye observed quietly.

"He is a very special young man," Aaron agreed, his voice a gentle murmur. "I think he gets a lot of that from June."

Skye noted how her companion's gaze sidetracked again to Luke's mother. At several points over the last few hours, she had caught something she thought might be longing in his gaze when he looked at the woman. It didn't happen every time but enough that she was curious. "Do I detect a missed opportunity?"

"Excuse me?" Aaron asked, startled.

"June. You look at her a lot, almost with regret."

"Noticed that, did you?"

"I did. So… what's the story?"

"Like you said. A missed opportunity. We dated for a little while a few years ago, after Erica died, but I wasn't ready to move on yet."

"So Luke might've been your stepson and that bun in June's oven might've been yours."

"I doubt it. She and Ben were meant for each other. Hell, the man *knows* how I feel—felt—about her, and he's not remotely jealous because she's his and he's hers. I'm grateful for that because June is still a very good friend." He gave a soft huff of laughter and studied the gently swaying couple for a few moments before returning his attention to Skye. "I used to know what that felt like, to be one half of a whole and so sure of my love."

The direction of the conversation made her squirm a little—because she obviously did *not* know what it was like to trust her spouse so completely—so she changed tactics, though the subject was far too fascinating to let it go.

"How did you meet her? June, I mean."

"My brothers and I went to college with her and Aeli in Devyn. I'm not ashamed to say that I was attracted to her from the start."

"She's a beautiful woman," Skye agreed.

"In every way. Henry and I had this idea we'd take them both out. That didn't ever happen, obviously. Back then, we were still a bit wild for their tastes."

"You were a partier? I don't see it."

He chuckled. "What can I say? I was young and dumb."

"What changed?"

"Erica. I finally realized that I loved her. I didn't need the parties or the drinks or the girls. I didn't need anything but her."

"She sounds like an incredible woman."

"She was."

The fondness and love in his eyes, undimmed by time and grief, touched something deep in Skye's heart. She couldn't imagine what it must be like to be loved like that, though she thought she felt a glimmer as she danced with Aaron. She had only just met him, but he made her feel treasured. Wanted. She particularly enjoyed the way he focused his attention on her with his hand resting lightly on her back and how the heat of him chased away the chill of the quickly cooling evening. "How did you meet Erica?"

"I didn't, really. We're both from Northstar, so we'd known each other since birth. I don't remember ever noticing her as more than a friend until Pat showed up in Northstar. Watching him and Aeli fall in love must've triggered something because the first time I ever asked Erica to dance was at the potluck a week or so before they got engaged. The rest, as they say, is history." He twirled her around. "How about you? How did you meet your ex?"

"Really? You want to talk about that?"

"Too soon?"

"Maybe." She sighed. "I'm still processing everything, I think. The divorce won't be final until next Monday, though it could have been done weeks ago if Darren weren't holding out just to spite me."

"Did he finally sign?"

"No, by Washington law, he doesn't have to, but the grace period or whatever they call it is almost up."

"How long were you together?"

"Eleven years, married for eight." She stared blindly around at the flickering candles that lined the dance floor. "I was so young and stupid. He was cute, funny, sweet… but he doesn't love me. Not how Ben loves June." She titled her head and studied her companion. "Or how you still love Erica. I honestly don't think he's is capable of that kind of love."

"I'm sorry. I really am."

Skye shrugged. "I just wish I'd figured it out sooner, before I'd wasted so much time and energy, and before I let him hurt me and change me."

Aaron frowned quizzically at her, and for a sickening moment, she thought he'd ask how Darren had changed her… and understood that that realization was one she hadn't yet begun to analyze. He must have seen the fear on her face because he gave an almost imperceptible nod and said, "I wish you'd figured it out sooner, too. Do you have any kids?"

She leaned back in his arms, surprised by the question. "N-no. Why do you ask?"

"You're so great with Jessie—so patient and attentive—that I wondered."

"She's a beautiful little girl." Skye replied, trying desperately to stem what felt almost like grief, though she didn't know why she felt the need to hide the effect this particular conversation had on her. Habit, she thought, because if anything, Aaron made her feel like she could open up and be honest about these things. For once. "I used to want kids, but now it's just one more thing that Darren ruined for me."

"Did *he* want kids?"

"He said he did. As soon as my business took off, he brought it up, but when he accused me of sleeping with my assistant, Joel, I began to understand that something wasn't right between us."

Aaron leaned away to stare at her. "He thought you had an affair?"

She nodded. Resentment trickled through her, and she felt the stinging threat of tears. "As they say, a cheater thinks everyone else cheats, too."

He opened his mouth to say something, then snapped it shut. The shock on his face said plainly enough that neither he nor Erica had ever suspected—or had reason to suspect—the other had been unfaithful. It also told her just as clearly that he would've remained loyal to his spouse to his dying breath. *How wonderful that must feel*, she thought with a sneer, envying Erica more than was right.

"Would you like to take a breather?" Aaron asked at

last. "Maybe have a drink?"

She laughed without humor. "A drink sounds fantastic, but I probably shouldn't because I don't want to get on your bad side, you being the local law and all."

"I can drive you home."

"I don't want to ruin your fun."

He shrugged. "Luke isn't the only one to be volunteered for extra duties today. I got volunteered for Vince and Evie's Taxi Service."

"In that case… I'd like another dance first, and then I'll take you up on that offer."

He tucked her more tightly against his body, and her pulse quickened delightfully in response. Whether he did it because the slow, romantic song warranted a higher level of intimacy or because some innate need to soothe her worries compelled him to hold her close, she didn't know. She didn't care, either. Tonight, it was enough to be the center of his attention, and she intended to savor each moment with him.

As evening deepened into full night, she sipped champagne, danced almost every song with Aaron, and took dozens more photographs of the newlyweds and their guests. At some point, Lindsay and Henry disappeared, and Skye gave them only a passing thought with the hope that a few hours enjoying Henry might soothe Lindsay's bruised confidence. If Henry was anything like his twin, he was exactly the kind of man Lindsay needed to spend some time with to see that not all men were like her callous, self-centered exes.

Finally, the party wound down, and after Vince carried his new bride to his truck and drove away toward the

Bedspread Inn to much cheering, the cleanup crew picked up the worst of the mess while the designated drivers drove the guests who'd had a little too much to drink home. Skye waited patiently for Aaron to come back for her, enjoying the slight buzz from the champagne that helped numb her ever-present thoughts about Darren. The respite was temporary, she knew, but she thought Aaron might provide a more effective distraction. When her mind took a sharp detour into a more carnal region of thought, she giggled. *Not that kind of distraction. At least, not yet.*

By the time the man centered so firmly in the forefront of her mind returned for her, she was yawning and beyond ready to get out of her bridesmaid dress. She helped a groggy Jessie into the car seat in the center of the backseat of Aaron's extended-cab pickup before settling into the passenger seat. The little girl was out cold long before they reached Skye's temporary home.

"I'm sure you've heard about Luke's football game on Saturday," Aaron remarked when they stood on the deck of her cabin.

"I have. I understand my friend Lindsay may be going with your brother Henry."

"He's hopeful," he replied with a bemused grin. "And maybe I'm hopeful, too."

"Oh?"

"If you're willing…." He hesitated, as if debating his words. "I'd like for you to come with us—specifically, with *me*—and I'd like to take you out to dinner after."

"Are you asking me on a date?"

"I am, if you're not offended. I know you said that maybe it's too soon, and to be honest, I'm not sure I'm—"

Impulsively, she kissed him, and the words he might've used to talk them both out of the date died against her lips. At first, he tensed, but slowly he relented to her persistence. She pressed her body against his, surprised and exhilarated when he clasped her face in both hands and kissed her back. He didn't let her give in to the wild urges surging through her but kissed her firmly with a startling combination of hunger and restraint that made her feel as if he were savoring every moment. Or trying to be proper but unable to resist her. The sensation was entirely new and incredible.

She pulled away, breathless. "If Darren ever kissed me like that, it was so long ago that I've forgotten. You, Deputy Hammond, are an excellent kisser."

"That's the champagne talking," he replied. His voice was sexily hoarse.

"No, it isn't. I haven't had *that* much to drink, thank you."

She tilted her head to kiss him again, but he leaned away and grazed his thumb over her lips, then pulled his hand away, trailing his fingertips along her jaw as if he were unwilling to let go.

"Skye. Your divorce isn't even official yet."

"I don't care." She straightened as a flash of anger burned away the faint blur of alcohol for a moment. "It's not like he's honored our vows. Why should I, now, when they mean *nothing*?"

With a faint smile and a startling gentleness in his gaze, Aaron brushed his thumb across her cheek so tenderly that she barely felt it. "The next time we kiss—if it happens again—I want it to be because you want to kiss *me*, not because you're trying to get back at your ex."

With that, he turned and trotted down the steps. She couldn't tell if he was angry, hurt, or if the kiss and her thoughtless remark had affected him at all. *Smooth, Skye. Real smooth.*

When the alcohol left her system, she was going to regret this. Not kissing Aaron—she'd do *that* again in a heartbeat—but ruining the moment by mentioning Darren. Maybe kissing Aaron was wrong, since she was still legally married, but there was no guilt, and try as she might, she couldn't bring herself to regret it. As far as she was concerned, her wedding vows had been nullified the day she'd walked in on Darren and Leslie. Anger and pain threatened to ruin what had been a spectacular day, so she stubbornly blocked the memory, but as she turned and headed inside, she wondered how long it would be until she was free from her ex's destruction.

* * *

Aaron shut the door of his pickup. "What the hell am I getting into?"

Skye was—technically—still married. What was he doing letting her kiss him… and kissing her back? Unlike Skye, he couldn't blame his actions on alcohol because he hadn't had a drop.

Memories of the evening and that entirely unexpected kiss captivated his mind for the duration of the ride back to his house. Even the cool summer night air wafting into the cab of his truck through the partially open windows couldn't chase away the flush of desire. Recalling how she'd felt in his arms as they danced, so graceful and willing, it wasn't too difficult to figure out why his baser needs had momentarily gotten the better of him. It was the spark of something he had still been too lost in grief to truly feel when he'd dated June, and it reminded him strongly of the moment at that auspicious potluck when he'd finally realized he wanted to be more than friends with Erica.

When he parked in front of his house, he climbed out of his truck and carefully lifted his sleeping daughter from her car seat. She murmured and sighed but didn't wake. With her head resting on his shoulder and her limbs dangling limply, he paused for a moment before heading inside. Sometime between the end of the party and now, the moon had risen. Only a day or two past full, it glowed brightly, brushing the sweeping landscape with silver light. He wondered if Skye had noticed and, hoping she had, if she was outside right now with her camera trying to capture the impossible beauty of it.

Erica had loved nights like this. Before her, Aaron hadn't often taken the time to appreciate the moonlight, but he had taken her advice to cherish the little things like that and the warmth of Jessie's breath against his neck. He tightened his arms around his daughter, keenly feeling the ache of gratitude for the most precious gift Erica had given him.

Sighing, he carefully ascended the steps to his deck. Instead of leaning down to reach the doorknob, he bent his knees and kept his upper body straight so he didn't disturb his daughter. It struck him, as he padded across the living room and down the hall to Jessie's bedroom, that he had become accustomed to doing everything himself. But it might be nice to have someone there in moments like this to open doors or fold down the blankets on Jessie's bed so he could simply lower her into it without twisting his body like an inept contortionist.

Jessie stirred as he was pulling off her dress shoes and groggily changed into her nightgown with some help. When he tucked her into bed, she wrapped her arms around his neck and squeezed.

"Skye is nice, isn't she, Daddy?"

"She is, but go back to sleep. We can talk about Skye tomorrow."

"Do you like her? I like her."

"Go to sleep, Jessie."

She yawned widely and curled her arms around her favorite stuffed moose. Her cat, Spook—a large, medium-haired black feline more like a dog in attitude—leapt onto the bed and promptly curled up against his mistress's back. Aaron reached to scratch under his chin and was rewarded with a purr that could rival a diesel engine. He'd never been a fan of cats beyond their usefulness as pest control, but Spook was an exception. The cat was a character.

"I love you, Daddy. Pooky loves you, too."

"And I love you both."

"And Chance, too?"

"Of course I love Chance, too. I need you to go to sleep so I can go let him in."

"Night night."

He leaned down and kissed her forehead before heading toward the door. "Sweet dreams, Jessie," he whispered.

He went to the back door to let their new dog in. The black Lab was still young—not quite a year old yet—and though they'd only had him a little over a month, he wiggled and squirmed for a good fifteen minutes before deciding

Aaron had been thoroughly greeted. Aaron smiled fondly and vigorously scratched under Chance's collar.

"I'm getting soft in my old age, aren't I?" he murmured. "First the cat, now you. At least Spook kills mice. What about you? Hmm? How are you going to earn your keep? Are you going to be a bird dog? Because you sure aren't a cow dog."

The black Lab cocked his head, listening intently, and wagged his tail.

"Tell you what. Since you were alone all day, how about we take you up to play with June and Ben's dogs tomorrow? I'll bet you'd love a good romp with Casey and Cheyenne, wouldn't you?"

At the mention of the Conners' dogs, Chance's tail wagged faster, nearly spinning in a circle. Aaron chuckled. "All right, propeller tail. Tomorrow. Now it's time for bed."

Chance trotted toward Aaron's room, paused in the doorway to make sure his master was following, and with a grunt, flopped on the big, fluffy dog pillow Jessie insisted he needed. Chance had largely ignored the pillow until Aaron had moved it from the foot of his bed to the side where he slept. He liked to be close to Aaron, but he also wanted to be able to keep an eye on Jessie's room. As young as he was, Chance already had the same protective tendencies June and Ben's dogs had, and Aaron wondered if it was inherent in the retriever breeds or if Chance had picked up the trait from spending time with the Conners' golden retrievers.

As he went through the motions of preparing for bed, Aaron's mind again drifted back to Skye and how she'd kissed him out of the blue. The mere memory of it made his heart race. Though he'd known her only a handful of hours, he suspected her husband was an idiot for letting her go. No, that wasn't right. Darren hadn't let her go. If he had, he would have signed the papers. He'd driven her away and realized his mistake too late. Aaron shook his head, unable to fathom why the man had accused her of cheating. He didn't think she'd ever been *tempted* to stray, but maybe his opinion was skewed because he'd never doubted Erica for a moment and didn't have a clue what it must feel like to suspect his lover of infidelity.

"And thinking like that'll just keep me awake," he muttered and slid into bed.

The sheets were cool and welcoming, and all at once, weariness settled over him. Reaching over the edge of the bed to give his dog one last pat, he rolled onto his side, facing the window. Moonlight streamed through the gauzy curtains Erica had picked out when they'd first moved into this house. The line between wakefulness and sleep blurred until Aaron wasn't sure if he was dreaming or awake.

He felt the mattress shift and dip as she slipped into bed beside him, and he looked into her smiling eyes.

The moon is pretty tonight, isn't it? she murmured.

Yes, it is, he replied. He wanted to reach for her, to tuck her snuggly into his arms and never let her go again, but he knew he couldn't because she wasn't really there. *I miss you, Erica.*

I know you do, but I'm still here. She placed her palm over his heart, and he could feel the warmth of her skin. *And I always will be.*

This isn't real. I'm dreaming.

She brushed her lips across his before curling into his

body with her back to his chest. He wrapped his arm tightly around her and breathed in her familiar and precious scent. She smelled of moonlight and mountain breezes, he thought. If this was only a dream, he never wanted to wake. But between one heartbeat and the next, Aaron jerked awake, and she was gone, leaving behind a cold hollowness.

Unwilling to believe his now-open eyes, Aaron reached across Erica's side of the bed, but his hand found exactly what his eyes saw. Emptiness and undisturbed sheets. Erica had not been here tonight or any night for nearly half a decade, so why did his heart still torture him with such brutally real visions of her? He lifted his hand to the spot where hers had been, trying to force his aching heart to understand that it was a dream.

The memory of a kiss lingered, but it wasn't the feather-light touch of Erica's lips he felt. He flopped onto his back and covered his face with his hands as guilt crashed through him like storm surge and demolished every thought he'd had tonight of moving forward with his life. He was stupid for thinking any woman, even one as compassionate as June or as compelling as Skye, would ever push Erica out of his heart. So maybe it was best if he cancelled his date with Skye, put an end to things before he could hurt her.

No. The defiance of the thought shocked him, and anger seeped through him, disintegrating the paralyzing grief. *It's been damn near five years. That's long enough.*

Chance gave a soft whine when Aaron climbed out of bed and tiptoed across the hall to peek into his daughter's room. In the dim light, he could see the shape of her curled beneath her blankets and, beside her, the black ball of fur that was Spook. Habit argued that he was only concerned for his daughter's happiness, but a voice deep in the back of his mind had more selfish reasons for wanting to keep his date with Skye. It was time to be honest with himself.

"I'm tired of being alone," he whispered, afraid that the admission would slip away if he didn't say it out loud. Once the words were out of his mouth, even though no one was awake to hear them, he was relieved. Yes, there were still times he wished he'd died with Erica, and he would always miss her, but damn it, he was only thirty-one, with a whole lot of life ahead of him, and he shouldn't have to live it alone.

He crawled back in bed, exhausted by the day's activity and his ongoing battle with his grief, and made a promise to himself. *I already gave up my chance at happiness with June, and if I have that chance with Skye, I will* not *let it slip away again.*

Four

SKYE'S MORNING DIDN'T START WELL. The finality of her divorce, which would be official in just two more days, had plagued her all week. Questions of what she'd missed, what more she could have done to save her marriage, and the doubt about her decision to leave Darren had greeted her with the newly risen sun, crushing her beneath a lead blanket of failure. When Aaron showed up at her front door dressed in a yellow Montana State Bobcats Gold Rush T-shirt with a matching shirt for her, she nearly backed out of going to the game. But he grinned and asked her if she was ready, and breathlessly, she said yes.

After their three-hour ride from Northstar to Bozeman, her dark mood had faded into oblivion, and now, standing with at least fifty people from Northstar and watching the marching band parade toward the field, she was glad she'd come. The electrifying energy of the pre-game activities was infectious, and her doubt vanished.

"I didn't think there'd be so many people from Northstar here," she remarked to Aaron.

He chuckled and lifted his daughter to his shoulders. "This isn't even everyone who came. The rest are either already in the stands or on their way. The Bedspread's restaurant is closed, and so is the Ramshorn because no one wanted miss Luke's first start as a Bobcat."

"Is *everyone* coming?"

"Pretty close."

"Evie wasn't kidding when she said Northstar is like one great big family."

"Nope, she wasn't. Have you ever been to a college game before?"

"My dad and Lindsay's are alumni of the University of Washington, and they have season tickets, so yeah, I've been to a few games." Skye grinned broadly. "Linds and I were both managers for our high school team, too. Well, I was more photographer than manager, but still."

Aaron broke out laughing, and Skye couldn't help laughing with him. "Henry wasn't joking when he said you both loved football."

"We used to be total tomboys. Back in those days, it was always jeans, a T-shirt, and a ponytail." She glanced down at her attire. "Almost exactly like today except for the makeup. I wouldn't have been caught dead wearing makeup back then, and now…."

"You make being a tomboy sound like a bad thing, but I, for one, am quite partial to jeans, T-shirts, ponytails, and no makeup. When did you decide to ditch the tomboy?"

"Darren wasn't fond of it, and I discovered that I got more business when I dressed up a little. I miss those days, though, when I got to hang out with the team and people didn't care what I wore as long as my pictures were good." She laughed. "We had a lot of fun, didn't we, Lindsay?"

Her redheaded friend turned to grin over her shoulder in reply. "Yes, we did."

"And you were impressed that I know how to dance," Aaron said. "Erica liked football well enough, but whenever I'd start talking about it, her eyes tended to glaze over. And I'm not even one of those guys who lives and breathes it."

"Did you play?"

"High school and college. Henry and Nick played, too. Of course, none of us were as good as Luke. The kid's a natural. What about your ex? I imagine he appreciated your interest."

"Not so much. He played—that's how we got together—but he quit his junior year. He didn't like the new coach, and he wanted me to quit, too, but I refused. He didn't like that, either."

"Your ex sounds like a real asshole."

"Daddy! That's a bad word," Jessie piped.

"Sorry, pumpkin. You're right, and I shouldn't have said it."

"It fits, though," Skye muttered. More loudly, she said, "Why do you think he's my ex?"

"Point taken. Here come the players."

At his words, Skye remembered her camera hanging ignored around her neck and her offer to June and Ben Conner to take pictures of the game so they could actually watch it. She lifted her camera, removed the lens cap, and waited for the five-wide line of players to approach. She felt the familiar jab of excitement as her eyes took in the golden helmets and navy blue and gold uniforms. Her grin widened at the clicking of cleats on pavement. It reminded her forcefully of her high school days when she'd been privy to all the behind-the-scenes action, something she'd dearly missed.

Luke wasn't difficult to spot. He was in the first row on the side closest to where Skye stood with his family and friends. She twisted the lens to zoom in and took a few shots before she spotted a small navy blue patch on his jersey just below the Nike swoosh. The letters MT-CL and the number three were embroidered in gold. None of the others had that patch, and it piqued her curiosity. She'd have to ask Aaron about it later. When Luke reached them and gave Jessie a high-five, she was glad she'd opted for one of her wide-angle lenses because she was able to get both of them and Aaron in the frame. Instinctively, she knew she'd captured a very special shot.

Once the players had passed, she turned to her date with energy buzzing deliciously through her. "Now what?"

"Now we head into the stands," Aaron replied. "You're going to love the seats. We're in the first row on the fifty-yard line."

"If I can't be on the field, that's the next best thing," she replied, and turned to follow Aaron through the throng of people. "I imagine June and Ben have something to do with that."

"And Pat and Aeli and Vince's parents. The rest of us chipped in, of course, but they're the ones with the club memberships. Most of the people from Northstar are in the cheap seats, but Henry and Lindsay, Nick, Beth, and Will, Evie and Vince, Andy, Jane, and Becky Epperson, and Marvin and Mary Struthers will be sitting with us and the Conners and O'Neils." He chuckled when she regarded him with lifted brows. "Don't worry. No one expects you to remember everyone in a day."

"That's a relief. Who are Marvin and Mary Struthers?"

"They own the Ramshorn. Well, they own it until they sell to June, Ben, and Luke, but it'll be a few years yet before that's official."

"Ah."

The rest of their party joined them with Lindsay on Skye's right side and Henry beside her. June and Ben sat on Aaron's other side, while the others sat in the row directly behind them. This was going to be fun, Skye decided, glancing at the posters her group had brought with Luke's number nine and "Pride of Northstar" written in bold.

June leaned around Aaron to address Skye. "Are you sure you don't mind taking pictures for us?"

"If I didn't want to do it, I wouldn't have offered. And don't you dare think about offering to pay me for them, either," Skye replied. "I don't get to indulge in my love of sports photography often enough anymore."

"Well, thank you. Again. There were a few of Luke's high school games I didn't really get to watch because I was too busy taking pictures."

"I used to do that when I was the photographer for the Vikings."

"You were a Viking, too?" June asked. "Ben, Aeli,

and I all graduated from North Kitsap."

"Small world."

"Have you ever met Aelissm's uncle, Bill Granger? You might've. Evie dated Aeli's little brother Kent in high school. We fondly refer to Bill as our center of gravity because he's largely responsible for bringing us all together."

"Aaron, would you mind trading me seats?" Skye asked, tired of leaning over him to talk to June.

"How about I go get us some refreshments and snacks before the concession lines get ridiculous?" he offered instead.

He took orders, and Linsday and Henry offered to help.

"Jessie, sweetheart, do you want to stay with me so you can watch the boys warm up?" Skye asked.

"Can I, Daddy?" the little girl asked.

"Of course," Aaron replied, kissing the top of his daughter's head before she bounced off his knee and crawled into Skye's lap. "I'll be back in a bit."

As soon as they'd left, Skye turned back to June and dove back into their conversation as if the interruption hadn't occurred. "I *love* Bill! Huh. I'm surprised that I never met Aelissm or you or Ben before now."

"Well, I think we graduated a couple years before you started high school."

"Yeah, that makes sense. Bill and Mary are wonderful people. They live right across the street from Lindsay's parents in Indianola, and they let us play volleyball in their yard below their house and let us use their stairs to the beach any time we wanted."

"They *are* wonderful people. Bill's the reason I have

Luke, and both Ben and Pat worked with him when they were at the sheriff's department, so we all owe him a lot. Not that he'd ever believe that. He's a rare breed and such a great man." June leaned a little closer, and the intensity in the older woman's insightful blue eyes startled Skye. "So is Aaron."

Skye opened her mouth to respond, then snapped it shut.

"I'm not trying to be nosey, and I hope I haven't offended you. I still care about him, and I want to see him happy again. I wouldn't say anything, but I haven't seen him look at a woman the way he looks at you since Erica died."

"I'm sure you're exaggerating because I've seen the way he looks at *you*. Sorry, Ben, but it's true."

"What can I say? My wife is an incredible woman," June's husband replied, smiling briefly before returning his attention to the football team.

"Aaron's right. He's not remotely jealous."

"He has no reason to be."

"I'm not used to that, I guess." Skye didn't add anything to clarify and sensed she didn't need to. Sympathy washed over June's face. "Would it be rude if I asked about you and Aaron?"

"Not at all. Honestly, there's not much to tell. We went on all of seven dates a few years ago, and it ended cordially when we both realized he wasn't ready to move on yet. Of course, we were friends for several years before we dated, so it was pretty easy to stay friends after."

"Yo!"

They all turned to see Luke standing just below them with his helmet dangling by its facemask on his wrist and four miniature blue-and-gold footballs tucked in the crook of his elbow.

"For Ant, Iris, Will, and Jessie," he explained. When his gaze landed on Skye, he grinned. "I'm glad you came, Skye. How were the shots I took of Vince and Evie's wedding?"

"They were great, Luke," Skye replied with a laugh. "And isn't that the last thing you should be worrying about right now?"

"Probably. Here." He tossed one of the footballs to her for Jessie, then lobbed the others to their intended recipients and turned his gaze on his parents. "Are we all still on for dinner in Butte after the game?"

"Yep," Ben answered. "We have reservations at the Pekin Noodle Parlor."

"Yes! I love that place. Hope you like Chinese, Skye, because the Pekin is the best."

"I love Chinese, actually."

"Hey, Luke," Becky called to her cousin. "Almost everyone from Northstar is here to watch—even the die-hard Griz fans are wearing Bobcats blue and gold—so you'd better win."

"Thanks for reminding me," he groaned. Then he grinned again. "I'm not going to make any promises. We've got this untested quarterback."

"Now, why does that sound familiar? Oh, right. That's the exact same thing you said before the Wolves won the state championship your senior year."

"You're not... nervous... are you, Luke?" Skye asked.

"Luke's never nervous," Aaron said, returning with

Henry and Lindsay and the food. He handed Skye her cheeseburger and drink.

"I might be just a little bit today." Luke glanced over his shoulder. "I gotta go. See ya after the game."

"Good luck!" their group chorused as he tugged his helmet back onto his head and jogged away. He lifted a hand in acknowledgement.

"He's the quarterback?" Skye asked June.

"Yep."

"Somehow, I'm not entirely surprised. No wonder he's a little nervous. That's a lot of pressure." From the corner of her gaze, Skye caught Aaron watching her and turned to look at him. The expression on his face was one of amusement and something else she couldn't quite put a name to. "What?"

"Darren is an idiot."

For the second time in twenty minutes, she opened her mouth to respond only to shut it again. She suspected there was a lot more to his statement than appreciation for her love of football, and she didn't quite know how to react to the implied compliment. The habit of responding to her ex's subtle and sly ridicule with silence or acquiescence prevented her from accepting the praise. "I'm sure I'm just as responsible as he is for our marriage falling apart."

"Do tell."

"I can be pretty independent and stubborn at sometimes, and I made it clear that my photography business was mine. Sorry, but I'm just not one of those women who gives up her dreams when she gets married."

"I repeat. Darren is an idiot."

The startling gentleness she was beginning to

understand was ingrained in him returned to his eyes, and one corner of his mouth lifted in a devastating mixture of sensitivity and roguish charm. Skye was assaulted by a torrent of unexpected gratitude and pleasure that he seemed to find appealing everything about her that Darren had despised. She also felt a flare of the self-confidence her ex had eroded, but most notable was an overwhelming desire to kiss Aaron again, right there in front of his friends and family. Heat flushed through her as she recalled their first kiss and how he'd kissed her back with that intoxicating mixture of hunger and restraint.

"You might want to get your camera ready," he murmured. "The team's about to run back out onto the field."

With a start, she jerked her attention back to the field to see that all the players had vanished back through the inflatable Bobcat tunnel. The stands had also nearly filled in the time she'd been talking with Aaron and June. It was a significantly smaller stadium—maybe a quarter of the size of what she was accustomed to, but that somehow made the experience more exhilarating. She suspected her companions and the fact that she knew one of the players had something to do with the thrill pulsing through her.

Before, when they'd walked out onto the field for warm-up, each five-wide row of the team had linked hands. Now, they rushed through the tunnel with Luke in the lead. Skye pressed the shutter button repeatedly until her camera had to pause to catch up, and then the cheer erupted from her. She would have been absolutely stupid to miss this, she thought, screaming with the rest of the capacity crowd when Luke threw a jaw-dropping sixty-seven-yard pass on his first possession of the game, and again on the next play when he handed the ball off to the running back, who dove into the end zone for the touchdown. On the Bobcats' second possession, the opposing players were ready for the pass, and Luke—demonstrating the quick thinking required of a quarterback—ran the ball thirty-five yards, sidestepping tackles with impressive agility and power.

"Looks like the other team may have underestimated the rookie quarterback," Skye yelled to June over the roar of the spectators.

"Wouldn't be the first time!" June replied, laughing. "If you'd seen him his freshman year of high school, when he played wide receiver, you would have thought Greg Wells was nuts for putting him on the varsity team. He was tiny. Five-two or three, I think."

"No way."

"I swear it's the truth. I was terrified he'd get trampled, but he is probably the sturdiest and most resilient person I know, and he's proven it time and again." June frowned thoughtfully at Skye. "It took you a while to let your excitement loose today—even though you obviously love football—like you have been bullied into suppressing your feelings. But I think you're resilient, like Luke. Given a little time and some space… and maybe a distraction or two…." June glanced at Aaron and Jessie, who remained oblivious of their conversation, and smiled. "You'll bounce back and be stronger for it."

Before Skye could even begin forming a response, Pat leaned down from the row behind them.

"She does this all the time," he said. "She had it figured out that I was in love with Aelissm long before I arrived at the same conclusion."

"Sometimes, it's easier to see things from the out-side," June remarked. "And for the record, Pat, *Luke*—at twelve—knew you were in love with Aelissm before you did."

"Can we please not traumatize Skye with the story of how he figured it out?"

June laughed. "Oh, but it's such a *fun* story. However, I don't want to make you blush, and I certainly don't want to traumatize Skye."

"Thank you," Pat replied.

"Sorry if I crossed a line," June said a moment later.

Having finally recovered a few of her wits, Skye re-plied. "You didn't, but you *did* take me quite by surprise."

It was easy to see why Aaron still harbored feelings for June Conner. Skye had never met anyone quite like her; she was as beautiful inside as out and startlingly insightful and compassionate. A little voice told her she should be jeal-ous of June, that she'd never be able to compete with her, but a louder voice took the woman's praise to heart and squashed the bubbling fear of inadequacy. She forced her attention back to the game just in time to see her new friend's son complete another pass for the Bobcats' second touchdown of the quarter.

At halftime, she leaned over and kissed Aaron's cheek. "Thank you for bringing me. I needed this."

"Needed what?" he asked with a lopsided grin.

"All of this. The excitement of the game, the love of your friends and family and you and Jessie. I feel appreci-ated. It's been a long time since I felt that."

She hoped he might kiss her then, but instead, he took her hand and pressed his lips to her knuckles, then whispered close to her ear, "You're welcome."

That first day in Northstar, she'd understood that her time in Montana would be good for her. Now she suspected that Aaron Hammond might just be the best part.

* * *

Aaron almost wished he and Henry had declined the Conners' offer to join them and Becky and the O'Neils for a post-game dinner at the Pekin Noodle Parlor in Butte. Almost. The urge to have Skye to himself—or at least, *mostly* to himself—was powerful, but he couldn't deny that the exhilarating day followed by delicious food and the company of good friends had him quite relaxed. Tonight, he wasn't plagued by the usual worries about whether or not he was doing enough for his daughter or the question of how much longer he'd be able to balance work for the sheriff's department and the ranch. He wasn't even troubled by the knowledge that Jerry Mackey was a free man again as of yesterday.

His gaze swept around the table at the smiling faces of his closest friends and family. Their party of sixteen crowded around the long table at the front of the second-floor Chinese restaurant, talking and laughing about the events of the day. The Bobcats had won the game with a respectable final score of thirty-five to seventeen. Luke had played a phenomenal game and scored the last touchdown late in the fourth quarter when he broke loose from a tackle that might've ended in a sack and darted twenty-seven yards into the end zone. That play alone had silenced the doubt of the radio broadcasters Aaron and Skye had listened to on the way to Bozeman this morning, and Aaron beamed with the pride shared by everyone at the table.

Appropriately, Luke was the center of attention, and Aaron was content to watch the others quiz him on the game. The adults paused occasionally to include Jessie and Ant O'Neil in the conversation, and Aaron couldn't help but notice again how patient Skye was with his daughter as she listened attentively to the little girl's questions and answered them in simple terms Jessie easily grasped. He found it quite amusing, as well, that the three people most engaged in the discussion about football were all female—Skye, Lindsay, and Becky. It didn't surprise him in the least that Ben's niece was excited; after all, Luke was her best friend, and she managed their high school team. But he loved Lindsay's and Skye's interest and suspected he and Henry had discovered a pair of rare gems.

"You seem pretty mellow this evening, Aaron," June remarked.

"Mmm. It's been a great day." He turned at her. "Thanks for inviting us out tonight."

"You're sure you don't mind hanging out with us instead of keeping Skye all to yourself?"

"It might be nice to get to know her one-on-one, but no. This is perfect. I can't believe how great she is with Jessie. And with Luke. I know it's not really my place, but I'll always have a soft spot for that kid of yours."

"You helped us more than I can ever say with that nightmare with JP. And with the aftermath. For that alone, it will *always* be your place. Of course, the fact that you've been my friend longer than I've had Luke solidified your place long before that."

"Thank you." He watched June's son indulge Will, Ant, and Jessie in a table-top re-enactment of a few plays before adding, "I hope I do half as well with Jessie as you've done with Luke. He's turning into a hell of a man, June."

"You are doing an amazing job with Jessie, Aaron. She's a happy, wonderful little girl, and I have every faith you will raise her to be an incredible young woman."

"Ugh. Don't say it like that. I still can't believe she'll be five in three weeks. I don't want to think about her growing up yet."

She snorted. "What are you complaining about? Luke will be *nineteen* in a week and a half. You want to talk about kids growing up too fast…."

"Okay! You win." He chuckled. "So, what do you think of Skye so far? Since you two were chatting it up most of the game, I assume you've had plenty of time to form a more in-depth opinion."

June gave him a smile that said she knew something he didn't, and his pulse quickened. "I reiterate what I said at Evie and Vince's wedding. I really like her. And the more I get to know her, the more I see to like."

Aaron watched his date with narrowed eyes. Physically, she and June were both attractive women, but where June exuded compassion and intuitiveness and unobtrusive confidence, Skye struck him as reserved and cautious. He thought he sensed a similar self-assuredness in her, too, but it was hidden beneath a layer of doubt, and he wondered how—more importantly, *why*—her ex-husband had buried it.

The waitress rolled their food down the long aisle between the coral pink, enclosed booths from the kitchen at the back of the restaurant, momentarily disrupting the conversations. Aaron tucked into his sweet-and-sour chicken and nearly purred with delight.

"Luke, you were right. This is amazing," Skye said. "What do you think, Jessie? Do you want to try some of my egg roll?"

Jessie nodded, so Skye cut off a small piece and plopped it on the little girl's plate. Aaron gaped when Jessie not only ate it but asked for more.

"I have never gotten her to try the egg rolls," Aaron whispered in Skye's ear, afraid that saying it any louder would jinx it. "She's normally a pork-fried-rice-or-nothing girl."

"Maybe she's just trying to impress me," Skye replied.

"Is it working?" he asked before he could stop himself.

"She impressed me when she first walked up to me and told me her daddy thought I was pretty."

Aaron wasn't sure if he should be horrified, grateful, or something else entirely, so he gave in to the first emotion that pushed its way to the front and laughed. "I love that little girl."

"That's quite apparent." Amusement and something softer danced in Skye's amber-colored eyes. "I know this was supposed to be a date, so I'm sorry I've been mostly ignoring you."

He tilted his head to study her and took another bit of his dinner while he tried to find the words to explain what he felt. Finally, he said, "I always thought it would be difficult, trying to date with Jessie. But you're making it so easy."

"Wasn't she invited along when you dated June?"

"Of course she was, and so was Luke, but June is a special woman."

Hurt flickered briefly across her face in the moment it took Aaron to gather the rest of what he was trying to say, and he felt a jab of guilt.

"I'm quickly getting the impression that you are, too," he added, relieved when a shy smile replaced the flash of pain. "He did a number on you, didn't he? Darren."

She dropped her gaze to her lap. "I guess he did."

"I'm sorry. I shouldn't have brought it up. We're having fun, and I just ruined it."

"No, you didn't, but you're right. The comment you made about June… it was an innocent remark, but I took it wrong."

"Why?"

"Because Darren says things like that, only he doesn't follow them with a compliment. When he says them, they aren't innocent. They're like needles, and you can only withstand being poked so many times before you start to wince even when there's no needle. I keep thinking about my psychology class in college, about an experiment my professor described in which a dog was repeatedly shocked and unable to escape the pain. Eventually, it simply endured the shock, and even when it could change the situation, it didn't. I feel like that dog."

"But you *did* change your situation. You're here now, aren't you?"

"Maybe. I still have my doubts about whether I made the right decision. Like this morning, before you picked me up. I realized my divorce will be final on Monday, and I just wasn't sure I'd really done everything I could to make it work with Darren."

"Marriage is a two-way street, and even when it's

great, you have to make compromises. It sounds to me like you were the only one trying to make it work."

"Maybe. I know I probably wasn't the wife he wanted."

"Why do you do that?"

"Do what?"

"Put the blame on yourself. If you weren't the wife he wanted, maybe he should have adjusted his expectations or married someone else. Life is too short to waste it on anyone who can't or won't love you for who you are." He inhaled deeply to rein in his emotions as familiar losses curled around him and made it hard to breathe. "Life is just too short."

"I imagine you probably know that better than anyone else here."

"I doubt that. There are several at this table who understand it too well. Without a doubt, that's the worst part about my job. Considering how small our county population is, I've probably seen more than my fair share of lives cut short. Aside from Erica, Mike Thompson and Carol Landers were the hardest. It doesn't seem like two years already." He leaned back in his chair and lifted his brows in surprise at the passage of time. "Wow. Mike had just graduated from high school and had a scholarship to play football for the Griz, and Carol would've been a senior that fall."

"What happened to them?"

"They were murdered. I found Mike in his brand new truck—his graduation present—out by the turn to Northstar. He'd been shot once in the chest, and his killer tried to make it look like a suicide. And Carol…." He shook swallowed the grief that rose with the memories. They had both been so young with such promise. "She was tied to a post and executed firing-squad style up by June and Ben's cabin."

"She was Luke's girlfriend."

It wasn't a question. Aaron nodded.

"Evie mentioned her. Did you find her, too?"

He shook his head. "Luke and Becky did."

"Oh, my God."

"That's why the people of Northstar are so support-ive and protective of him—of them both—and why almost everyone from the valley was at the game today." He forced a smile. "Well, that and the fact that he's just a great kid."

"And a gifted athlete."

Some of the tension drifted away, and Aaron's lips lifted again, willingly this time. "That, too."

"I meant to ask this earlier, but I think I know the answer now. The patch on Luke's jersey… it's for Mike and Carol."

"Yes, it is."

The rest of the meal passed pleasantly with friendly chatter and lots of laughter. The evening news came on the television in the front corner of the room as they were pol-ishing off the last of the delicious food, and a cheer rose from their table when a snippet of Luke's post-game inter-view was shown. The reporter called the game a "stunning debut of a promising new quarterback." The ruckus from their table attracted the attention of the restaurant's other patrons, some of whom quickly noticed the young man on the TV was sitting in their midst. When a man came over to congratulate Luke, Aaron decided it was probably time to head out. He glanced at his watch. It was already a quarter after seven, anyhow, and it took two hours to drive back to Northstar.

"Are you about ready?" he asked Skye. "I hate to cut this short, but I have to get up early for work tomorrow."

"I am but certainly not because I'm tired of your friends' company." She glanced down at Jessie, who had again made herself comfortable in Skye's lap. "I think you're probably ready, too, aren't you, sweetie. It's been a busy day, huh?"

"Uh-huh," Jessie replied. "But lots of fun."

Aaron headed to the back of the restaurant to pay his and Skye's portion of the bill, then returned the table and paused behind Luke's chair. He dropped a hand to the kid's shoulder and leaned down to say, "Great game today, Luke."

"Thanks for coming, Aaron."

"I wouldn't have missed it for the world." To everyone, he said, "G'night all. See you back in Northstar."

"Good night!" they chorused.

Jessie bounded down the long flight of stairs to the street from the Pekin, and Aaron hung back with Skye, smiling at his daughter's antics. He surprised himself when he hesitantly reached for Skye's hand and took hold of one of her fingers. She returned his gesture with a shy smile, and he surprised himself again when he raised her hand to his lips and kissed her palm.

"Thank you for coming with me today," he murmured. "I know it's probably too soon for you, but I've really enjoyed my time with you. If you're up for it, I have something else in mind that you might enjoy."

"Oh?" she inquired, climbing into the passenger side

of his truck after Jessie had crawled into her car seat.

"We're stacking hay next weekend, and I thought you might want to come down to the ranch to take pictures. I imagine you probably haven't seen many beaverslides in Washington."

"I don't even know what a beaverslide is."

"Then you have to come see one in operation."

"Sounds like fun."

They lapsed into comfortable conversation about their lives—her photography business and his life growing up on the ranch. Golden hour painted the tumbled landscape between Butte and Devyn with sharp contrast, and Aaron listened as Skye explained about it being her favorite time for landscape photographs. He let her ramble on, smiling occasionally when Jessie joined in the conversation with some tale or other, but shadows darker than those now caressing the land crept into his mind.

Why, after the wonderful day he'd had, should thoughts about Jerry Mackey intrude on his happiness? The man had been released yesterday, and though Aaron had neither seen nor heard anything else about him other than confirmation of his freedom, he suspected it was only a matter of time. He didn't hope Jerry had finally gotten over his belief that his brother was dead because of Aaron, and if Aaron were completely honest with himself, he couldn't even blame the kid. Joseph had been the only family Jerry had left. Now he had no one but his dirtbag cousin, and from what Aaron had heard, there hadn't ever been any love between them, and any there might've been had been obliterated when Jerry had first ratted on Zach and then testified against him in court.

"You're awfully quiet," Skye remarked.

At her interruption, he realized with a start that he'd already left the interstate south of Devyn for the two-lane highway out to Northstar. The sky glowed with the fading remnants of sunset, but he couldn't recall the height of the fiery display. He glanced in the rearview mirror to see his daughter just sliding into sleep.

"Sorry. I was just thinking," he replied.

"Seems like some pretty serious thoughts."

"You could say that."

"Want to tell me about it?"

He started to tell her he didn't want to burden her with it, but when he opened his mouth, entirely different words spilled out. "Jerry Mackey's out of prison. Got out yesterday."

"Okay. Who's Jerry Mackey?"

"A kid I arrested—for the first time—almost five years ago in connection with a large drug ring."

"Are you worried he might come after you?"

"It wouldn't be the first time. He was in prison this last time for assaulting me. Don't know what he was thinking because he didn't have a snowball's chance in hell of beating me. Kid's half my size, and he's no brawler."

"Then why are you worried?"

"I'm not worried. It's more that I understand too well why he hates me."

"And why is that? Because he did jail time for breaking the law?"

"No, because his brother shot my wife and then turned the gun on himself."

Silence filled the cab of the truck for several long

moments as Skye processed what he'd told her. He glanced at her momentarily, and the shock was plain on her beautiful face.

"I hadn't heard how she died."

"Joseph didn't mean to pull the trigger." He inhaled deeply. "It was our anniversary—only our second—and we were in Devyn heading to dinner. He accosted us in the middle of the road, threatening me, telling me to let his little brother go. Then the gun went off, and Erica was hit. She died in my arms… right there in the street."

"My God, Aaron. I am so sorry."

He continued as if she hadn't spoken, unable to accept her sympathy at the moment. "Joseph put the gun to his head right after, taking with him the last person Jerry had to rely on. So, yeah, it isn't so hard to understand why Jerry hates me. Not hard at all."

They lapsed into silence again, and Aaron focused on the darkening road. Though she didn't say it, he knew Skye must be thinking it wasn't right that Jerry Mackey blamed him for Joseph's death. He didn't try to explain why he felt responsible because he couldn't even explain it to himself.

When he turned into the driveway of the rental cabin and parked his truck, he realized he wasn't ready to end the day. He sat behind the wheel for a moment, staring at the cabin, then stepped reluctantly out of the truck to walk Skye to her door. "So, we're on for haying next Sunday, right?"

"You bet. Aaron?"

"Hmm?"

"I want to kiss you again."

Lowering his gaze to her, he sighed. "We've been through this."

"I want to kiss *you*. I want to feel again how you made me feel that night after Vince and Evie's wedding."

He knew he should probably turn and walk away, but he couldn't. Instead, he lingered on the deck, awkwardly staring up at the stars twinkling in the fading twilight. Then, as if possessed by some unstoppable compulsion, he returned his gaze to Skye's face, saw the desire hazing her eyes, and tilted her face up. He kissed her lightly at first until she angled her body into his with her fingertips tentatively touching his arm. Then he drew her into him and kissed her more thoroughly, giving in to the hunger that had been gnawing at him all day. He pulled away when they both started to get carried away, groaning low in his throat as he did.

"I've been waiting all day for this," she purred, echoing his thoughts so closely he wondered if she'd heard them. "I love the way you make me feel. Not just now, but… whenever I'm with you."

"And how is that?" he asked, touching his lips briefly to hers again.

"Wanted. And respected." She tilted her head and held his gaze. "You're holding back, but… but not like you don't want more."

"You're definitely right there. I *do* want more." He kissed her again, lightly. "But we should call it a night because I really do have to get up early for work."

"All right. Good night, Aaron. And thanks again."

He only smiled, then turned and headed out to his truck with need pulsing through him. Skye Hathaway was a compelling woman.

* * *

Skye leaned against the closed front door and tipped her back, grinning smugly. The smile faded when she thought back over her day and returned to the conversation she'd had with Aaron about his late wife. He had described her death so plainly, as if he were giving a report, but she had sensed the deep well of emotion beneath his words. She couldn't begin to imagine the agony of losing someone she loved as much as he had obviously loved Erica, let alone holding them and watching them die, powerless to stop it. It was easy to see why he still grieved for her.

Sighing, she straightened and walked into the downstairs bedroom where she'd set up her office. The clock on the wall said it was a quarter after nine, and though she knew if she downloaded the files from her camera now, she'd be up half the night going through them, she sat down at the desk and lifted her camera out of its bag.

Before she could even connect the cable, the phone rang. Frowning, she wandered into the kitchen and looked at the caller ID. With a groan, she told herself not to answer it; she'd had a great day, and there was no point in ruining it by taking the call. But the habit of eleven years had her hand shooting toward the cordless phone.

"What do you want, Darren?" she asked flatly.

"One of your clients stopped by today."

"I highly doubt that." Skye had given her assistant all the necessary contact information and instructions for what to tell clients. If a client truly had stopped by Darren's house.... No. Her clients all went directly through her office or her website now, and both Joel and her site would've told anyone that she was away for at least a month and how she could be contacted. Besides, she'd cleared her calendar and notified all her clients of her sabbatical.

"She wanted to know when you'd be back. Said she wanted to make an appointment for her son's senior pictures. I told her you'd be back in a couple weeks. That wasn't very professional of you, up and leaving without giving your clients so much as a heads up."

"I *did* give my clients a heads up. And I may not be back in a couple weeks. I haven't decided yet when I'm coming back." *Or if I'm coming back.* The thought materialized out of nowhere and nearly popped out of her mouth. She inhaled deeply to keep it locked inside. "Look, Darren, I don't know what you're trying to pull, but I had a great day, and I'd rather it didn't end on a sour note."

"And, what, talking to me about your clients would do that?"

"Yeah, it would. It already has. I have a bunch of pictures from the game today that I want to at least skim through before I go to bed, so—"

"Game?"

"Yes, a football game. Aaron took me out to watch a local boy's first college game."

"Who the hell is Aaron?"

Too late, she realized her mistake and searched frantically for a way to salvage the situation. "He's my landlords' son."

"So, what, you're sleeping with him?"

"No, I haven't slept with him. Not everyone is like you, Darren." *To hell with it.* "Not that it's any concern of yours, but I did *kiss* him. And you know what? He kisses me like you never did… like you never *could* because the only person you care about is yourself."

"Jesus, Skye. We're still married."

The rebuttal sounded weak, and Skye wondered if she had finally managed to turn the tables on her ex and made him feel just a tiny prickle of the humiliation he'd wrapped around her for most of their life together. A slim smirk lifted her lips, and she said with sugary politeness, "Legally, we're only married until the day after tomorrow, but as far as I'm concerned, our marriage ended the day I walked in on you and *Leslie*. What I do or whom I kiss is not—and has not been for months now—any of your damned business."

She badly wanted to end the call, but she waited a heartbeat, then two. When Darren didn't respond, she pumped her fist in the air and grinned triumphantly. For the first time ever, she had rendered him speechless. "Goodbye, Darren."

Gently, she pulled the handset from her ear and pressed the call-end button. With the same light touch, she settled the cordless in its cradle and strode back to her computer. While the pictures downloaded, she replayed the conversation in her head and was amazed at herself. Gone—if only temporarily—was the self-effacing, dutiful wife. In her place was a woman Skye scarcely recognized, a woman with the same determination as the girl who hadn't cared what people thought and signed up for the unfeminine position of football team manager simply because she loved the sport. A woman with the same independent spirit of the artist who'd relentlessly built her client base and constructed a business around her passion for photography.

With that self-confidence burning brightly, she got to work. When she came to the shot of Luke giving Jessie a high five, she decided to break her long-standing tradition of using one of her landscapes as the desktop image on her laptop. She'd framed the shot perfectly, but she added a touch of vignetting to the corners to really make the young pair and Aaron stand out. Skye felt Aaron's love for both his daughter and June's son radiating from the image and wondered at the thought that had popped into her head when she'd told Darren she wouldn't be coming back to Washington in a couple weeks. It was a silly idea, that she could stay here, but it was persistent, and she was amazed that Aaron's attentiveness had already had such a powerful effect on her. Was she so starved for respect and attention that she would melt into trembling mess of gratitude at the slightest display of either? Had Darren damaged her so deeply?

Slamming the door on the thought, she vowed to take everything one day at a time and relearn how to be that independent and confident woman—as had been her intent when she'd decided to extend her stay in Northstar—then set the photograph as her wallpaper and called it a night.

Five

"SO, THESE THINGS are called beaverslides," Skye remarked, staring up that the large, wooden contraption. "And they're used for making those big haystacks I see all over the valley?"

"Yep. They're also called dereks." Aaron pointed to the tilted deck. "That's the slide. The two panels coming off the sides there are the wings, and the back panel they join with to make the box is called the backstop. The teeth there on the bottom are the basket, and that's what the hay rides up the slide."

She listened attentively as he described the rest of the parts, including a roofless old pickup attached at a right angle by a cable to the basket's pulleys. Aaron said it was the hoist and described how his father could put a load of hay into the front, middle, or rear of the box simply by driving the hoist truck slower or faster.

"Someday, one of us will get to drive the hoist," Henry said, "but Dad makes it look easy, and he enjoys it, so we keep letting him work it."

"You *let* me?" John Hammond retorted. "As I recall, the last time I let you try the hoist, we had to throw two more stackers in the box to level your mess of a pile."

Henry scrubbed his hand through his blond hair, grinning at his father's jest. "Well played, Dad." Turning to Skye, he said, "When Dad finally decides to pass the torch, it'll be to Nick or Aaron. I'm a buckraker at heart."

"What's a buckrake?"

"Those two tractors over there are buckrakes—the ones with the spikes on the front," Aaron answered. "We use those to push the hay onto the basket. If we had more help today, we'd probably get the third buckrake going. But it's a small field, so we'll make do with a small crew."

"How long will it take to stack all this?" Skye asked, gesturing around at the hay, which had been raked into long rows.

"Half a day. We'll probably get six or seven single stacks out of this or three double stacks."

"All right, let's get to work," John said. "Ben, Luke, you two up for stacking again?"

"Yep," Luke replied and grabbed two pitchforks. He kept one for himself and handed the other to Ben. "We've got a pretty good system worked out, don't we, Dad?"

"Yes, we do," Ben replied.

"You get one day at home a week, and you choose to spend this one stacking hay?" Skye inquired.

"What can I say?" He shrugged, smiling. "I'm a

glutton for punishment."

"Not as much of a glutton as Jake," Henry said with a laugh.

"Really, Henry? Do we have to bring that up every time we stack?"

"But it was such a memorable day."

"Yeah, not the kind I *want* to remember."

"What happened?" Skye inquired.

"We had a ranch hand who used to harass Luke relentlessly," Aaron said. "We were stacking hay two years ago—shortly before Carol and Mike were killed—and Luke finally had enough."

Ben cleared his throat. "Let's just say that Jake bit off a lot more than he could chew, and leave it at that."

"Thanks, Dad," Luke said. "It's certainly not something I'm proud of, so if it's all right with everyone, can we get to work?"

"Sounds good to me," John said. "Pat, you're raking around the slide, as usual."

"Any last-minute instructions?" Skye asked Aaron as he turned toward the buckrakes.

"Um… stay out of the way so you don't get hurt and have fun."

He added a wink to the second instruction and jogged over to one of the tractors with the wicked-looking spears on the front. Skye popped her lens cap off and tucked it into the back pocket of her jeans. She watched Aaron drive the first load of hay onto the teeth of the basket. With that, stacking was in full swing, and John Hammond and his crew worked with seamless precision. Henry's words about his father's skill on the hoist quickly became clear as John dropped load after load of hay exactly where it needed to be in the box. Ben and Luke worked well together pitching hay, and Pat kept the pulleys clear with an efficiency that told her they'd been doing this together for a long time.

The whole thing fascinated her, and the fire of ambition pulsed through her as she framed her shots to best capture it all. She looked for the wide-angle shots, close-ups of the machinery, and candid shots that would capture the camaraderie of the crew. Despite the lung-clogging swirl of hay dust, the men joked and laughed as they worked. Try as she might, she just couldn't picture Darren participating in the friendly teasing. He'd probably scowl the whole time and hate every minute of this.

The morning was cool. Cooler, she noted, than it had yet been. Though the air here was always drier than what she was used to, today it was even more so. It was… crisp. She wondered if that meant fall was just around the corner. Evie *had* said the fall colors peaked the last week of September, and with the first week already gone, the end of month wasn't far away.

Faster than she would have imagined, the hay crew finished the first stack. Luke and Ben gave it a nice, rounded top that made it look very much like a loaf of bread before riding the basket down the slide. *Well, that answers the question of how they get down.* Skye pressed the shutter button a dozen more times.

The Hammond twins pulled the derek forward with their tractors. Apparently, this would be a double stack with the single stack now creating the backstop—the panel had been dragged out of the way. She continued to take pictures and waited until they'd finished this second stack and begun a new one several dozen yards away before excusing herself to go photograph the other side of haying—the kitchen. The light out here was no longer ideal, anyhow, as the sun neared its zenith.

She hopped on the four-wheeler John and Tracie had told her to use and drove back to the main house. Surrounded by breathtaking mountain views, it was impossible not to grin like a fool, and she paused several times in her ride to take more pictures of the fields, willow-lined creeks, sagebrush hills, and towering mountains. It would be so easy to live here, and she knew that she had already fallen in love with Northstar. Without Darren around to tell her what she was doing wrong or ask impatiently if she was done taking pictures *yet*, the constant tension was gone, replaced by a serenity that allowed her to truly immerse herself in her craft.

Long before she reached the front yard of the main ranch house, she smelled it—the mouthwatering fragrance of the baby back ribs Tracie, June, and Aelissm were smoking for lunch… or whenever the men were done stacking hay. It was a tradition, they'd told her, and one everybody looked forward to.

She parked the four-wheeler in front of the house and made her way around to the backyard where she found the three women shucking ears of sweet white corn at the picnic table. The open smiles on all their faces and the occasional laughter reminded her forcefully of her two best friends. It had been too long since she'd really indulged in anything like that, she thought, covertly studying the trio. Evie had been here in Northstar for most of the last two years, and both she and Lindsay had been so busy making a living that they hadn't made enough time to get together. When they had, Darren usually saw fit to interrupt with a phone call, tersely asking Skye when she was planning on coming home, and she'd slunk away like a beaten dog, feeling guilty for spending time with her friends.

It's not right, she thought stubbornly. *But I let him do that to me. I let him keep me from enjoying time with my friends.*

She doubted any one of the three women she observed had ever felt that same guilt, and wondered if she'd ever be lucky enough to find a man who supported her. Unbidden, her gaze drifted over her shoulder toward the hayfield. She could hear the rumble of the tractors and the almost rhythmic sliding of the basket up and down the slide. With such supportive friends and family, surely Aaron couldn't be anything like Darren. He had not shown even an inkling of the mistrustful tendencies that defined her ex-husband. He could be exactly what she needed and what she had always wanted in a man—someone to love her as she was and to share her life as her partner and best friend.

Shaking her head, she started toward the picnic table. She would only be in Northstar for a few more weeks, but there was no reason why she couldn't let the peace and friendship offered so freely here help her rediscover herself and no reason why she shouldn't indulge in a little feminine companionship. With a twist of her lips, she admitted that she wanted to indulge with a little masculine companionship as well. Whether it was wise to do so, she couldn't say, but what harm was there in seeing where her undeniable attraction to Aaron Hammond led her?

"The ribs already smell wonderful," she remarked,

joining the women. "And I bet they'll taste even better."

"We certainly hope so," June replied. "How goes the stacking?"

"They were almost halfway done with the second double stack when I left."

"They'll probably finish around one or two then," Tracie said. "Perfect. Are you enjoying yourself, Skye?"

"Absolutely. I think I may have found a subject for a book."

"A photography book?" June inquired.

"Yeah. One of my regular clients has a friend who owns a small publishing company, and they've both been after me for a couple years now. Originally, I wanted to do one about sports traditions, but I'm too out of that loop anymore. Everything else I came up with just didn't feel like the right subject. So this… this'll be great."

"Well, you be sure to let us know when it comes out, so we can be the first in line to buy copies," Tracie remarked.

"You can have as many copies as you want, but I'm not going to let you buy them." She sat on the bench of the picnic table and tipped her head back, smiling as the sun warmed her face. "I could get used to this."

A laugh from Aelissm brought Skye's attention back to her companions.

"Remind you of someone?" Tracie asked June and Aelissm.

The other three women exchanged knowing glances, but no one elaborated on the joke.

"Definitely," June replied.

Skye's curiosity got the best of her. "What? And

who?"

"Pat and Luke," Aelissm answered.

"How do I remind you of them?"

"I daresay you're getting attached to Northstar already." June tilted her head and smiled. "Just like Pat and Luke when they first arrived."

"What about Ben? I thought you said he went to school at North Kitsap with you and Aelissm."

"He did, but like Aeli here, he was born in Devyn. He spent his first eight years here in Northstar, so when he came back, it was more a homecoming than an introduction. Still, he and Pat and Luke and Aelissm and I…." She gestured around at the mountains and the valley. "We all found everything we wanted, right here."

Skye glanced between the two longtime friends. When her gaze momentarily dipped to their bellies, she immediately looked away, uncomfortable. How incredible it must be to grow a new life. She didn't begrudge them their happiness, but neither could she suppress the twinge of envy at the unintended reminder that the family she'd always wanted was still far out of reach. And might always be.

"I can certainly see why," she said finally. "This place is amazing, and all the people…."

"Let the betting begin." Aeli gleefully rubbed her hands together.

"Are you sure you want to start betting, Aeli? You don't exactly have the best track record."

"Hush up. It was one bet, June, *one* bet that I lost to my husband."

"What about the bet with Luke about when Ben would propose?"

"I was smart enough not to take that one."

"What bet did she lose?" Skye inquired.

"How tall Luke would be," June answered.

Aelissm laughed again. "Six years, and they still won't let me live that one down. But that's all right. Let's me know I'm loved, because if they didn't love me—"

"We wouldn't waste the time and energy to tease you."

Skye snapped a picture of the two friends with their arms around each other's shoulders and smiles that spoke of a lifetime of friendship. "So, when are you due?"

"Middle of October. June's a week ahead of me, though." Aelissm's gaze softened when she smiled at June. "The journey hasn't exactly been what we expected, but somehow we've still managed to get to where we always wanted to be. Raising our families together here in Northstar, surrounded by mountains, fresh air, and—best of all—great people."

It sounded like a fairytale, Skye thought, or a dream that came true only for others. She had believed it would happen for her when she'd said yes to Darren's proposal, but now she was newly divorced and starting over nearly from the beginning. Maybe she wasn't exactly too old for it to yet happen, but after wasting so much time on Darren… she was doubtful. What if she was one of those women destined to choose the same breed of loser over and over, who couldn't find a good man if he was standing right in front of her? Again, she glanced over her shoulder at the hayfield. She suspected that Aaron was firmly in the latter category.

"Your divorce is final now, isn't it?" June asked.

Skye nodded, trying to figure out what subtle clues

the insightful woman had used to gauge her thoughts.

"How's it feel to be a free woman?"

"When you put it that way…." Skye forced a smile. "Pretty good."

"But…?"

"I still have a long ways to go before I feel free."

June reached across the table to squeeze her hand. It was a simple gesture but full of sympathy, and Skye was glad for her friendship, even though she'd known the woman for two weeks. She knew she would keep in contact with her, and with Aelissm and Tracie, even after she left Northstar. When she lifted her eyes to meet June's gaze, she noticed the frown of concern pinching the older woman's brows together.

"I think maybe you should join us at the Ramshorn for dinner and a swim tonight to celebrate," June said. She glanced at her other companions. "What do you say, Aeli? Tracie?"

"I think that's a wonderful idea," Tracie agreed.

"Yes, it is," Aelissm added.

"Celebrate?"

"My birthday is tomorrow, and Luke's is Tuesday, but we're celebrating early while everyone is together."

Out of habit, Skye started to object. "That's really not necessar—"

"Please," June interrupted. "Join us."

"I can't intrude on your family gathering."

"You're *not* intruding. We want you there, and I'm pretty sure Aaron and Jessie want you there, too. Unless you don't want to come…."

"Of course I want to come." Maybe she should feel

annoyed by the way they pressured her, but honestly, she was grateful that they weren't allowing her to back out because she loved their company and because it was time she stopped avoiding things she wanted to do. She smiled. "I'll be there."

"Excellent. Now, either get your butt back to taking pictures or help us with lunch."

Skye opted to help the women cook, though she frequently stood back to take pictures of them, too. The rest of the morning passed quickly and delightfully, and by the time the men were done haying, Skye's cheeks ached from smiling and laughing so much. June, Aelissm, and Tracie were charming women, and she needed their brand of camaraderie.

Everyone gathered around the picnic table, and Skye hovered around with her camera, but it wasn't long before the tantalizing aroma drove her to take her seat. The meal was delicious. The baby back ribs had been smoked to perfection and were accompanied by a sweet and spicy homemade barbecue sauce, coleslaw, corn on the cob, and mashed potatoes. Wedges of perfectly ripe watermelon served as desert. The women had prepared just enough for everyone—leaving no leftovers—and when Skye voiced her admiration, Tracie only remarked that they'd done this a time or twenty.

All through the meal, Skye soaked up the relaxing air of love, only marginally pained by the easy intimacy the married couples displayed. They weren't blatant with their caresses—a lingering hand against a neck here or a quick kiss there—but it made Skye very aware that she and Darren had never had that sort of comfortable, effortless relationship.

When Aaron took her hand and kissed her knuckles with a light smile dancing on his lips and adoration playing in his beautiful blue eyes, she struggled to keep breathing because the promise of that very kind of relationship sat right in front of her, but could she, after Darren's emotional abuse, believe she deserved it?

"Having fun?" he asked.

"Mmm-hmm."

After lunch, the O'Neils and Conners headed home, and Aaron showed Skye the big barn. She was in heaven. There were saddles, lariats, antique harnesses and plow equipment, tractors, and a wide assortment of other good-ies, and the filtered light in the barn set the mood perfectly. Jessie, at her father's request, let Skye work, watching her with fascination. Occasionally, Skye glanced at the little girl and noticed that she was nearly vibrating with the two dozen questions swimming in her inquisitive mind. Skye felt a little twinge of guilt for ignoring her, but she was grateful to be able to work without interruption. She'd probably have enough pictures from today alone to fill a book, she thought when her camera beeped to tell her the memory card was full. She exchanged it for an empty one and imme-diately dove back into her spree.

She began to wonder when Aaron would get bored like Darren always did. Actually, Darren would have started complaining a long time ago, she knew, amazed at the vast differences between her ex and Aaron Hammond. Waiting for Aaron to say something grew into a distracting tension, so she finally turned to face him, only to find him watching her with a lopsided smile that showed no trace of irritation, only patience and a surprising interest in what she was doing. Her heart jumped a little at the sight of that endearing expression. She hesitated, waiting for him to say something, but he didn't, so she asked, "What?"

"You're beautiful," he said.

Skye blushed and looked away to hide the smile she couldn't stop.

"So intent. It's like you see all this stuff in a completely different way than I ever have. It's... amazing."

"Thank you," she replied quietly. "But it's my job to look at things differently, to find the beauty in my subject."

"How did you get started in photography?"

"My dad gave me his old film SLR when I was in junior high. He taught me how to use all the settings—the aperture, shutter speed, and whatnot—and I fell in love with it. I used to take pictures of everything. Taught myself how to compose my shots using the rule of thirds and leading lines and all that."

"And how did you come to take pictures for your high school football team?"

"I was watching practice one day, experimenting with action photography, and the head coach saw me and asked to see the shots when I got them developed. He loved them. He still hadn't found a manager yet, so he asked if Lindsay—who was already a *huge* football fan—and I wanted the job. Lindsay, of course, didn't need any convincing, and when Coach Carson said I could be the team's photographer, well, that was all I needed to hear."

"And that's how you met Darren. Through football, right?"

"Yep. He asked me out that first season, and he was cute and popular, so like the naïve girl I was, I said yes. He had a lot of talent—started on varsity as a freshman—but he didn't have the drive or motivation or heart. When Coach Carson retired and they hired Coach Harmon our junior year, Darren decided he didn't want to play anymore."

"Why?"

"Coach Harmon didn't put up with his BS, and Darren didn't like it when Harmon benched him the first game for showing up to practice late."

"But Coach Harmon kept you on as manager and photographer."

Skye nodded. "I really liked him. I respected that he was fair. I liked Coach Carson, too, but he let players like Darren get away with too much. Looking back, I should have realized Darren was trouble when he quit something he loved because he didn't want to follow rules."

"The more I get to know you, the more you amaze me."

She blushed at his blatant praise and lifted the camera to snap a picture of him before that wonderful smile of awe left his face. By the time she lowered her camera, it had vanished, replaced by a quirky grin of amusement. In that moment, he was devastatingly sexy and disarmingly thoughtful. She wanted to curl herself around him, kiss him again. And more.

"Good thing Jessie is here," she murmured.

"How come?" the little girl asked.

Horrified that she's said it out loud, she stuttered out, "Because I want to take some pictures of you two together in here. Some candids."

"What's a candid?"

"A picture of people doing whatever they're doing. Like… I don't know."

"Want to give Remington a treat?" Aaron asked his daughter.

"Yeah!"

Skye took some pictures of the father and daughter as they grabbed some oats out of a bin near the door and headed toward a stall just inside the far door. It was then that Skye realized the barn was almost empty of animals. There were a couple of barn cats hanging around, but otherwise, all the stalls were empty. Or so she'd thought. As soon as Aaron and Jessie reached the last stall, a gorgeous, summer-sleek bay stallion thrust his head over the stall door. His ears swiveled forward, and he let out a soft huff. Such large, intelligent eyes, Skye thought, zooming in for a close-up of his face. Then Aaron hoisted Jessie off the ground, plopping her on his hip so she could hold the bucket of oats out to the horse. Though she'd spent her entire life around horses, Jessie was obviously delighted.

"Let me guess. Horses are your favorite animals. Right, Jessie?"

"Uh-huh."

"Marginally," Aaron replied. "She just loves animals. Which is why we have a house cat and a dog who doesn't know the first thing about working on a ranch."

"Black Lab, right?"

"Right."

"So, how come this guy is in here instead of outside with everyone else?"

"He's recuperating."

"From what?" Skye joined her companions at the

stall door. Immediately, she noted several long, half-closed gashes on the horse's shoulder. There were more on his rump, and if she had to guess, they looked like claw marks.

"Mountain lion. Had one try to take a calf, but Rem here put an end to that."

"You poor boy," Skye said, hesitantly stroking her fingers down the bay's cheek.

Remington pushed his velvety nose into her palm and let out a soft huff of air. She nearly stepped back despite the wooden stall door between them. He was so big. She'd never been this close to a horse before, but he seemed so gentle.

"He likes you."

"You sound surprised." Skye glanced over the horse, but she sensed nothing dangerous about him; he was the picture of relaxation.

"Rem is Nick's horse, and as such, the only person he genuinely loves is Nick. Beth is probably his second favorite person. Or Will." Aaron patted the horse's neck, and Skye figured Remington was pretty fond of him, too. "Consider yourself charmed because he doesn't like many people, and some he hates outright."

"I presume mountain lions fall into the latter category."

"Definitely. Don't feel too bad for him. He's been getting the royal treatment since it happened, and as bad as it may look, it's actually quite minor compared to some of the injuries I've seen a mountain lion inflict on a horse or a cow."

"Still...."

"He'll be just fine. And thanks to him, the calf will be

fine, too. The cat… not so much."

"Did you see it happen?"

"Not all of it, but we heard the commotion. By the time we got up to the tree-line along the upper side of the pasture on the four-wheelers, it was all over. The calf and its mother were standing several yards away, and Rem stood between them and the carcass like a good guard horse. Weren't you, handsome?"

"He killed it?" Skye asked in disbelief.

"Yep. He's a tough old boy. Extremely protective and sharply intelligent. Anyhow, I hate to cut this short—really, I do—but if we're going to meet everyone at the Ramshorn for dinner and swimming, we should probably get going. I still need to take a shower to get all the hay off me, and I imagine you'd probably like to go home to get your stuff."

Skye glanced at her watch and her eyebrows shot up in surprise. "I didn't realize it was that late."

"It is. You've been taking pictures for two hours." He tilted his head and regarded her with a faint smile of fascination. "You really get lost in your work, don't you?"

"I do. I'm sorry."

"Nothing to apologize for. It was fascinating to watch you. Wasn't it, Jess?"

"Yeah! Can you teach me how to take pictures?"

Skye laughed as a delightful relief washed over her, obliterating the habitual tension left over from Darren's selfish impatience. "You bet, sweetheart."

* * *

Aaron lounged near the stairs in the larger, cooler pool at the Ramshorn, watching his daughter play with Skye,

Luke, Becky, the O'Neil kids, and Nick's son, Will. Skye, Becky, and Luke had their hands full launching the youngsters, but by the grins on their faces, Aaron suspected they were having nearly as much fun as the kids. Beside him, sitting on the steps, June and Aelissm chatted away with Beth and Tracie about some party the Ramshorn was hosting in a couple weeks. Aaron passively listened to the conversation, but his attention was mostly on Skye. She wore a simple but flattering one-piece swimsuit the same shade of red as her bridesmaid dress from Evie's wedding. The color looked good on her, emphasizing the deep red, natural highlights in her dark hair and bringing forth a warm glow from her honey-colored eyes. Although, maybe it was more the happiness in her gaze than the color of her suit that brought out that warmth.

Ben, Pat, John, and Aaron's brothers returned from the hotter pool to join Aaron and the ladies at the steps.

"Is it just me, or does the air feel a little fall-like today?" Pat asked.

"I'd say it feels a lot fall-like," Aaron replied. "I'm ready for it. Summer was too long and hot this year."

"Agreed," June said. "So, tell me, Aaron. Is Skye getting sick of us yet?"

"I don't think so. I hope not."

June gave him a knowing wink before pushing off the steps and swimming into her husband's arms. Aaron's gaze again drifted to Skye, and he excused himself from his companions to join her, Luke, and Becky.

"Tired of this yet?" he asked her. Unable to resist, he pressed a quick kiss to her cheek. "I mean, it seems like every time we're together, we're always with my friends and family. I don't want you to feel… I don't know. Pressured. Or overwhelmed."

"Why on earth would I be tired of this?" she asked. "I love your family. And your friends. They have all been so welcoming. Truly, Aaron, it's been a long time since I've been able to just hang out with people like this. We—Darren and I—never really did this sort of thing much."

"Whyever not?"

"Well, most of my friends can't stand him, so naturally, he doesn't like them, either. And I don't care for most of his friends. They all like to go out and drink and party, and I prefer something more like…." She gestured at their surroundings. "Like this."

As she spoke, the sadness he was beginning to associate with her reminiscences about her marriage crept into her voice and darkened her amber eyes. Instinctively, he gathered her in his arms with her back to his chest and leaned against the wall of the pool. He wondered if he was overstepping his bounds, but she didn't flinch or tense up. In fact, he thought he heard her sigh in contentment.

The momentary flicker of concern for how his daughter might react vanished in an instant when Jessie glanced at him from her perch atop Luke's shoulders. Her grin of amusement shifted into one of pure happiness. She might be too young to understand the intricacies of adult courtship, but Aaron knew she understood that Skye made him happy. She'd remarked as much last night. *When Skye is with us, you're not so sad,* she'd said when he tucked her in. *You smile a lot more.* He had to agree with her innocent observation.

"I can't imagine how lonely you must've been,"

Aaron said softly. "I don't know what I'd have done without this—without *them*—when Erica died. I'm not saying I'm a total people person, but there is something wonderful about a small, close-knit group of people who love each other and look out for each other."

"There is," Skye agreed. She turned her face to him and smiled. "This is nice, too."

"What is?"

"This. I've become so accustomed to handling everything on my own that it's nice to know you're there to catch me if I fall, as they say."

"I guess that means I'm not crossing a line."

"Not at all. I'll admit that I felt a little guilty for kissing you *twice* before Darren and I were officially divorced—because maybe it's sort of scandalous—but I know that's stupid."

"It's not stupid. I think I might've felt the same, though I tried not to think about it like that." He inhaled deeply and let it out slowly. "Like you said, it's not like he was true to your vows, so I don't think us kissing was bad."

"Good thing you were in control," she remarked with amusement thick in her voice. "Because I certainly wasn't. I wonder what might've happened…."

He frowned thoughtfully. "You've already thought about…?"

"Maybe. You're an attractive and considerate man, Aaron."

"Well, thanks."

She sighed again. "Who am I kidding? I was never one to jump into bed. Hell, Darren's the only man I've ever been with, and our sex life hasn't exactly been anything to get worked up over." She glanced at him again. "And that's probably way more than you ever wanted to know."

"No… not really. Just more pieces to the puzzle. If there's one thing I learned from my wild youth—"

"Your wild youth?"

"It's my tale, so let me tell it."

"Yes, sir."

"Anyhow, I can tell you that sex in general can be good, but with the *right* person, it's amazing."

"Let me guess. June and Erica."

"With Erica, absolutely. June, no. She and I never made it past a couple of kisses. She's all Ben's."

"Somehow, I'm not at all surprised. I used to think I'd be that woman, but…."

"You were, and you always will be, Skye."

"The virginity ship sailed, Aaron. I will never be that woman again."

"I'm not talking about virginity. I'm talking about loyalty. That's what matters. Even after everything Darren put you through, you remained loyal until the end." He tightened his arms around her. "Now, quit being so humble and enjoy the attention, would you?"

She laughed softly and curled her fingers around his forearms. When she inhaled, he thought she was going to argue, but instead, she exhaled in a sigh and let her head fall onto his shoulder, tucking her face against his neck. Need shuddered through him, and he closed his eyes to drive it away. This was neither the time nor the place for anything along the lines of what his body wanted, but even if they were alone, her divorce was still too fresh. If she'd felt guilty for kissing him, he could only imagine the torture she'd put herself through if he let them get carried away before she was ready.

A small voice in the back of his mind argued that *he* wasn't ready, but it was barely more than a whisper, drowned out by a much more insistent one eagerly listing reasons why it was time to let go of Erica. Try as he might, he couldn't deny his attraction to Skye—either the physical or the emotional. Every argument for why it would be best to keep his hands and eyes to himself was met with a more rational reason why he shouldn't.

Skye Hathaway was intelligent, sexy, and humble. She was strong and independent but not so much so that she would push him away in favor of doing things her way. Best of all, Jessie loved her, and she seemed to love Jessie. His friends and his family all adored her, and they were—every last one of them—finicky about who they chose to bring into the circle.

Aaron kissed the top of her head. *How in the hell could Darren look at this incredible woman and find nothing but flaws?*

* * *

Skye flopped in the chair at the desk in the downstairs bedroom, frowned at her laptop, then decided to adjourn to the living room and the comfort of the couch so she could watch full night descend over the valley. She unplugged the computer, slung her camera bag over her shoulder, and packed both into the open living space. Setting the camera and laptop on the coffee table, she paused briefly in front of the big front windows to admire the western sky as twilight faded into night. The brightest stars were already coming out in the darker parts of the indigo arch. Behind the dark smudges of the clouds that had, only three-quarters of an hour ago, burned vibrantly with sunset, a scattering of pale blue wisps dusted the sky, and she thought they might be noctilucent clouds. If she recalled correctly, they were rare, even in the northern continental US, so she took her camera in hand, grabbed her tripod out of the bedroom, and headed out onto the deck.

She took several long exposures with her remote so she wouldn't jar the camera by manually pressing the shutter button and enjoyed the ethereal beauty of the phenomenon. As the minutes ticked by and more stars appeared in the fading twilight, Skye wondered if Northstar wasn't conspiring to keep her here. Between the hundreds of shots she'd taken on the Lazy H earlier today and now this, she was in heaven. Since her business had taken off, she hadn't had as much time to play with her photography, to remind herself of why she'd fallen in love with this art form.

When the last strands of luminescent gossamer faded into star-strewn cobalt, she turned and went back inside to begin the hours-long process of downloading, sorting, and selecting photos. She hovered over the couch, but before she lowered herself onto the inviting cushion, she decided it was probably time she called her parents. She hadn't talked to them since the night of Luke's football game. She dialed their number and pulled a bottle of water out of the fridge while it rang. She was nearly back to the couch when her mother finally picked up.

"Hello?" her mother asked.

"Hi, Mom."

"Skye, honey! Tom! It's our daughter."

She heard the clatter of another phone on the same line being picked up, then her father's voice greeted, "About time you called again. How have you been, pumpkin?"

She smiled, amused that her dad still called her by the same nickname Aaron called his daughter. "I'm good. What have you two been up to since last week?"

"Oh, you know," her mother replied. "The usual. Work. But your father did take me out to a lovely dinner last night. Out of the blue. It was wonderful, wasn't it Tom?"

"It was. We should do it more often."

Listening to her parents' playful banter, she wondered how she had ever fallen for Darren Fitzhugh. She'd always heard that women tended to marry men in the image of their fathers, but Darren was so different than her dad. Then again, it hadn't exactly lasted forever, either. Aaron, on the other hand, reminded her a *lot* of her dad. He had her father's easy-going patience, and she suspected, a very similar compassion.

"How about you? What adventures have you had this week?" her dad asked.

"Plenty. Mostly, I've been taking it easy. I think I've driven half the roads in the valley and taken a couple thousand landscape shots. It's nice to be able to take pictures just for myself again."

"Now, you said something about helping out on your landlords' ranch today, didn't you?"

"Yeah. I didn't really help much, but I took a lot of pictures of them stacking hay. I'll have to email you some pictures. It's fascinating how they do it. They have this thing called a beaverslide, and they—"

"A what?" her mother asked.

"A beaverslide. Oh, I'll just send you the pictures. I

don't know if I can really explain it, anyhow. After lunch, when they were done stacking, Aaron showed me the barn, and…. Let's just say it'll take me hours just to sort through all the pictures I took today."

"We can't wait to see some," her father said.

"Even better… I think I finally found a subject for that book Faye and Eloise have been begging me to put together. Northstar ranch life."

"Oh, honey! That's wonderful."

Skye smiled. Her parents had always been so encouraging, even when she'd told them she wanted to make a career of the hard-to-get-into field of photography. In contrast, Darren had derided her choice. Why had she wasted so many years on him? She shook her head. It was done and over now. No point in beating herself up over a past that couldn't be changed.

"Tell us more about this Aaron fellow." Her dad's voice had a touch of fatherly protectiveness, and she smiled. She might be twenty-six years old, but it was nice to know he still wanted to shield her like he had when she was a little girl. "You talk about him a lot."

"He's great. His whole family is, and so are his friends. They're all so kind and inviting, and they've all really made me feel at home. Especially Aaron."

"You sound so happy, pumpkin."

"She does, doesn't she, Tom. Remind me to thank that young man."

"Mom…."

"It's been a long time since we've heard that excitement in your voice. You've been excited about your work, sure, but not so much about life."

"Well, don't go overboard, okay, Mom? I'm not looking for anything permanent. Right now, I just want to enjoy my freedom and learn to enjoy life again. Do something for me for once."

Even as she said it, she felt like she was lying. Maybe she wasn't looking for anything permanent, but she certainly hadn't decided she would ignore this thing—whatever it was—between her and Aaron. In fact, she was quite interested in exploring it. As she thought back over their day together, her mind caught on the handful of moments in the pool at the Ramshorn when he'd held her and so effectively driven Darren from her mind. It had been wonderful to be held like that by a man again. Again? She couldn't remember ever finding the same comfort and relaxation in Darren's arms.

"It's your life, Skye. You're the only one who can live it. Just know we love you and we want you to be happy."

There was something in her mother's voice, something more than motherly affection. It told her to grab on to this chance at happiness with both hands.

"Thanks, Mom. I love you both."

"We love you, too. Good night, sweetie."

She ended the call and returned to her work, but her mind refused to focus on the task at hand. It was too busy analyzing the differences between Aaron and Darren. There were many. The more she thought about it, the more she wanted to get to know Aaron. What if she only felt this way because she was starved for the kind of reassuring attention he offered? The question that followed directly on the heels of that one was supremely smug. *Does it matter?* With a decision to let happen whatever was going to happen, she put her camera and laptop away and prepared for bed. As she slipped under the blankets of the bed in the loft, she sighed with the same contentment she'd felt earlier in Aaron's embrace.

Six

PEARL DROPPED HER CAR KEYS and purse on the counter and turned to Aaron. "You remember that conversation we had this morning about not seeing hide nor hair of Jerry Mackey?"

"Yeah," Aaron replied warily. "I take it he's turned up."

"I bumped into him just now as I was finishing my lunch."

He studied her face for a moment, trying to glean clues from her perplexed expression. "Oh?"

"He didn't have two words to say to me. Just nodded once—so I know he saw me—then ducked his head and scooted by. It wasn't exactly enough to figure out whether or not he's gotten the fool idea of revenge out of his fool head, but it did confirm that he's back in town."

"Which we already heard from his PO."

The phone rang, interrupting their conversation. Aaron waited while Pearl answered it, though he wasn't sure what else there was to say. Her admission only reminded him of that tragic day, and though he knew she was looking out for him, he really didn't feel like ruining the rest of his day with thoughts of Jerry Mackey and Erica's death.

"He's standing right in front of me, but you almost missed him, Nick," Pearl said to the caller.

Aaron frowned. Why was Nick calling the sheriff's department instead of his cell phone? Moments later, when he pulled the phone out of his pocket, he saw why. It was dead.

"I'll tell him. Mmm-hmm. You, too. Buh-bye." Pearl lifted her eyes again. "That was your brother."

"So I gathered. What'd he want?"

"He asked if you would pick up some screen and spline and also if you would mind fixing the screen door on the rental cabin after work since neither he nor your father have been able to get away from the ranch all week. He also said that the tenant—Skye, is it?—knows you're coming, so just head on over to the cabin."

Aaron's heart quickened and his lips curved at the thought of seeing Skye this afternoon. Fixing the screen door would give him the perfect excuse to visit her again, and he wondered if she would want to come over for dinner and to watch the Bobcats' game. Memories of the Gold Rush game, now two weeks' past, enveloped him with a dizzying combination of contentment and excitement. It struck him then that the mere thought of Skye had pushed Jerry Mackey clean out of his head. Interesting.

"Now, that's a smile I haven't seen on your face in quite some time," Pearl observed. "I'd hazard a guess you found yourself another lady friend. Your parents' tenant?"

Her words only made him grin more broadly, but he didn't confirm her suspicion. "I'll see you on Tuesday, Pearl."

"Mmm-hmm." The silver-haired dispatcher winked knowingly.

Lifting his hand in a wave of farewell, he trotted out to his pickup and headed for the hardware store. The anticipation of venturing over to Skye's cabin mounted as he gathered the supplies to replace the ragged old screen on the kitchen door. After a moment's hesitation, he splurged on the larger rolls of screen and spline, figuring he or Nick would likely be replacing the rest of the screens on the cabin before too much longer. He chuckled, amused that he had just created another excuse to visit Skye. He tossed a spline roller onto the counter with the rest of the materials because he didn't feel like wasting time digging in his garage for his. Any time he spent searching for the long-lost roller would be time he didn't spend with Skye.

While he waited for the cashier-in-training to ring up his sale, he wondered if Skye'd had a chance yet to go through her photos from Vince and Evie's wedding, Luke's first game, and hay stacking last weekend. From the few glimpses he'd had of her work, he knew she was talented, and admittedly, he wanted to see those events through her gifted eyes.

He headed home to change out of his uniform before driving to the cabin without stopping to pick up his daughter from his parents'. Nick would have undoubtedly passed on the word that he'd be late to get Jessie, knowing it would be easier for Aaron to repair the screen door without having his daughter under foot. When he parked his truck beside Skye's SUV, his heart beat faster with the anticipation at seeing her.

Stepping out of his vehicle, he noticed a distinct change in the air. What had been a subtle touch of autumn cool in Devyn was, here in Northstar, a biting crispness driven in by a brisk north wind. He inhaled slowly and caught the sharp scent of snow. Finally, he thought, studying the soft, fine gray clouds gathering around the mountains. He'd noticed a few springing up over the peaks on his drive home, but in his excitement to see Skye, he hadn't paid them any attention. With winter poised to exhale the first breath over Northstar, it would be a perfect evening to light a fire in his woodstove, graze on a homemade pizza, and snuggle on the couch with Skye and Jessie while they watched Luke's football game.

He bounded up the steps to the deck and knocked on the door. His excitement fizzled when Skye didn't answer. He knocked again, but still there was no response from within. Maybe she'd gone out with Vince and Evie. That seemed likely, since the newlyweds had arrived home from their honeymoon only last night. Undoubtedly, Skye would want to spend as much time with her best friend as she could while she was in Northstar.

Aaron ignored the trickle of disappointment brought by the thought of her leaving the valley, and with his tools and materials tucked under his arm, he let himself in. The front door was locked, confirming his suspicion that she'd gone out with Evie. The moment he stepped inside, he noticed that the cabin was chilly. Had she not turned on the furnace yet? He strode across the open living area, passing by the open door of the downstairs bedroom.

His heart lurched with surprise and something hotter when he spied Skye sitting at her desk with her back to the door. She appeared to be engrossed in her work, and craning his neck, Aaron saw the white cords of her ear buds and understood why she hadn't answered his knock. He let her be for the moment to settle his tools and the screen beside the kitchen door. Before he went back to the bedroom to let her know he was here, he checked the furnace located on the narrow wall between the bathroom and pantry.

He swore Nick had said he'd checked the level on the propane tank, but maybe he'd been wrong to assume his brother had also lit the pilot light on the furnace because there was no telltale blue glow in the little round window. Aaron stood and snatched the canister of long matches from the cupboard above the refrigerator.

With the dilemma of the furnace solved, he returned to the bedroom and lifted his hand to knock but hesitated. Skye, still sitting with her back to him, wore a figure-flattering, glittery gold sweater. The neckline dipped in a shallow V in the back, and her rich, dark hair was pulled up in a messy bun, affording him a tantalizing view of the elegant nape of her neck. For a moment, he couldn't find the breath to call her name. When she leaned down to look more closely at her computer screen, the bright glow from the window twisted and danced on her soft skin, drawing his gaze to the hint of the feminine ridges of her shoulder blades. Talk about a kick of desire right to the gut.

At last, he forced himself to break the trance and

knocked.

With a start, she jerked around in the chair, but smiled when she saw him.

"Hi," she said shyly. "Nick said you'd be by this afternoon. I guess I didn't realize how late it was."

"You *did* seem pretty engrossed. Your pilot light's lit, so you can turn on the heat now."

"Thank you."

"What are you working on?"

"Oh, just going through my shots from last weekend, picking out the best ones, and making some adjustments to enhance certain aspects of the shots I really like."

He stepped into the room and leaned over her shoulder with his hand braced on the back of the chair. He thought he spied Luke's Bobcat uniform peeking out from behind the window of the shot of the beaverslide she was working on. The photo in the window was spectacular and had been taken before they'd gotten to work. The light and shadow of early morning brought out details of the derek he normally didn't notice.

"That's a great shot," he remarked.

"You think this one's great, take a look at this one," she replied and opened another of the beaverslide, this time in action.

Aaron narrowed his eyes and studied the shot a little more closely. Somehow, she had captured the essence of hay stacking. A load of hay was just spilling over the top of the slide into the box, where Luke and Ben stood with pitchforks in hand and their faces turned away from the plume of hay dust. John Hammond sat in the driver's seat of the hoist, looking back over his shoulder while Aaron pushed the next load of hay toward the derek. Pat was busy clearing the pulleys of hay.

"That really captures… everything. Can I have a copy of this one?"

"Sure. I have another shot you'll probably want a copy of. Here."

She hid her photo-editing program, revealing her neatly organized desktop. The image on it was of Aaron, Jessie, and Luke before the Gold Rush game when Luke had given Jessie a high five on his way to the field to warm up. It was an incredibly poignant shot, especially when he considered everything Luke had accomplished to earn that uniform. The kid had come so far and overcome so much in his nineteen years, and Aaron was as proud of him as he knew Ben and June were. His gaze shifted to his daughter. The delight on her young face was exquisite. She looked so like Erica in that shot that his chest tightened.

"I definitely want a copy of that one," he murmured, nearly choking on the words. He cleared his throat. "The Cats are in Pocatello, Idaho, but the game'll be televised, and I'm hoping you'd like to come over and watch it with Jessie and me. Dinner's included, of course."

"I'd love to. What are we having?"

"Homemade pizza. Probably pepperoni, since that's Jessie's favorite."

"It's mine, too. That sounds great, Aaron. I can't wait."

"In that case, I'd better get the screen door fixed right quick."

Twenty minutes later, the screen door was done. Aaron gathered his tools and gave Skye a quick kiss on the cheek before stepping out onto the front deck. She followed him out.

"When did it get so chilly out?" she inquired. "It wasn't this cold when I went to lunch with Evie and Vince. Think it'll snow tonight?"

The excitement in her voice brought a smile to his face. "I'm betting so. Feels like snow. Smells like it."

"So, how much time should I give you before I head over to your place?"

"Oh, probably twenty or thirty minutes, depending on how long it takes me to detach my daughter from my nephew."

"I'll see you then. Wait. You're the house at the end of Aspen Creek Road, across the creek, right?"

"No, that's Nick and Beth's place. I'm the second to last, just before the road drops down to the creek."

"Oh, you have that beautiful wood-sided place with the red trim, wrap-around deck, big front windows, and a view to die for!"

"That's the one."

"I can't wait to see it."

"Then I'd better get out of here. See you in a bit."

It was more difficult than it should have been to turn away from Skye. Aaron made do with another quick kiss to her cheek and forced himself to walk down the steps, reminding himself that he'd see her again soon.

He stopped at his parents' house only long enough to get his daughter. He snuck out the door before his nephew realized Jessie hadn't returned from the bathroom to continue their game of bowling, but before he finished buckling Jessie in, he heard his mother call him from the front door of the ranch house. With an impatient sigh, he straightened and turned to face her.

"What's the rush?" she asked.

"Skye's coming over to watch the game with us."

"She is, is she?" Tracie smiled broadly. "In that case, I won't keep you. I assume you got the door fixed."

"I did. And lit the pilot light on the furnace for her."

Tracie touched a hand to his cheek. "Have I told you lately how proud I am of you?"

He shifted his weight restlessly, wondering what was on his mother's mind. "I'm sure you have. You've always made sure I know."

"Good. You're a good man, Aaron, and a wonderful father. I just wish you were happier."

"I *am* happy, Mom."

"Not like you were when Erica was alive. But… I see hints of that kind of happiness in you again. I just hope you won't get your heart broken if Skye isn't ready to jump into another relationship."

The topic made him uncomfortable. With his relationship—if he could even call it that yet—with Skye being so new, the last thing he wanted to think about was the likelihood that it would never have much chance of turning into something lasting. Her home and her career were in Washington, and she was only here for certain through the end of September. Only two more weeks, though she had mentioned more than once a desire to stay a bit longer.

"I'm not telling you to stay away, honey," Tracie said gently. "I'm just asking you to be careful."

He couldn't find the words to express his love and gratitude for his mother's support, so he just wrapped her in a hug that he hoped said it for him.

"Go. Have fun tonight."

"Thanks, Mom."

On the ride home, Jessie chattered on about her day with Will and their grandmother, and though Aaron listened with the appropriate nods and smiles and half-hearted questions to prompt her story when she faltered, he couldn't block the sadness that weighed down on him. He knew his mother was only looking out for him, but he wished she hadn't said anything about Erica, especially not after Pearl's mention of Jerry Mackey. He'd been looking forward to a fun night in with his daughter and Skye, a tasty pizza, and a football game, but now… he wasn't sure he'd be able to pull himself out of the old funk. The familiar, suffocating grief closed in around him like the clouds thickening around the peaks of the mountains above him.

"Are you okay, Daddy?" Jessie asked.

He glanced at her and tried to smile, but when she frowned in concern, he knew he'd failed. "I'm okay. Just thinking about your mommy again."

"Think about Skye instead," she suggested. "Because I don't want you to be sad tonight. I don't like it when you're sad."

He took her hand and kissed the back of it. "Thanks, pumpkin."

"Is she really coming over tonight? I heard you tell Grandma she was."

"Yep, she is," he replied. "In fact, she'll probably beat us home. You don't mind sharing our pizza with her, do you?"

"Nope! Are we gonna watch Luke's game on TV,

too?"

"That's the plan."

As he'd predicted, Skye had already arrived by the time he parked his truck in front of his house. She stood on the front deck, wrapped snuggly in a jacket, gazing up at the mountains with camera in hand. Despite the nagging sorrow, he couldn't help but notice how beautiful she was. The weak, golden light shining through holes in the deepening cloud cover ignited her loose-flowing hair, coaxing deep red highlights from the dark mane, and in the cold wind, her cheeks were rosy. As usual, it was her eyes that held his attention longest. There was such open, almost innocent wonder in them as she studied her surroundings, looking for the best shots.

Aaron glanced at the mountains. The peaks were now nearly hidden behind the clouds, and the first plumes of snow curled over the higher ridges, proving his weather forecasting skills correct. He watched Skye lift her camera and twist the lens to zoom and focus. Quietly, so as not to disrupt her, he helped Jessie out of her seat and asked his daughter to let Skye take her pictures. The command didn't work any better now than it had at Vince and Evie's wedding, and she raced up the steps and threw her arms wide in expectation of a hug. Skye obliged, beaming, and Aaron wished *he* had the camera so he could capture the moment.

"Welcome home," she said when he reached the deck.

For the second time in half an hour, he found himself overcome with emotion and unable to respond. It had been so long since a woman had stood on his deck to greet him after a long day at work, and though she wasn't Erica, her greeting was as endearing to him as any Erica had ever offered.

"You were right," she remarked, gesturing at the curls of snow drifting over the mountains. "Will it fall down here, too?"

"Probably, but we won't get much more than an inch or two, and it'll likely melt off by tomorrow afternoon."

"Snow in September." She shook her head and smiled. "I don't think I've ever seen that before."

"Well, now you have. I'm going in to start a fire in the woodstove and get the pizza going, but you're welcome to stay out here and take pictures as long as you like."

She glanced at her pinkening fingers and flexed them, then laughed softly. "Something tells me I won't be out here long."

By the time Skye came in, Aaron had let Chance in, started the fire, turned the TV on to the appropriate channel, and pulled the fixings out for pizza. She set her camera and bag on the dining room table—safely out of danger from the black Lab's exuberant prancing—and spent a few minutes getting to know the dog before joining Aaron in the kitchen. Jessie asked if she could throw the ball for Chance in the yard. Aaron agreed and watched the pair out the window for a few moments before turning his attention to dinner.

"I love this open floor plan," Skye remarked, gesturing around at the large area that included the living room, dining room, and kitchen in an airy, high-ceilinged L.

"Me, too. I'll give you a tour as soon as the pizza's in the oven."

"Sounds great. How can I help?"

He nodded to the pizza crust. "You're on sauce, and I'll get some cheese grated."

They worked quietly, which gave Aaron far too much time to think. After Pearl's news and his mother's comments, it was difficult to shake the memories of Erica. They flirted with him, beckoning him back to the shadowy world of grief. He wondered, as he always did, what he could have done differently, if there was something more he could have said or done to save his wife. He knew it was useless to ponder such questions, but that didn't stop them from tormenting him.

Absently, he passed Skye the pile of cheese he'd already grated so she could start spreading it on the pizza. He grabbed another chunk of cheese, but on the first slide down, his knuckles grazed the grater, and he swore. He couldn't remember the last time he'd tried to shred his own fingers, and tossed the grater and bowl into the sink before excusing himself. He'd managed to cut three knuckles, and by the time he reached the bathroom, blood began to trickle from the wounds. He cleaned and dressed them, then returned to the kitchen.

"Sorry about that," he said. "Gimme a second, and I'll…. Never mind. You already washed them. Thank you."

"You're welcome," Skye replied. "Are you all right?"

His lips twisted in chagrin. "I'll live."

"You seem distracted tonight, Aaron, so I'll ask again. Is everything all right?"

He regarded her wearily, hesitant to reply. This was supposed to be a fun night, he reminded himself, and he had no right to ruin it for Skye by bringing up his late wife. She didn't deserve to be relegated to the back seat. Not tonight, not ever. He started to shake his head and tell her not to worry about it, but the concern in her gaze stopped him. In this instance, perhaps honesty was best. Then she could decide if she was willing to get tangled up in his mess.

"Jerry Mackey's back in town."

"You saw him?"

He shook his head. "Pearl, our dispatcher, bumped into him. I don't know why it's bothering me so much. I already knew he was back in Devyn, but I guess Pearl seeing him just makes it more real. And, inevitably, thinking about Jerry Mackey makes me think about Erica… and that day."

Skye slipped her arms around his neck and held him tightly. A sigh shuddered through him, and he hugged her back, grateful beyond words for her support.

"I'm so sorry, Aaron," she whispered.

"Me, too. I didn't mean to ruin your evening."

"You haven't. I just wish I could help you."

"You are," he replied around the lump in this throat, clinging to her. "More than you know."

* * *

As promised, after the pizza was in the oven, Aaron gave Skye a tour of his house. It was a single-story, three-bedroom, two-bath home, and Aaron explained that his eldest uncle had built the house and lived in it until his divorce and subsequent decision to leave Northstar two years before Aaron and Erica's wedding. Aaron and Erica had bought the house from him for next to nothing.

The hall branched off from the center of the L of the main living space. On its right were the two smaller bedrooms with a bathroom separating them. The first was obviously Jessie's room, and the second appeared to be a rarely used computer room. On the left side of the hall was the master bedroom, which had its own bathroom.

At the very back of the house were a laundry and utility room and an enclosed porch that opened out onto the back portion of the wrap-around deck. A doggy door had recently been installed on the outer door of the enclosed porch, and the deck offered a commanding view of and access to the large, newly fenced backyard. She had no trouble imagining Chance as the pampered pooch, an image that was confirmed when she and Aaron returned to the living room to find both him and Jessie curled up on the recliner together. Aaron lifted a brow at the pair and shook his head, smiling.

"Yeah, I'm getting soft," he muttered before turning away to check on the pizza.

While he was distracted, Skye continued her perusal of his home. The décor was distinctly Western with a color scheme of red and wood tones, weathered-wood picture frames, an old wagon wheel hanging above the front door, and many other artifacts from around the ranch. Erica's feminine touches were still everywhere, from the red pillows on the big beige couch to the coordinating drapes, but the space was equally masculine. It spoke of harmony and balance, and Skye got the impression that Aaron hadn't changed much of anything since Erica's death, not because he was trying to keep her memory alive but because the style suited him. Skye found the house to be very warm and welcoming despite the niggling sense that this was another woman's home and she had no right to harbor any feelings beyond friendship for that woman's man. She folded her arms tightly across her chest and glanced sidelong at Aaron.

That she *did* feel something more than friendship for him was undeniable.

The feeling of trespassing on Erica's territory evaporated when she perused the family pictures arranged in a seemingly haphazard jumble on the wall separating the living room from the master bedroom. With medium brown hair and lively hazel eyes, Erica Hammond had been a beautiful woman, the kind who smiled with her whole being, confident but compassionate and giving. Skye couldn't imagine a woman like that would begrudge her even a romantic relationship with Aaron.

"She was gorgeous," Skye murmured when Aaron came to stand behind her.

He didn't say anything, but she looked over her shoulder to find him watching her with a faint frown, and his eyes said everything she needed to know. *You're beautiful, too*. He stroked his fingertips lightly down her neck, then gently tucked them beneath her jaw to turn her face more fully toward him and pressed his lips to hers in a featherlight kiss.

"Your daughter's watching," she murmured against his lips.

"I don't care," he whispered. Then he chuckled. "Besides, I'm pretty sure we've had her blessing since Vince and Evie's wedding."

He pulled her against him and lowered his lips to her neck. She shivered with pleasure, wishing she could beg him for more. The buzzer on the oven timer sounded, interrupting the tender moment, but he didn't seem to hear it.

"Aaron…."

"Yeah, yeah. I hear it."

"How can I help?"

"You," he answered, planting another quick kiss on her neck, "can help by plopping your shapely backside on the couch and getting comfortable."

She obeyed and curled up against the arm of the couch with her arms folded on the back and her chin resting on her forearms. With Aaron's attention directed elsewhere, she was free to watch him without him knowing. It fascinated her endlessly how comfortable he was in the kitchen. His combination of masculine power and effortless grace was irresistible. He wore a pair of faded jeans, and though they weren't the classic Wranglers, they hugged his narrow hips and classic cowboy backside in a most distracting way. The long-sleeved T-shirt he wore was tight enough to show off his toned upper body, and the muscles of his back, shoulders, and arms flexed beneath the soft, navy-blue fabric as he worked. Skye's lips quirked upward in appreciation. What she wouldn't give to run her hands over his body. Darren was more heavily muscled, but his musculature was entirely the product of the gym, and the conceit that came with it greatly detracted from the visual appeal. For reasons Skye had no hope of explaining, it was gratifying to know that much of Aaron's physique came from hard work on the ranch.

The object of her fascination glanced over his shoulder and caught her watching. "See something you like?" he asked.

"Yes, I do. You know, I never imagined a man in the kitchen could be so… sexy. Then again, maybe it's just you because Darren was a train wreck when it came to cooking."

Aaron offered her that charming one-sided grin.

"Well, thank you, ma'am."

He carried the pizza and some paper plates into the living room and set everything on the log coffee table. "Dig in. No, Chance, not you. Get off the chair, dog, and go lie down."

Chance slunk off the recliner and flopped on the floor in front of the television with a grunt. Moments later, a black cat ambled into the living room, lifted his head to sniff, and joined the dog.

"That's Spook, or as we usually call him, Pooky," Aaron said. "He thinks he's a dog."

"I can see that," Skye remarked, noticing how the big cat eyed the table with the same intent expression as the black Lab.

Half an hour later, when the game started, they were still grazing on the delicious pizza. Aaron sat with his back propped against the back of one side of the plush, L-shaped couch and his legs stretched out on the shorter bench. Skye had—at his invitation—snuggled up to his side with her back against him and his free arm tucked casually around her shoulders. Jessie frequently glanced in their direction, grinning slyly each time as if the sight of her father and Skye curled up together was most pleasing.

In contrast to the excitement she'd felt being in the stands at the first game, Skye was now utterly mellowed by the snow falling outside and the blissful warmth of the fire in the woodstove. She watched the game almost passively, enjoying the company more, amazed by how comfortable she was with Aaron. Setting her empty plate on the coffee table, she tucked her arm around Aaron's chest, grateful for the balm of his patient, soothing presence.

Moments later, Jessie crawled alongside her father, wedging herself between him and the couch cushions. She met Skye's gaze and grinned.

"Feel loved yet, Aaron?"

"Mmm-hmm," he replied. "I like it."

They watched the game like that, cuddled together on the couch almost like a family. Briefly, Skye wondered if it was smart, allowing herself to get so attached to Aaron and Jessie because it would only make leaving Northstar to return to her life in Washington that much harder. Unwilling to sour her perfect evening with those thoughts, she firmly closed her mind to them and concentrated on the game. It was a tense one, with the lead flip-flopping between the Bobcats and the Idaho State Bengals.

With only twenty seconds left in the game, the Bobcats were down by a field goal and deep in their own territory. Skye watched the players return to the field after their last time-out, and knew what was coming as soon as the two teams lined up. Luke would pass, but the Idaho State defense would undoubtedly go for the blitz and the sack. Sure enough, there it was. Luke quickly made the pass and shot down the field. When the receiver lobbed the ball back to him, he was wide open.

"He's at the thirty, the twenty, the ten! Touchdown Montana State!" the announcer cheered. "Now, you all know I'm a die-hard Bengals fan, but I gotta hand it to the Bobcats' quarterback. That kid is quick."

"Damn right he is," she remarked, beaming.

When no one responded to her comment, she glanced up at Aaron and smiled. Despite the intensity of the final quarter of the game, both he and Jessie were sound asleep. She had taken enough pictures of dads asleep with their kids that the poignancy of it shouldn't still affect her so deeply, but as she sat up to study Aaron and his daughter, something stirred deep in her heart. Unlike the posed images, this was real and precious. Tonight felt so right. There was something powerful between her and Aaron that had been missing in her marriage—an openness and honesty she and Darren had never shared.

Aaron and Jessie weren't hers, but she wanted them to be. The fact that she'd met them only three weeks ago seemed inconsequential. Skye glanced at the pictures on the wall above her. More worrying than the short time she'd known Aaron was the possibility that he might never be able to let go of his wife.

"Aaron," she whispered, nudging him.

His eyes flickered open. "Hmm?"

"The game's over, and your daughter's asleep."

He frowned, then kissed the top of Jessie's head and carefully pulled himself more fully upright. "What'd I miss?"

"Well, I'm not sure. But the Bobcats pulled off an offensive blitz, and Luke ran in for the winning touchdown with no time to spare."

"Damn. I might have to see if June and Ben recorded the game so I can see that." He yawned. "Sorry we fell asleep on you."

"That's okay."

"Give me a few minutes while I get Jessie into bed, and I'll be back out."

"How about I help?"

He opened his mouth to speak, and for a fleeting

moment, Skye thought he would object. Then he said simply, "Thanks."

Skye slid off the couch to get out of his way.

"Jessie, honey," he crooned. "Time for bed, pumpkin."

When the girl murmured and snuggled more tightly into her father, he swung his legs over the edge of the couch and simply lifted her with him as he stood. Skye followed him down the hall to Jessie's bedroom and grabbed a nightgown out of the top drawer of the dresser. As soon as the little girl realized Skye was still there, her eyes sprung wide, and she launched into an interrogation about the game. Skye obliged, detailing the plays as Jessie changed into her nightgown and headed into the bathroom to brush her teeth and hair, then helped Aaron tuck his daughter into bed. She leaned against the dresser while he read Jessie a bedtime story.

"Can I have a kiss, Skye? Right here?" Jessie asked, pointing to her cheek.

"You bet, sweetie." Skye leaned down and pressed her lips to the little girl's silky cheek. When she straightened to meet Aaron's gaze, there was something in his eyes that made her heart trip; beneath the exhaustion, she saw a shadow of pain wrapped in a glimmer of hope.

"Good night, Jessie. Sweet dreams," he whispered and ushered Skye out of the room. He turned the lights off, but left the door open.

They retreated to the kitchen, and Aaron leaned against the counter, staring in the direction of his daughter's room. He took a deep breath and let it out with a shudder. Skye curled her arms around his ribs, holding him tight as she rested her head on his shoulder, and wished she could erase the sorrow from his eyes.

"I am so tired of being alone."

"You're not alone right now," Skye murmured. "I'm right here."

With a thumb under her chin, he tipped her head back and lowered his lips to hers. As he kissed her tenderly, she slid her hands up his chest, delighted by the feel of smooth muscle beneath her palms. Daringly, she dragged her fingertips down again before slipping her hands beneath his shirt. His skin was warm and soft, and when he broke the kiss to let out a low groan of pleasure, desire rippled through Skye. It had been a long time since sex had been anything more than an obligation and even longer since she'd wanted a man like she wanted Aaron. The shock of that realization made her jerk back.

"I'm sorry," she sputtered. His eyes were closed and the muscle in his jaw twitched. Guilt gnawed at her, and she wondered if his groan had been of pleasure or disgust. "That was such an invasion of your privacy."

"Do you hear me complaining?"

When he opened his eyes, desire had burned away every last trace of sorrow. His irises were slim threads of blue rimming dilated pupils, and when she tentatively rested her hand on his chest again, she felt his heart racing. Those obvious signs of desire reignited her own.

Breathlessly, she remarked, "I feel like I should think we're moving too fast, but everything about this feels right."

He didn't respond but instead wrapped his hands around her upper arms and kissed her again with a distracting intensity. Suddenly, he pulled away.

"I have to stop now," he muttered. "Or I won't be able to."

Skye was about to beg him to keep going, but sanity returned. "Jessie."

He nodded. "I doubt she's asleep again yet." With a laugh, he added, "I *knew* dating as a single father couldn't possibly be as easy as it's been so far."

Because she wasn't quite ready to leave, she offered to help him with the dishes and refused to take no for an answer. They flirted and teased each other, and by the time the dishes were dried and put away, it was after ten. He walked her out to her car.

Tiny snowflakes swirled around them, glittering in the glow of the porch light, but the ground was still mostly bare. She shouldn't have any trouble getting home, though the thought of her empty cabin was not appealing after her evening with Aaron.

"See you soon?" he asked, leaning in her open car window.

"You bet," she replied and kissed him. "Are you free tomorrow?"

"I have to help move cows tomorrow, but I should have the evening free. Shall we go out—just you and me?"

"Jessie is more than welcome to join us," Skye replied.

"I know, but I want you to myself for once."

"All right, then. See you tomorrow evening." For good measure, she kissed him one more time.

Seven

A GIDDY SMILE LIFTED SKYE'S face as she read the email from her client's book-publishing friend. Eloise had loved the sample images Skye had sent of the Hammonds' ranch and had given her the go ahead to gather the photos she wanted to use, suggesting the book focus specifically on the Lazy H Ranch. Eloise wrote, *Let's call it "Modern Traditions: Keeping the Traditions of Montana Ranching Alive" or something along those lines.* Skye briefly wondered how the Hammonds would feel about having their ranch featured in the book. They'd given her permission to take as many photographs as she wanted and to use them, but that was a little different than having their ranch spotlighted. She made a note to ask Aaron on their date this evening.

She opened the next email. It was from her assistant, detailing the goings-on back home with the business. Skye's mouth fell open. Twenty-five clients for senior pictures and twelve weddings to schedule? As she continued down the list of requests Joel had sent her, the realization hit her that she needed to take a trip back to Washington to deal with it all. Really, she should probably just end her vacation and head home early, but she wasn't ready to leave Northstar. More to the point, she wasn't ready to say goodbye to Aaron and Jessie. It might be foolish, but she wanted to see if this thing building between her and Aaron was something special, or if it was only a wishful illusion rising from the ruins of her broken marriage.

No, she thought. It wasn't an illusion. At least, not entirely. There was something between her and Aaron, something more than the undeniable sexual attraction that set Skye's body to humming whenever she was around Aaron, but after her failed marriage to Darren, she didn't entirely trust her feelings. He was patient and compassionate, laid-back and charming, and the exact opposite of Darren. What if she was only falling for him because he was so different from her ex?

She snorted. There was no use denying that she *was* falling for him, but what if the novelty wore off and nothing remained to fill the void?

In that case, a trip to Washington to deal with her business might be a good thing. It would give her time to clear her head a little, to ponder what she felt for Aaron without being distracted by him. If she were honest with herself, the fear that she was plunging ahead too quickly was very real. For the first time in her life, she was free to do as she pleased—more importantly, she was free to rediscover herself—and the last thing she wanted to do was jump into another serious relationship before she was ready.

Skye stood and wandered out into the kitchen. With a twist of her lips, she pushed through the screen door Aaron had fixed only yesterday and stood on the ramp just outside. The inch of snow that had fallen in the valley overnight had long since melted, but the mountains were still dusted with white, and though the sun had beamed all day, the crisp bite of autumn was still in the air. Everything was fresh and clean, and the world smelled amazing. She inhaled deeply the fragrance of damp sagebrush and pine and narrowed her eyes, noting the sharp clarity of the light. It was as if the snow had cleared away every last particle of summer's haze. When she turned her gaze toward the stand of quaking aspen behind the cabin, she spotted a few clumps of leaves that were already turning. She had to come back for their autumn show; there was no arguing that point. The thought firmed her decision to go back to Washington for only a few days and return to Northstar to finish her vacation.

Hearing the rumble of a truck and the crunch of tires on gravel, she turned and went back inside. Aaron was early, and she hadn't even started getting ready for their date. She stepped into the bathroom and stared at her reflection for a moment, at the simple ponytail and the makeup-free face. Aaron wasn't Darren, she reminded herself, and he didn't seem to give a damn about whether or not she wore makeup. In fact, he seemed to like her without it better, and besides, they were heading to the Ramshorn with the plan to take a dip in the hot springs after dinner.

A knock sounded on the front door.

"Come on in!" she called as she snatched a towel

from the bathroom before racing upstairs to grab her swim-suit. She glanced over the log handrail of the loft, and the corner of her mouth lifted as he walked inside. *Hello, sexy.* How was it that he could look so good in a long-sleeved T-shirt and jeans?

"Are you ready?" he asked.

"Almost. Just gotta grab my swimsuit, and I'll be right down."

Ten minutes later, Aaron parked by the brick-red log building that was the Ramshorn's pool house. He gallantly opened Skye's door and offered his hand to help her out. She didn't let it go as he shut the truck door behind her, and with their hands entwined, they walked down the packed dirt driveway to the lodge. The heat of his skin against hers warmed away the autumn chill and kindled a slow-burning blaze of desire. Before they ascended the ramp to the door of the restaurant, Skye pulled Aaron to a stop and tucked herself into his willing arms. Standing on her toes with her hands pressed against his back, she kissed him. Without hes-itation, he kissed her back, and she smiled against his lips.

"Feeling a little frisky, are we?" he inquired.

"Maybe just a bit. It must be the fall air."

"Mmm. I love this time of year."

The door of the lodge creaked open, and Skye glanced up to see Luke standing on the covered porch with a dishrag tossed over his shoulder. Grinning, he said, "Do we need to book a room for you two?"

Skye laughed. "I already have a cabin, remember?"

The young man chuckled and braced his forearms on the porch railing. Skye guessed he must be taking a break.

"Hey, that was a great last-second play last night," she

said.

"Thanks," he replied. "Your table's ready for you, whenever you're ready for it."

With an amused shake of his head, he went back inside.

Skye looked up at Aaron and pressed her lips briefly to his again before taking his hand and leading him inside. Sure enough, the Conners had reserved a table for them beside the northernmost windows, complete with an arrangement of fall-colored flowers accented with a twig of golden aspen leaves and a flickering pillar candle.

"Was this their idea or yours?" Skye asked.

"A little of both. My idea but their design."

"It's perfect."

Aaron pulled out her chair for her, and moments after he'd taken his seat, Luke came over with their menus.

"Welcome back to the Ramshorn," he greeted.

"Football star, photographer, and waiter," Skye remarked. "How on earth do you have time for a social life?"

"I don't," he replied. There was a faint trace of bitterness in his voice, but his next words and the charming smile he flashed her contradicted it. "But I don't particularly want one right now, either. What may I bring you to drink?"

Skye glanced at Aaron, wondering if she'd crossed a line with her attempt at humor. He shrugged. "I'll take a Coke," she told Luke.

"Aaron?"

"Same."

"I'll be right back."

Skye leaned across the table to whisper, "Did I say something wrong?"

Aaron shook his head. "No. Luke likes to stay busy. Keeps him from thinking of less pleasant things."

Time to change the subject, Skye told herself. She leaned back in her chair and decided now was the perfect time to bring up the book. "So, I heard back from my client's book-publisher friend—she sent an email this morning. She loved the shots and gave me the go-ahead to put the book together. She suggested I focus on how you and your family are 'keeping the traditions alive.' Too cheesy? And do you think your parents would mind…?"

"I'm sure they won't mind at all, and no, it's not too cheesy. But if you're going to do that, you should probably include a few other ranches because we aren't the only ones. The Royal R probably does even more."

"The Royal R?"

"Jim and Jessie Robinsons' place—they're Erica's parents. It's up in the Crystal Valley just over the pass. The Royal R is still a working ranch, but they opened the place up to guests a while back, and they teach their guests about ranching and let them help with basic chores. People seem to get a kick out of that."

"Ranch work has changed a lot in the last few decades, hasn't it?"

"Yeah. With all the new equipment—like the round baler my dad was hesitant to buy—a guy can do a lot more work. We don't need to employ as many hands, but we still do. There are a few men in this community who still earn their living as cowboys, and if ranchers like my father were to let go of those traditions, many of those men would be out of a job." Aaron leaned back and knitted his fingers behind his head. "It's a way of life, so yeah, we try to keep the traditions going. We still stack a lot of the hay we use—mostly in the old-fashioned way, even though we use tractors now instead of horses—because it's something we want to hang on to."

"And what about you? You help with the ranch, but it's not your life. You have your job with the sheriff's department. Did you decide the pursue that avenue because you couldn't make a living on the ranch or because you wanted to?"

"I wanted to." He frowned for a moment. "I'm glad I didn't quit when Erica died because I do love my job."

"Did you almost quit?"

He nodded. "I had a hard time getting past the fact that if I hadn't been a sheriff's deputy, I wouldn't have been the one to arrest Jerry Mackey and his cousin and Erica might still be alive."

At the mention of his wife, Skye flinched. His tone was so full of regret that she wondered if he'd actually gotten past that belief. "I assume you took some time off."

"Yeah. About four months. I damned near didn't go back, but Pearl—our dispatcher—and Pat were rather adamant about me not giving up."

"I, for one, am glad they convinced you to stay on," Luke remarked, returning with their Cokes.

"Thanks, kid."

"All right, what can I get you? The special tonight is prime rib with real mashed potatoes and steamed broccoli."

"That sounds fantastic," Skye said. "I'll just take the special."

"Make that two," Aaron said.

During dinner, Aaron graciously humored Skye as

she quizzed him about his family's ranch. At one point during a brief moment of quiet in the restaurant, June, Ben, and Luke joined them, but otherwise, Skye had Aaron entirely to herself. She rather liked it.

After dinner, they headed to the hot springs. The crisp autumn weather was perfect for soaking, and as much as she loved the feel of Aaron's arms around her as they sat together in the smaller, hotter pool, there were too many people—including several locals who stopped to chat—and she selfishly wanted him all to herself. So, after a short thirty minutes in the hot springs, Skye suggested they head back to her cabin.

"Are you sure?" he asked.

"Mmm-hmm," she purred, straddling his waist for a moment. She kissed him, then slipped away to get changed.

When they arrived back at her cabin, Skye didn't immediately go in. Instead, she stood on the deck, staring at the mountains and chewing on her bottom lip. With a sideways glance at Aaron, she understood what she wanted. Last night, when she'd impulsively slipped her hands under his shirt, she'd awakened a desire she hadn't felt in years, and it hadn't cooled in the intervening hours. But she was afraid he would find her lacking, as Darren obviously had, and didn't know if she could handle that kind of rejection so soon after the finalization of her divorce.

"What's wrong?" Aaron asked, slipping his arm around her.

"Can I be completely honest with you?"

"Of course."

She shifted her gaze from the mountains to his concerned face. After such a short time, she shouldn't be able to find such comfort or familiarity in that handsome visage, but she did. It was as if they'd been friends for years, and she knew instinctively that she could trust him with her secrets and doubts, that he wouldn't judge her.

"Intimacy has never been easy or natural for me," she said slowly, trying to find the right words to adequately explain how she felt. "I've always been self-conscious, and with Darren, I always felt like I was doing it wrong. I always felt… awkward… with him. Maybe it's stupid, but I can't help feeling like I drove Darren to sleep with those other women because I couldn't satisfy him."

Without warning or restraint, Aaron turned fully toward her, clasped her face with both hands, and kissed her with such fierce demand that she forgot what she was worried about and gave in. She sank into him, sliding her hands up and around his ribs and digging her fingers into the meat of his back. At his growl, she pressed her breasts against his chest. There was no doubt, no shyness, no reserve. Only blatant and raw need. Delighted by how the length of Aaron's hard body fit against hers, she let her hands play, exploring the lines and contours of his back, arms, shoulders, chest, neck, jaw… everything she could reach.

He leaned against the railing and, with his hands under her rump, he hoisted her off the ground. She gripped his waist with her thighs and threaded her arms around his neck. The desire that dilated his eyes was intoxicating, as was the way he tipped his head back and let his eyelids slide closed as she combed her fingers back through his dark blond hair.

"I call bullshit," Aaron whispered, opening his eyes again. "You are… incredible."

She trailed her lips along the line of his jaw, and he gripped her upper arms to push her away.

"Skye."

The plea in his voice simultaneously begged her for more and commanded her to stop. She met his gaze, confused.

"We have to stop."

"Why?"

"I don't want to do anything before you're ready."

Taking a deep breath to cool the fire, she allowed herself a few moments to consider his words. She should be appalled at herself for her uncharacteristically brazen physicality. After all, she had still been married only a few weeks ago. Instead, she realized that she wanted Aaron like she'd never wanted Darren. Even those first few, hormone-driven encounters when she and Darren were in their late teens paled in comparison to what Aaron made her feel and want with the lightest touch. She probed the thought, searching for cracks and finding none. Far more intriguing, there was no fear that she would disappointment Aaron. Where there had always been pressure, now there was only contentment and a sense of rightness… and curiosity.

She leaned back in Aaron's arms, tilted her head, and studied him first with a photographer's eye. The westering sun limned his blond hair like a glowing halo, creating a breathtaking picture. Right then, he wasn't just sexy. He was beautiful in every sense of the word.

He was giving her an easy out, but she didn't want it.

"I want this," she murmured. "I want you."

For a moment, she thought he'd argue, but instead, he widened the V-neck of her sweater with infinite tenderness to bare her shoulder. Cool air hit her naked skin, and goose bumps rose. Then, with a supporting arm wrapped still around her shoulders and a hand buried in her hair, Aaron lowered his head to kiss her neck and collarbone, and the warmth of his lips sent an entirely different kind of shiver through her. She arched into him. Even if they never spoke again after tonight, she knew she would never regret sleeping with him.

"Are you sure?" he asked.

"More sure than I've been of anything in a long time."

"At any time, if you want me to stop…. If you change your mind…."

"Something tells me I won't. And lucky for us, I'm still on the pill."

"Why?" Aaron asked, frowning in concern.

His tone told her that he suspected her ex's influence in that decision. She briefly considered giving a blasé response but couldn't bring herself to do it. "Until my divorce was final, I wasn't too sure I would actually go through with it, so I figured it was better to be safe than sorry. And after it was a done deal…." She wiggled her brows. "Well, I met this sexy Montana cowboy, and I guess I was hopeful he might someday take me to bed."

He set her down gently, and as soon as her feet touched the deck, she went to the front door to unlock it and step inside. She twined her fingers with Aaron's and pulled him toward the stairs before her habitual shyness returned. He yanked on her hand before they'd crossed the living area and spun her toward him with the same agile grace he'd demonstrated at Vince and Evie's wedding.

Instead of continuing the dance, he took her face in his hands again and kissed her with the same restrained hunger he'd had that night. Skye's pulse tripped deliciously.

"I don't care what lies your ex-husband told you." He lightly kissed each cheek, then her lips again. "You are an amazing woman, Skye Hathaway."

She stared into his eyes, dazzled by the emotion shimmering in their blue depths. "How long has it been for you, Aaron?"

"A while."

"I know you said you and June never…. Has there been anyone since Erica?"

He winced at the mention of his wife. "Only one. And it meant nothing."

The bitterness that crept into his voice told her that he wasn't trying to make her feel better or marginalize the experience but rather that he wished it *had* meant something. She had been entirely correct in thinking there was nothing quick or shallow about Aaron Hammond. Whatever youthful frivolity he might've once possessed had long since been left behind.

And what about this? Us? Do we mean something? Skye was afraid to ask the question, though she desperately wanted the answer. Before she could find the courage to give voice to her concern, he kissed her again, then tucked an arm behind her knees and swept her off her feet. Her heart pounded with anticipation as he carried her up the stairs.

"Are you still sure about this?" he asked huskily, lowering her onto the bed.

"Absolutely."

Relief washed over his features, and he laid her down

and proceeded to slowly and tantalizingly remove her shoes and socks. He spent a few moments to massage her feet and rub his hand up her calves and shins. Positioning his hips between her knees, he shifted his attention—and his hands—to her torso, diving under her shirt. With leisure and reverence, he pushed her shirt up, smoothing his hand over her skin and leaving a path of kisses from the low waist of her jeans up her belly and ribs. Gradually, as his touches shifted from an unhurried adoration to a more aggressive exploration, the tingles dancing along her nerve endings grew into an aching heat.

She wiggled beneath him and pulled her sweater over her head. When she tossed it to the floor, he tucked his arms along her sides with his hands beneath her shoulder blades and continued his increasingly demanding ministrations. Her bra soon followed her sweater onto the rug, and she inhaled sharply as Aaron cupped her naked breasts in his hands, massaging her to aching need. When he gently flicked her nipple with his thumb, she swore under her breath.

Eager to explore the planes of his body—with permission this time—she tugged at the hem of Aaron's shirt.

"Off," she said.

With a chuckle, he obeyed, sitting back on his heels as he yanked the shirt over his head and cast it aside. Giving her newfound confidence free reign, Skye sat up and pushed him down onto the mattress. Swinging a leg over him, she straddled his waist, and heat exploded. Even through his jeans, his arousal was plainly evident. For a moment, she ignored it and gazed at him, enchanted by how the evening sunlight streamed through the loft's dormer window and painted his body with golden light and sharp shadow.

"You are so beautiful," she murmured, tracing her fingertips along the lines between light and dark on his torso. She followed the paths of her fingers with her palms, then her lips, thrilled when his skin prickled with goose bumps.

"And you are breathtaking," he whispered, snatching her hand and brushing his lips across her palm before relinquishing it so she could continue her exploration.

As she played, he freed her hair from its ponytail to let it fall loose over his chest. He threaded his fingers through it, then curled up to kiss her. When he wrapped her in his arms, nearly crushing her, an unfamiliar emotion rushed through her. It was more potent than the most intimate caress because it went straight to her heart.

"I need you," he whispered with his cheek pressed against her chest.

Somehow, she knew he wasn't talking about sex, though his erection was ample evidence that he needed her in that way, too. His voice was thick with raw vulnerability, and she clung to him. She shimmied out of her jeans and panties, then tugged his jeans and plain navy boxers down his long legs before tucking herself back into his embrace. The muscles in her thighs tensed as she hovered over his lap, and the warmth of his skin against hers, combined with the anticipation of what was to come, had her aching for him. There would be time later to further explore his body. Right now, her own demanded release. Boldly, she curled her fingers around him to hold him in position as she sank into his lap and took him into her.

The relief of penetration was exquisite. She was ready

for him, so there was no pain or discomfort. She gathered him into her arms and kissed him gently.

"You feel so good," he said softly.

"So do you."

Sinking back onto the bed, he slid his hands over her shoulders and down her back to grip her hips. She let him guide their pace, suddenly shy and unsure of herself. When her old doubts began to creep into her mind, she slammed the door on them and let her body do the thinking. She concentrated on how he filled her completely and reveled in the feel of skin against skin.

"Come on, sweetheart," Aaron whispered. "Let go. Just feel."

Sensations like she'd never experienced crashed through her, and she gripped him with her legs, falling into an undulating rhythm. She pushed down and drove him deeper into her, rose a little, then pushed down again, searching for release. When he lifted his hips to meet her, she moaned, and a pleased smile curved her lips. He slowed their pace, allowing her to more fully enjoy the feel of him buried deep inside her, then, with rising urgency, thrust more quickly. Pressure built until she thought she would fracture, and finally, she plunged over the edge. She trembled with the force of her orgasm. Half a heartbeat later, Aaron groaned as he too found release. She pulled him up and into her arms as he throbbed inside her, clinging to him to keep upright as her body continued to quiver.

Skye wondered suddenly and unexpectedly if she was falling in love with him. So newly divorced, she didn't know if it was possible. Hell, she didn't even know if she would recognize real love, but she felt something for Aaron that was far stronger than anything she'd ever felt for Darren. Was this insatiable need to be near Aaron love or was it only gratitude for how he was helping her recover her sense of self-worth?

Unable to answer the questions swarming in her mind now that the fervor of lovemaking was fading, she pulled away from Aaron so she could lie down beside him. Maybe her answer was right there in her need to be close to him. She wrapped her arm across his chest with her hand tucked beneath him, her head on his shoulder, and her legs entwined with his, in no hurry to end this wonderful experience.

"I've never fallen into bed before," she remarked.

"That wasn't falling into bed," Aaron replied. "I *have* fallen into bed—when I was young and stupid and didn't know any better—and that can't begin to compare with this."

"It's never been like this for me," Skye said. "If I'd known sex could be like that...."

She let the sentence hang, unwilling to ruin the moment by mentioning Darren.

"It matters who you're with. There's only one other woman who has ever made me feel like you just did."

"Your wife."

Aaron didn't respond, but he didn't need to, and Skye chided herself for mentioning Erica. So much for not ruining the moment. To his credit, Aaron only tightened his arms around her. She wondered what he was thinking but couldn't bring herself to risk a glance at his face, afraid that she would see memories of his wife swimming in his eyes. Right now, she didn't want to share him with anyone, especially not the woman who still owned his heart.

* * *

Aaron wished Skye hadn't left the metaphorical door open for Erica to walk through. As guilt pummeled him, he was glad they were in the cabin and not his house. He tightened his arms around the woman in his arms, trying to ignore the confusion and irritation stirred by his conflicting thoughts. Erica was gone, and what Skye made him feel—not just physically but emotionally as well—had the potential to rival the love he'd shared with his wife, so it wasn't too hard to figure out why he felt like he'd betrayed Erica. But dammit, it had been more than long enough, and like he'd told Skye last night, he was tired of being alone. He refused to let his grief destroy another chance at happiness.

"I wish you could stay," Skye said. "I kind of like this. But I know you have to go pick Jessie up."

He turned his face to her and kissed the top of her head. "I have the early shift again, so she's staying with my folks tonight."

"So… you can stay?"

"I probably shouldn't. I have to get up at two, and I don't want to wake you. Besides, something tells me that if I stay, I won't be getting much sleep."

She smiled at him but sighed. "Damn."

He lingered in bed with her until the sun disappeared behind the western peaks, then flipped the covers back, trying hard not to look at Skye's gloriously naked body. And failing miserably. She was stunning. Slender and toned but with delicate features that contrasted the strength she possessed. Her legs were long and elegant, her waist was trim, and her breasts were firm and perfect. He longed to skim

163

his hands over her gorgeous body again, to take his time exploring each and every feminine curve of her, and to see that radiant desire ignite in her eyes again. Another round was damned tempting, despite the guilt still pulsing through him, but as it was, he'd be lucky to get four hours of sleep by the time he got home and got everything settled for the night. As he dressed, he fought to keep the thoughts of Erica and questions about his feelings for Skye at bay. If he gave in to any of them, he wouldn't be able to sleep at all.

When he sat down on the edge of the bed to pull on and lace up his work boots, Skye scooted over to him and curled herself around him, folding her hands against his chest and resting her chin on his shoulder.

"Are you all right?" she inquired.

He kissed her over his shoulder, searching for the right words. Unable to find them, he replied, "Yeah. Why?"

"You seem a little… solemn."

"Just tired."

"Don't tell me that little bit of exercise wiped you out."

He chuckled and kissed her again. "Well, I did just turn thirty-one a few weeks ago. Can't keep up with a young thing like you."

She splayed her fingers and dragged her hands sensuously over his chest, and he nearly groaned. "I highly doubt that."

"Well, thank you, ma'am. Honestly, though, I do need to get some sleep. Two o'clock isn't that far away."

He pulled his long-sleeved T-shirt over his head and stood. Ignoring the desire that flared at the sight of her naked body, he leaned down to kiss her again before heading for the stairs. It felt wrong, leaving right now, but he *did* need to get home and get to bed so he wouldn't be completely exhausted at work tomorrow.

Skye dressed hurriedly in her pants and sweater without bothering with her undergarments and followed him downstairs. He pulled her into his arms and smoothed his thumb across her cheek.

"I should get going," he said.

"I know."

With his arm tucked around her waist, they stepped outside. Aaron inhaled deeply, soothed by the cool, fresh air, but he didn't smile. Instead, he tightened his arm around the woman at his side.

"Are you okay with this?" she asked, frowning as she pulled away to look at him.

"Please don't."

"Don't what?"

"Ask that," he replied. "I'm a little raw right now, and I don't want to say anything to hurt you. That's the last thing I want."

Her honey-colored eyes narrowed in understanding. "Ah."

"Making love to you was incredible, but what I feel for you brings a lot of things to the surface. Things I wish weren't there." Aaron swore under his breath. This was exactly what he *didn't* want to happen. "I don't want to feel this way, Skye. I want to be able to give you everything I have and everything I am, but—"

"It's been almost five years, Aaron. If Erica loved you as much as I know you still love her, I can't believe she'd want you to continue suffering." Her chin trembled. "I don't regret being with you, but if you can't let Erica go, please tell me now because I will *not* compete with her. I've been competing with other women for Darren most of my adult life, and I won't do it anymore. I deserve better, and thanks to you, I actually believe that now."

"Skye...."

"I need to head back to Washington for a few days to take care of some business. Maybe that'll give us both some time to think about what we want to do now."

With tears brimming in her eyes, she turned and went inside, closing the cabin door quietly behind her. He winced. A slam would have been preferable, though the snick of the lock jarred him just as thoroughly.

He stared at the closed door for several long moments, knowing it was probably a bad idea to let those thoughts ferment but understanding that she was right. The pervasive feeling that he'd somehow betrayed his wife meant that he still had a lot to come to terms with, and he didn't want to drag Skye through the mess of trying to sort it all out. At last, he turned away and walked out to his truck with a heavy heart, vowing to do as Skye suggested and hoping it wasn't already too late to undo the damage he'd just caused.

Eight

SKYE STOOD AT THE GLASS front door of her photography studio a few blocks north of downtown Poulsbo and watched Eloise Philips stride out to a Lexus sedan so new it still had temporary stickers in the window. Though the senior editor and CEO of the small publishing house wasn't someone Skye would normally spend much time with, she was excited to be working with Eloise on the photography book. She doubted she'd make much money off it, but it'd be a nice addition to her résumé and the list of her accomplishments on her website. More to the point, though she didn't want to admit why, this book project was close to her heart.

When Eloise drove off, Skye paused to stare up at the Douglas firs that towered over her studio. Even after three days back in Western Washington, their height still felt foreign to her eyes, which had become accustomed to the shorter, slimmer lodgepole pines that blanketed the mountains around Northstar. She'd grown up here, made her life here, but she couldn't shake the nagging sensation of being a visitor.

"Joel, what would you do if I decided to stay in Northstar?"

"What do you mean, boss?" the young man asked.

She turned to face him and crossed the room to his desk with deliberate, pointed steps. The question had come out of nowhere, but now that it was out, she couldn't ignore it. Looking through the images she'd selected for the book with Eloise had stirred a poignant longing and a regret that she had left Northstar without talking to Aaron again. It had been four days since they'd made love, and she could still feel every breathtaking sensation. Her cheeks flushed, and she forced those memories to the back of her mind, but not quickly enough. Joel's brows lifted, and he her flashed a grin.

"Interesting," he said. "This wouldn't have anything to do with a certain hunky sheriff's deputy Lindsay mentioned?"

"Dammit, Linds," Skye muttered, far more amused than annoyed. Sighing, she replied, "Yes."

"You're serious about him, then," Joel observed. "Lindsay wasn't sure."

"Honestly, I don't know how serious we are."

"We?"

"Well, I'm not sure if he's ready to let go of his wife yet. And being with him means I would eventually have to relocate to Northstar—he'd never come here, because he just belongs there—and I don't know that I'm willing to give up my business. I worked hard to build it into what it is."

"Yet you ask me what I'd do if you went back to Montana and stayed. Besides, you're talented, and you've built it once, so you can build it again. Better because now you know what to do and what not to do."

"There isn't nearly as much of a client base there, Joel."

"Then I guess you'll just have to live off his salary and the proceeds from the book of photographs you took on his family's ranch."

Skye laughed. "You are incorrigible. And you still haven't answered my question, so I'm going to tell you what you'd do."

"Okay. What will I do if you don't come back?"

"You'd take over Hathaway Photography."

"I'm not ready for that, Skye."

"Like hell you aren't. You've been more or less running it while I've been in Montana, and I went through some of the pictures you've taken this past month. They're beautiful, Joel." She smiled at her assistant. With dark hair, piercing dark eyes, and a slight frame, he reminded her very little physically of Luke Conner, but the two young men had much in common. Both were charismatic and talented, but also humble and caring. "And, in the likelihood that I don't decide to stay in Northstar, I want to bring you in as a partner. Sooner rather than later."

"I'm honored."

Before Skye could say anything further on the matter, the front door opened. She turned to see a longtime client stride inside—Eloise's friend.

"I'm so glad I caught you before you left!" Faye said.

"You just made it. I was about to head out the door," Skye remarked. "Lindsay and I are supposed to be meeting for dinner one last time before I head back to Montana."

"Speaking of heading back, when are you planning to be back for sure? I have some events coming up at the inn in mid to late October—I know we've already booked you for that wedding on October fourteenth, but we have a fiftieth anniversary party the week before that, and they'd like a professional photographer. Also, we *have* decided to host an autumn costume ball again this year."

"I'm glad to hear that business is booming. I can't say exactly when I'll be back just yet. I have the cabin through the end of the month, and Eloise wants some shots of the fall color for the book, so I'll probably stay long enough to get them. Word has it the peak for color is the last week of September, which should put me back in plenty of time to shoot your events."

"Fantastic."

"I hate to run, but I should have left ten minutes ago. Besides, right now, Joel knows the schedule better than I do, and he'd be happy to help you."

The owner of the Agate Bluff Inn eyed the young man with skepticism, and Skye bristled. She liked Faye well enough, but she didn't have much tolerance for her occasionally snooty attitude. Joel was more than capable of photographing the events at the inn, but Faye wanted *experience*.

"Oh, Skye, it'll only take a moment," Faye said. "Are you sure you can't—"

"As I said, I'm already running late. I'll be in touch

soon to let you know exactly when I'll be back to work." Skye leaned over to whisper in Joel's ear. "Don't let her push you around."

Joel chuckled. "Sure thing, boss."

She ducked out the door before Faye could try to stop her. Thoughts of handing over her company to Joel fizzled, not because she didn't think he could handle it but because so many of her regular clients were like Faye. They trusted Skye, were comfortable with her, and might have a hard time adjusting to working with Joel, regardless of how talented he was. She'd spent too long mentoring him to just dump him into the deep end of the photography pool and watch him sink. What had she been thinking, dangling the possibility of his own company in front of him? Had her time in Northstar—more specifically, her time with Aaron—skewed her perception of reality that much? As she'd told Joel, she'd worked hard to build her business, and she loved what she did for a living. Everything she had dreamed of in high school and college… she had it.

Not everything.

Inexplicably, Jessie's beautiful young face popped into her head, and Skye realized she missed the little girl as much as she missed the girl's father. She had spent the past three days stubbornly ignoring how much she wanted to see them both again, and now that she'd finally given in to the thoughts about them, she couldn't force them away again.

"Who are you kidding, Skye?" she asked herself as she drove away from the studio. "You're never going to replace his wife."

With a growl, she headed around the end of Liberty Bay through Poulsbo Junction and headed south toward

Silverdale. She'd hoped to run home to freshen up a bit before heading out to dinner with Lindsay and Noah, but she hadn't exactly done anything physically taxing today—scheduling jobs might be mentally exhausting, but she hadn't spent more than twenty minutes away from her desk—and besides, the time alone would only give her conflicting thoughts about Aaron a stronger foothold. So really, it was probably a good thing she was behind schedule.

She spotted Lindsay's car in the parking lot of their favorite Mexican restaurant and hoped her friend hadn't been waiting too long.

"And I thought *we* were running late," Lindsay remarked as soon as Skye walked through the door. She and her eight-year-old son were still standing in the waiting area, and had apparently just arrived.

"Hi, Noah. How are you, kid? And how's school going?"

"I'm good," he replied. "School's okay I don't like him."

"I'm sorry to hear that. But you gotta get through it, and before you know it, you'll be done, and maybe next year, you'll get a teacher you like."

"Yeah. I guess."

The hostess showed them to their booth beside a window that overlooked the parking lot, set their menus on the table in front of them, and poured them some water before returning to the front desk.

"I'd apologize for being late, but since you two just arrived, I don't feel so bad," Skye said. "Eloise stayed longer than I'd thought she would, and then Faye Marcus stopped in right as I was about to head out the door. I had to push her off on poor Joel. And speaking of my assistant, what's this I hear about you gossiping about me and Aaron?"

"Who's Aaron?" Noah asked before Lindsay could defend herself. Curiosity flashed in the vibrant green eyes he'd inherited from his mother.

"A man I met in Montana. We've gone on a few dates."

"But didn't you and Darren just get divorced?"

Skye winced. How many times had she told herself she shouldn't get involved with Aaron because it was too soon? Stubbornly, she refused to regret anything that had happened, and promised herself she would *not* believe any of it was wrong.

"Noah!" Lindsay snapped. "That was rude."

"What?" the boy asked innocently. "It's just a question."

"It's all right, Linds," Skye said, offering a placating smile. "Yes, Noah, we did just get divorced—*officially*. Unofficially, we've been divorced for months."

Noah bounced on to his next question, satisfied by her response and unbothered by the thoughts of inappropriateness that plagued Skye. "Is he a cowboy like the guy who took Mom to the football game?"

Skye glanced sharply at Lindsay. Lifting her water glass to her mouth to hide her lips from Noah, she mouthed, *You told him about that?*

Lindsay gave a subtle nod, so Skye said, "They're brothers. Twins, actually. Aaron and Henry Hammond. Their family owns the largest ranch in Northstar, the Lazy H. In fact, I'm putting together a photography book about their ranch."

"Cool! Did you get to ride any horses yet?"

"No, but I did get to ride a four-wheeler and watch them stack hay with this big wooden contraption called a beaverslide. When I come back in a couple weeks, I'll show you the pictures if you want."

Noah's head bobbed in enthusiastic affirmation, then he blurted, "Mom, I'm gonna go play the arcade games. Grandma gave me a buncha quarters." He zipped away from the table without waiting for permission.

Lindsay growled in frustration. "He's getting to be such a handful these days," she said. "He's like this every time he comes back from his dad's. Doesn't listen, thinks he can do whatever he wants."

"That's probably because Max is an arrogant piece of crap," Skye remarked. She could see Noah at the arcade games in the waiting area from the booth if she stretched her neck a little. "He and Darren are two peas in a pod."

"God, yes. And we were so damned stupid to get hooked up with them."

Skye nodded and stared outside for a moment, feeling a little claustrophobic in a town that she had once considered to have a relatively small population. "Did it feel strange, coming back here after being in Montana? Like… you didn't belong here anymore?"

"Yeah. It took a couple weeks before I felt like I could breathe again, and I'm not talking about the difference in altitude. I wasn't in Northstar long enough to get acclimated. It's more that I never thought I'd like the wide open spaces as much as I did."

"I wonder how much of that has to do with the people we met, particularly the Hammond twins." Skye smiled and shook her head, still half-lost in disbelief at the power of her desire to return to Montana. "I can't believe you told Noah about Henry."

"I want to be as honest with him as I can be. Oh, I didn't give him any details. I just told him a nice cowboy invited me to a football game, and he understood that. I certainly didn't tell him about dinner, or what happened after."

At those words, Skye's attention snapped fully back to Lindsay. "What do you mean, 'what happened after'?"

Blush stained the redhead's cheeks and neck.

"You didn't…? You did."

Lindsay nodded. "Maybe it was the excitement of the game, but…. He offered to drop my off at my hotel, but we went home to his place instead. And he took me to the airport in the morning."

"Lindsay! I am shocked," Skye said laughing. "One night stands are not your thing."

When her friend dropped her gaze and a shy smile crept over her features, Skye leaned back in genuine shock. The dozen teasing remarks that sprang to mind blinked out just as quickly as they had arrived. Was it possible? Could a single night of lust have spawned something more lasting?

"It wasn't just a one night stand," she observed. "Or, at least, you hope it wasn't. Have you talked to him since?"

"A couple times a week."

"Wow. Who initiated that?"

"He did. So, what about you and Aaron? Sounds like you two are getting pretty serious. You talk about him a lot when you call. Have you two… you know?"

It was Skye's turn to feel the heat of embarrassment

and remembered passion. "The evening before I left for here."

"And?"

"It was amazing. Sex with Darren couldn't hold a candle to it, not even back when we were horny teenagers." Her pulse quickened as memories of her one interlude with Aaron played in her mind. She hesitated to speak her heart, but if she couldn't be honest with Lindsay, who could she tell? "He makes me feel things Darren never did. And I'm not talking about sex, as incredible as it was. With him, I don't watch every step, or carefully consider every word before I say it, afraid that I'll do or say the wrong thing. I can't tell you how liberating it is to be with someone who appreciates me for exactly who I am."

"Oh, honey."

"I think I'm falling in love with him."

Lindsay frowned. "But…?"

"I don't know if he's ready to commit, and I'm not willing to compete with his dead wife. After putting up with Darren's crap for so long…." Skye shook her head, unable to put the words together to make Lindsay understand. "Besides, I'm rather liking my independence, so it's for the best that my time in Northstar is almost done. Really, I'm only going back to get some more shots for the book. Eloise wants some fall pictures, so I—"

Skye's voice abandoned her when she checked on Noah and saw Darren striding toward her. When she met his gaze, he smirked.

"Shit," she muttered. "Jackass at six o'clock."

Lindsay twisted in her seat and sneered. "What the hell are you doing here, Darren?" she asked.

"Hiya, Linny-linds," Darren remarked with sugary mockery. "I thought that was your rugrat playing the arcade games."

"You're such an asshole, Darren," Lindsay snapped. "Go away."

"Not until I talk to Skye."

"What is there to talk about?" Skye replied through clenched teeth.

"Plenty, sweetheart."

"Why are you here?"

"Dinner. We *are* in a restaurant after all."

"Yeah, but why are you standing beside our booth? The bar is much more your style, so spit out whatever bull-shit you think I want to hear and leave us alone."

"My little darling grew some fangs in Montana, I see. Looks like you might have a little fight in you, after all. I like that." He braced his forearm on the back of her booth and leaned in close, leveling what he must think was a sultry gaze on her. "It's sexy. Come on, sweetheart. You've had your fling, but now it's time to come home. You're not going to find anyone better than me."

"I've done plenty of thinking about that, Darren, and I'm more sure than ever that I made the right choice." She smiled, and with utter politeness, added, "I've already found someone better than you. Actually, I've found someone who's made me realize I couldn't do any *worse* than you." She paused to give those words a moment to sink in. Her sweet smile never faltered, even when she realized that his spell over her was well and truly broken. She felt no fear or shame at his words, only irritation at his interruption. "Is there anything else you feel the need to get off your chest, or was that useless attempt to bully me into coming back to you all?"

"You'll come crawling back, Skye. Just wait."

She laughed, and the iciness of it made her shiver. "Yeah, that'll happen sometime between hell freezing over and never, so have fun waiting. In the meantime, have a nice night, Darren."

Miraculously, he accepted the dismissal and stalked back through the waiting area toward the bar. As soon as he was out of earshot, Skye laughed gleefully. "That felt good!"

When she realized Lindsay wasn't laughing with her, she glanced at her friend. Lindsay watched her with brows lifted and a faint smile tugging at the corners of her mouth.

"Tell me again that you can walk away from Aaron, just like that."

She tried to say it. And couldn't. "I don't want to walk away from him, but I may have to. I won't settle for less than the kind of devotion he's capable of… and can't give yet."

"Lemme ask you a question. Has Aaron ever treated you like Darren did?"

"No. He's pretty much the polar opposite of Darren."

"Then I think you'd be stupid to walk away without giving him the chance to try."

* * *

"Hey, Pearl. Are you ready?" Aaron asked, folding his arms on the high counter of the dispatcher's desk.

Pearl explained a couple of her notes to the afternoon dispatcher before gathering her things and turning her attention to Aaron. "Why does it matter whether I'm ready or

178

not?" she inquired.

"I'm taking you out to lunch."

"You are, are you?"

"Yep. I hope you're in the mood for some Papa T's fried chicken."

"My husband's going to be a jealous man," Pearl remarked, slipping her hand around Aaron's offered arm. "He knows I have a weakness for a man in uniform."

Aaron chuckled. "So *that's* why you decided to be a dispatcher."

"You know it, honey. Have a quiet afternoon, Jamie."

After walking Pearl out to her car, Aaron braced his forearms on the frame of the open window and asked, "See you at Papa T's in five?"

"You bet."

Three minutes later, Aaron sat in his truck in the small parking area across the street from Papa T's with his hands on the steering wheel in a white-knuckled grip. He'd been back to his and Erica's favorite restaurant dozens of times since she'd died right there in the street in front of it, but he still had to swallow the nausea every time. Today, though the sun beamed from a cobalt sky scattered with fluffy clouds, it took him longer than usual to peel himself out of his truck.

If Erica loved you as much as I know you still love her, I can't believe she'd want you to continue suffering. Skye's words echoed in his mind, as clear as if she'd just spoken them.

He inhaled deeply. She was right. About him still clinging to the memories of his wife, about forcing Skye to compete for his attention. About all of it. And it wasn't fair to Skye. Or to Erica's memory, to Jessie, or to himself. He knew he didn't want to be alone anymore, and he knew Skye was an incredible woman. When he was able to push away the feeling that he was somehow betraying Erica by being with her, it was easy to picture himself spending with the rest of his life with her. And Jessie loved her.

But he was a coward, too broken and scared to take a chance.

That damning thought pushed him out of his truck and across the street. Pearl arrived half a step behind him, and he held the door open for her. The large, high-ceilinged room was packed, and Aaron followed Pearl to the only open table, which sat against the far wall to the left of the door.

"Aaron, Pearl," their waitress greeted. "Do you even need menus?"

"No, Irene," Pearl said. "We'll split the four piece chicken bucket."

"French fries, Jo-Jos, or cottage fries?"

"Cottage fries," Aaron replied. "Unless you want Joe-Joes today, Pearl."

"Lord, no. You know I always go for the cottage fries."

"Anything to drink?"

"Water's fine for me, dear," Pearl responded.

Aaron very nearly ordered a beer, but the mood he was in, he doubted one would be enough to take the edge off, so he settled for water.

"So, is Skye back yet?" Pearl asked as soon as Irene left them to tend to other customers. "You haven't mentioned her once, other that to say she was heading back to Washington for a few days. Everything all right?"

"She's supposed to be back tomorrow."

"Okay, that answers my first question. What about the other?"

After hesitating for a moment, Aaron told her what had happened on the night before Skye left—omitting, of course, the more intimate details, though he knew Pearl would put the clues together.

"She's right," he said. Admitting it aloud was more difficult, and his chest tightened, making it hard to breathe. "Why am I so afraid?"

"Once burned, twice shy, they say. You lost the love of your life, Aaron, and *how* she died makes that pain a thousand times worse. I don't think it's that you can't let go of Erica. I think you're afraid of loving Skye because you couldn't take it if something happened to her, too. It may not be logical, but the heart rarely is." Pearl started to say something else, but snapped her mouth shut as her eyes locked on the door.

Aaron turned around in his chair to see what had captured her attention just in time to take a fist to the jaw. He nearly fell out of his chair, but caught it only to send it tumbling a moment later when he shot out of his seat. Jerry Mackey charged him with fists swinging wildly. Aaron sidestepped him, and Pearl ducked out of the way as the kid stumbled into the wall. Before Jerry could fully turn around to face his target, Aaron had him pinned against the wall with a forearm across the kid's chest and a fist drawn back to strike.

"When are you going to learn that you can't beat me in a fight?" Aaron growled.

For several long moments, the dining room was

utterly silent. Aaron quivered with the rush of adrenaline, and his heart pounded, but he had absolutely no desire to fight. Jerry's eyes flashed with anger, but beneath the hatred was fear and something Aaron recognized all too easily. Guilt.

"Christ, Jerry. You *just* got out. Do you really hate me so much that you'd go back just to get in a good punch?"

"Go to hell."

"Been there for most of the last five years," Aaron replied. "Just like you."

"You don't know a damned thing about me."

"Like hell I don't. I'm curious to know, Jerry, what you think you can do that can possibly hurt me worse than holding my wife in my arms as she died, knowing I couldn't do a damned thing to save her."

"Go back to your meals," Pearl told the other diners. "Deputy Hammond has this handled."

Aaron narrowed his eyes and studied Jerry. As the fight in the kid slowly sputtered and died, there was little left in him but despair, so Aaron didn't believe him when he muttered, "Joseph's dead because of you."

"You don't really blame me, do you, Jerry."

Resentment flared in his hazel eyes, but he didn't deny it.

"You blame yourself," Aaron observed. Finally, deflated by the ebb of adrenaline, he lowered his fist and loosened his hold on Jerry, though he didn't yet release him. "I know that feeling, kid. Damn, do I. Not a day goes by that I don't blame myself for Erica's death, wondering if she'd still be alive if only I'd had my sidearm, or if I'd stayed more completely between her and your brother...."

Jerry's eyes rounded.

"Do you think I was glad when I looked up to see Joseph lying dead in the street? Do you think I felt vindicated, like Erica's death had been avenged?"

The kid opened his mouth, then closed it again.

"I didn't. I felt empty, and all I could think was that another life had been pointlessly wasted. I've never hated Joseph for what happened, and I sure as hell never hated you."

"Why?" His voice was so faint a whisper that Aaron more saw than heard the question.

"Because the sad truth is, Jerry, that what happened is nothing more than a terrible accident. I'm not to blame, and neither are you. You were a dumb kid, you made some dumb choices, and you've paid for them, but what happened to Erica and Joseph wasn't your fault."

"Yes, it is. If I hadn't—"

"Jerry, stop. Look at me." Aaron removed his arm and gripped the kid's skinny shoulders. The tears shimmering in Jerry's eyes sent a spear of sympathy straight to Aaron's heart. "It is *not* your fault."

With the tears spilling over, Jerry slid to the floor and buried his face against his knees. Aaron squatted beside him and wrapped an arm around his shoulders. Jerry leaned into him and cried, reminding Aaron that, though he was twenty-one now and had done time, Jerry Mackey was still just a scared, lost kid. A lot like Luke Conner but without a loving family to support him. Aaron stretched his legs out in front of him and sat with the kid who had—only moments ago—punched him. Absently, he rubbed his sore jaw and glanced around at the other diners. They watched covertly, curious but trying not to stare.

"P-please for-g-give me," Jerry said, his voice hitching with his sobs.

"There's nothing to forgive," Aaron murmured. "But if you need to hear it, then yes, I forgive you. Do you forgive me?"

"N-nothing to f-forgive, but y-yes."

Aaron glanced at the kid, and a corner of Jerry's mouth lifted. He wiped the tears from beneath his red-rimmed eyes, and after a while, when it seemed like Jerry was starting to get hold of himself, Aaron asked, "What are you going to do now?"

"I don't know. I'm staying in the apartment over Joseph's old girlfriend's garage, but I know she doesn't want me to stay there much longer. And I need to find a job. I haven't been able to get one. No one w-will to hire me." New tears threatened, and Aaron gave the kid a reassuring squeeze.

"What do you know about livestock?"

"Not m-much. Why?"

"If you don't mind some hard work, I think I can get you a job on my family's ranch. We've been looking for an extra hand."

"Why would you do that?"

Aaron considered his response for a while before he spoke. Pearl was wrong. He wasn't afraid of falling in love with Skye only to lose her like he'd lost Erica. Well, maybe he was, a little, but that wasn't the heart of his problem. "Pearl here thinks I can't commit to this new woman I've been seeing because I'm afraid I'll lose her, too, but that's not entirely true. I can't move on because I haven't forgiven myself for what happened to Erica, Joseph, and yes, Jerry, even you. You were just a kid, and yeah, it was a friggin' stupid thing that you did, letting your cousin drag you into that deal, but what choice did you really have?" Aaron scrubbed a hand through his hair. "I feel responsible for you, kid."

"You don't have to do that."

"Yes, I do. I'm not saying it's going to be easy, but it's a job, and it'll come with room and board."

"I don't know what to say."

"Sure you do."

Jerry let out a soft laugh. "Thank you."

"Truce?" Aaron asked, extending his hand.

Jerry shook it. "Truce."

"Great. Let me buy you lunch. Then I'll take you out to the ranch." Aaron found the heart to laugh. "I imagine your probation officer will get quite the shock when we tell him you're working for the same guy who put you in jail. Twice."

"Yeah, that is pretty ironic."

While they ate lunch, Aaron leaned back in his chair and knitted his fingers behind his head. Once or twice, he caught Pearl looking at him with something akin to pride in her eyes, and he dipped his head momentarily to acknowledge it.

When lunch had been eaten, Aaron told Jerry he'd meet him out at Joseph's old girlfriend's house, then turned to bid Pearl farewell.

"Other than causing quite a scene," Pearl remarked, "I'd say that some serious progress was made today."

"I think you're right. I know it probably sounds corny

as hell, but I truly feel like a weight has been lifted off me."

"I am so glad to hear that, Aaron. You're a good man, and you deserve to be happy. See you tomorrow, dark and early."

"Yep."

As he headed to collect Jerry, Aaron swore he could almost feel the pieces of his shattered heart coming back together at last. If he had known it would be so simple to derail Jerry's anger, he would have done it when the kid had stupidly attacked him the last time, but in this moment of clarity, he came to a realization that reminded him forcefully of June Conner. Neither he nor Jerry had been ready to forgive each other or themselves then. Now that they were, he knew he might have finally found the courage to take a chance on another shot at love. As soon as Skye returned to Northstar, Aaron vowed he would tell her exactly how he felt about her, and show her that she was the only woman in his heart now. He'd always love Erica, and he'd probably always miss her, but she belonged in his past. Skye, it appeared, might just be his future.

Nine

"BE HONEST," EVIE SAID, taking the cup of coffee Skye offered. "You're glad to be back."

Skye led her friend out onto the deck of her rented cabin and peered at the stand of aspen behind it. Patches of pale gold already mottled the once-emerald canopy of the grove. As her gaze wandered up the slopes of the mountains, she noticed splashes of vibrant yellow amongst the black-green of the pines. She turned back to Evie and took a sip of her coffee to delay answering. It was perhaps a little late in the day for coffee, as it was now after one, but the cool air warranted a hot beverage.

Was she glad to be back in Northstar? Absolutely. She'd arrived back yesterday, Friday, and breathed a sigh of relief and contentment when she'd mounted the stairs to this very deck. She had missed the wide-open spaces—the embrace of the guarding mountains and the sweep of the valley. She'd also missed the people. At lunch with Evie at the Bedspread, Pat and Aelissm O'Neil had greeted her as warmly as they would an old friend. Though she was conflicted, it wasn't too difficult to admit that returning to Northstar felt more like coming home than resuming her vacation.

She hadn't yet seen Aaron because he was still on the early shift, and she had arrived too late last night to call him, but he'd left a message on her answering machine inviting her to come over for dinner and to watch Luke's game tonight. The anticipation of seeing him again was potent.

"All right," she said at last. "Yes, Evie, I'm glad to be back."

"I know you told me that you haven't seen Aaron yet, but are you going over to his place tonight to watch the game?"

"Yeah." Unbidden and unstoppable, a smile quirked the corners of Skye's mouth.

"Damn. I was hoping you'd come watch it with Vince and…. Wait. Forget I said anything. I haven't seen that look on your face since high school…. Have you and Aaron…?"

Cursing the blush that warmed her cheeks, Skye let her gaze again wander over the landscape.

"Oh, you have! Do you love him?"

Abruptly, Skye yanked her gaze back to Evie. "Where did that come from?"

"Well, you're not exactly the kind of girl who jumps into bed. I know I teased you about taking a roll in the hay with him, but…."

The grin that spread across Evie's cherubic face was

clear indication of the thoughts running through her head.

"Don't go planning a wedding, now, Evie Carlyle. It's not like that."

"Then what's it like?"

Skye opened her mouth, then closed it. Finally, she said truthfully, "I don't know yet. But something was made quite clear to me on my trip back to Washington. Even if I decide to stay here and hand my company over to Joel, I can't do it right away because many of my best clients are snobs and they aren't ready to trust him yet."

Evie's mouth fell open, and she stared at her friend for several long moments. "You've actually thought about staying here and leaving your company to Joel?"

She'd thought about little else during her twelve-hour drive yesterday, but she wasn't about to share that because Evie wouldn't be able to leave such a tantalizing detail alone. "Well, I'm a freelance photographer, so I can technically do that where ever, right? I'm sure people here need photographers occasionally, too."

"You're not hearing me, Skye." Evie's shock shifted quickly to smugness. "You've only known Aaron for a month, and you're already thinking about staying here with him."

"No, I'm considering—if you can even call a fleeting thought that—staying here because I like it here."

"Uh-huh. Somehow, I don't think that's even a tenth of the reason why you're thinking about staying here."

"Evie, you're seriously making me regret telling you that."

"Hey, best friends are supposed to look out for each other, and Aaron is a great guy."

"I'm not denying that. But he may not be ready to have another woman in his life yet, and he may never be."

The sound of a vehicle approaching diverted Skye's and Evie's attention. Aaron's truck rolled to a stop beside Skye's SUV and the man himself climbed out, looking quite dashing in his brown and tan uniform and grinning like a fool. Skye's heart tripped in her chest as she drank in her first sight of him in almost a week. It wasn't that she'd forgotten how attractive he was, it was that the real thing was so much better than a memory.

"Afternoon, ladies," he greeted, bounding up the steps.

"Hi, Aaron," Evie replied. "Looks like you just got off work."

"I did. I haven't even picked Jessie up from her grandparents' yet. I couldn't wait to get home to see Skye. Do you mind...?"

Without waiting for a response from either woman, he clasped Skye's face, pulled her against him, and kissed her soundly. Skye melted into him, undeniably glad to feel his warm arms around her again and his passionate lips against hers. When they broke apart, they turned as one to see Evie watching them with an amused grin. Turning her gaze back to Aaron, Skye noticed a bruise on his jaw. Concern sent a shock of adrenaline through her.

"What's this from?" she asked, frowning and brushing her thumb over it.

"I ran into Jerry Mackey."

"Jerry Mackey? What happened?"

"I'll tell you about it later. Right now, I'm hoping you'll come with me to pick Jessie up. She's very excited to see you, and I thought it would be a nice surprise for her," Aaron said. To Evie, he added, "That is, if you don't mind if I steal Skye."

"I don't mind one bit," Evie replied. "Just let me put my cup inside, and I'll be on my way."

Skye gave Aaron a quick peck on the cheek, reluctant to let go of him. Finally, she pulled away and followed her friend inside the cabin. In the kitchen, Evie turned to her with a serious expression Skye had rarely seen on her face.

"Not ready for another woman my ass," she stated.

Before Skye could argue, Evie gave her a hug and zipped across the living area and out the front door. Skye watched her bid goodbye to Aaron, then turned to rinse out the cups and joined her lover on the deck. He took her into his arms again and held her tightly. She sighed happily and rested her head on his shoulder, content and soothed by his sturdy strength.

"I really missed you," he murmured.

"I missed you, too. And Jessie. So, shall we get going?"

Moments later, Skye was buckled into the passenger seat of his truck, detailing her trip. It was nice to be able to talk to him and know that he was listening. When she let slip her observation about the difference in vegetation and that Kitsap County hadn't felt like home, he chuckled.

"You sound like Pat O'Neil," he remarked.

"I thought we were going to pick Jessie up," Skye said when he reached the intersection of Elkhorn Road and the main road through the valley and turned right instead of left toward his family's ranch.

"We are. It was Grandma and Grandpa Robinson's

turn to have her."

Robinson? Right, Erica's parents. Skye only nodded and chewed on her bottom lip, not sure why the idea of meeting his wife's family made her uncomfortable. It was one more reminder that she would always be competing with Erica's memory if she pursued a serious—okay, *more* serious—relationship with Aaron. She straightened in her seat and vowed that she would enjoy today and her remaining time in Northstar and let things take their natural course without trying to force it. The promise would undoubtedly be harder to keep than it was to make, but she would try.

The conversation waned as Skye took in the sights while Aaron drove up the winding pass between the Northstar and Crystal Valleys. Before she knew it, they were turning onto a dirt road and passing beneath a tall log gate proclaiming the lands beyond to be the Royal R Ranch. A sign on the right pole welcomed guests and asked visitors to check in at the main house half a mile ahead. Gravel pinged on the underside of Aaron's truck, and Skye thought the washboard of the road might rattle her joints apart. A plume of pale dust marked the truck's passing.

"That house there is the home of Ben's sister, niece, and brother-in-law, who is the ranch foreman," Aaron said, pointing to the left.

Skye spied the quaint yellow house with pristine white trim sitting at the edge of the pines, looking over the sprawling alpine meadow and pastures. *What a beautiful spot*, she thought to herself. She nearly jumped when Aaron reached over and curled his fingers around hers, then gave his hand a squeeze, amused and gratified by his simple gesture.

The ranch road angled to the right, and shortly after, the main ranch house and a ring of small guest cabins, outbuildings, and barns came into view. The ranch house was exactly what she'd expect—a two story structure with rough-sawn pine siding and a covered, wrap-around porch.

"So, this is where Erica grew up."

"Yep," Aaron replied. "Those are the guest cabins over there, and the full-time ranch hands' cabins are over there, closer to the barns."

"Do they have a lot of guests?"

"They do a pretty good business, and the word is spreading. Jim and Jessie only got into the dude ranching thing about seven years ago. Jim was a little reluctant, but well, Jessie's a pretty persistent woman, and he couldn't argue with her logic." Aaron chuckled. "He won't admit it, but I think he likes meeting all the new people because he has a captive audience that hasn't already heard his stories two dozen times."

"Too funny."

Aaron parked in front of the main house and climbed out. Skye joined him hesitantly, and it gave her a smidgeon of confidence when he again took her hand. Why was she so nervous about meeting Erica's parents? Was it because she thought they'd hate her for moving into a position that was still obviously their daughter's? She shuddered, and Aaron must have felt it, because he let go of her hand for a moment to wrap a supportive arm around her shoulders.

"They don't bite," he murmured.

Taking her hand again, he led her inside through the front doors. The interior was rich with wood tones, deep red, navy, and evergreen accents. The scent of something delicious and barbecued wafted in from the kitchen, making Skye's mouth water even though she'd eaten just over an hour ago.

Standing at the island and pulling the meat from what appeared to be three cooked-to-perfection chickens was a woman with silvering brown hair and kind hazel eyes. Though she was slender and attractive, the more accurate descriptive was stout. Skye didn't doubt for a minute that Jessie was one tough lady who spent her days working side by side her rancher husband and loving every minute of it.

When she realized she had company, Jessie Robinson beamed and said, "You're a little earlier than I'd expected. Ah, you must be Skye. Aaron has told me a lot about you. Give me just a moment here."

Jessie turned around to face the sink and washed her hands. After drying them, she extended a hand to Skye, who shook it.

"Pleased to meet you. Aaron's told me quite a bit about you, too. This is a beautiful place you have here, Mrs. Robinson."

"Please," the older woman replied with a snort. "Call me Jessie. We're not that formal around here."

"Smoked some chickens, I see," Aaron remarked, leaning over to snatch a piece of dark meat. Jessie swatted at his hand, but he popped the meat in his mouth. "You've outdone yourself, Jessie. Skye, you have to try this."

He fed her a piece, and Skye couldn't help but nod in agreement. The chicken was amazing, juicy with a delicious smoky flavor, but she again felt the prickle of discomfort. Jessie studied her with narrowed eyes for just a moment before turning away to take a pot of homemade barbecue sauce off the stove.

"I assume you haven't eaten yet, Aaron, since you're early."

"Nope. I was in a hurry to get home. Skye just got back from Washington last night, and I didn't want to wait to see her. Besides, I figured Jessie wanted to see her, too."

If his comments bothered his daughter's namesake, the woman didn't show it. In fact, she smiled knowingly. "That she does. She's asked me about a dozen times today if I knew exactly when Skye would be back. So, why don't you run out and get her while I fix you both some lunch. Skye, would you like a sandwich?"

Skye swallowed the panic that rose at the thought of being alone with Erica's mother, and replied, "I just ate lunch not too long ago, but I'd love a bit more of a taste."

"I assume my daughter is out in the barn with Jim?" Aaron asked.

"Of course. One of the barn cats had kittens this week, so you may want to get her out of there before you ended up with another half dozen cats."

With a roll of his eyes, Aaron darted out of the house. Skye looked out the window over the kitchen sink and watched him jog across the yard to the barn.

"Here you go, sweetheart," Jessie said behind her.

She took the offered plate, nearly groaning when she forked a bite into her mouth. Without the sauce, the chicken had been amazing, but with it…. Skye thought she might have just found a new favorite dish. "This is truly incredible, Jessie. Thank you."

"Aaron tells me you have a deal for a photography book about his family's ranch, and that you might be wanting some shots and info on the Royal R."

"*I* do, but my publisher seems pretty set on focusing on the Lazy H." She gave a sniff of laughter. "Somehow, I get the feeling she'd change her mind if she saw this place. I imagine she might even book a trip out here to see it herself."

"Well, if she changes her mind, you're more than welcome to take whatever pictures here you need. You just let us know, and Jim or I or Jane or Andy will be happy to show you around."

"I may have to take you up on that, if only for myself."

Silence fell between them as Jessie focused her attention on fixing sandwiches for Aaron and her granddaughter. Skye shifted her weight, unsettled by the quiet. Without the distraction of conversation, she again began to think that she was trying to move into someone else's territory. Jessie glanced up at her again with that same, curious expression, and Skye felt like an open book.

"Are you all right, dear?"

"I… It's a little uncomfortable, meeting you."

"Ah. Is it about meeting me… or meeting Erica's mother?"

"Definitely the latter."

"Don't let that bother you, sweetheart."

"But I feel like I'm trying to take Erica's place in Aaron's life."

"Don't be ridiculous. You and Erica are two different women, and you each have your own place in his heart."

"But—"

"Do two children have the same place in their

parents' hearts? No, they each have their own place. The heart has infinite room for love, and each new person who comes into our lives has their own spot in our hearts." The sheer and limitless kindness in Jessie's wise eyes was disarming. "I will always miss my daughter, but I've had my time to grieve. Aaron is and will always be my son-in-law, and as such, I want him to be happy. If you're the woman to make that happen, how can I feel anything but love for you, too?"

Perhaps she should have been surprised when Jessie hugged her, but all she felt was gratitude and the sting of tears. "Thank you," she whispered. "If Erica was anything like you, it's very easy to see why Aaron still...."

She choked on the words, confused by what she felt. Before she could try to make sense of it or form the words to express rest of her thought, the younger Jessie burst into the kitchen.

"Skye!" she squealed.

She lifted the little girl and was rewarded by a shockingly strong bear hug.

"I missed you!"

"I missed you, too, pumpkin."

Skye couldn't be sure, but when Jessie Robinson leaned over to Aaron, she thought she heard, "You found another good one, and you better hold on tight this time."

* * *

Aaron stood in the doorway of Jessie's bedroom with his arm tucked around Skye's waist, staring into the dark room at his sleeping daughter. Sighing, he turned away and headed into the kitchen to clean up the mess from their supper nachos. When Skye joined him and offered to dry the dishes, he thought that this was becoming a routine of theirs; finger-food dinner while watching Luke's football game on TV, snuggling on the couch, tucking Jessie into bed, and cleaning up together. He liked it. Despite the exhaustion that weighed down on him, he'd forced himself to stay awake so he wouldn't miss even one precious second.

They had stopped back by her cabin so she could drive her SUV to his house—considering the likelihood that Jessie wouldn't be able to stay awake through the whole game—so they wouldn't have to wake the little girl to take Skye home. With the dishes done, the kitchen cleaned, and both their eyelids getting heavy, it was about time for Skye to leave.

"Stay with me tonight," Aaron heard himself say.

The invitation startled her as much as him, and she whirled on him, staring blankly. "What?"

"Stay here tonight," he repeated, tucking his arms around her waist and pulling her to him. "With me."

"Aaron... I don't know if that's a good idea."

He tilted her head up and kissed her gently. He wanted to feel her body against his again, skin to skin, and if the way she kissed him back was any indication, he wasn't the only one who wanted to be together. Not necessarily sex, though he couldn't deny that he wanted to explore every stunning line of her again—the memory of her body had haunted him every waking moment since she closed the door on him that night, even more so after his encounter with Jerry Mackey, as if a wall had finally crumbled. No, he thought, as exquisite as making love to her again would undoubtedly be, he could wait. Right now, he just wanted to spend the night with her in his arms.

"I need you, Skye," he whispered. "Please stay."

"Are you sure?"

"Absolutely sure."

"What about Jessie? Will she be okay with—"

"Jessie will probably be ecstatic." He held her at arms length and frowned. "Skye. If you don't want to stay, just say so."

"I *do* want to stay, but I probably shouldn't."

"Why?"

She opened her mouth, closed it, then said, "I don't know. I keep feeling like this can't possibly last, that it's too soon for us both."

She sighed heavily and paused for a moment. Aaron's heart fell, certain she was going to pull away.

Suddenly, she grinned and said, "Foolish though it may be, I *will* stay... because I really, really want to."

Giggling like a pair of teenagers, they turned off all the lights together and prepared for sleep. When Aaron dove for his bed to pounce on Skye, his black Lab bounced around like this was some kind of fun new game. He let out a yip of excitement, and both Skye and Aaron hissed, "Shh!"

"Don't you dare wake Jessie up, you silly dog," Aaron said with a chuckle. "Why don't you go guard her door? Skye will keep me safe."

Chance cocked his head with his ears perked, then collapsed on his dog pillow on Aaron's side of the bed. Aaron shook his head at his dog, still laughing. Then Skye straddled his waist and pushed him down.

"I thought you adopted Chance to be Jessie's dog."

"I did. But I guess he figures Pooky does a good enough job defending her from the evils of the night, so it's his duty to protect me."

"What about me? Am I an evil of the night?"

Aaron pulled her head down to kiss her soundly. "Most definitely not."

She lay on him chest-to-chest with her hands curled around his shoulders. A light frown creased the enchanting features of her face. She trailed her fingertips over the bruise on his jaw, and he winced. The frown deepened as worry darkened her eyes.

Still tender, he thought, prodding the bruise.

"It's later. Are you going to tell me how you got this? Because it looks like someone punched you."

"Someone *did* punch me."

"Who? And why?"

"Jerry Mackey, and I'm sure you can figure out why."

She swore under her breath. "What happened?"

"We finally bumped into each other on Thursday. It started out like it did the first time, but it ended… very well. We had a good heart-to-heart, got some things off our chests… and I offered him a job on the ranch."

"What?!"

"He's a good kid at heart, Skye; he's just had a shitty time of it. I figured, after everything we've been through, I needed to put us on the right course this time."

"You always tell me how amazing I am, but I don't think you have a clue how amazing *you* are. Not many men would be able to do what you did."

"Well, we'll see if I'm able to hold to it."

"You will."

The same relief he'd felt in the restaurant after once again deflecting Jerry's attack now washed over him, and before Skye could further question the incident, he took her face in his hands and kissed her. He was at peace right now, and he didn't want to ruin it by over-thinking things.

It didn't take long for that simple kiss to turn into more. Her body was every bit as beautiful as he remembered. More so because he knew it now—the softness of her skin and the firm muscle beneath it, the feminine curves, and the intoxicating heat of her. Last time, he'd eagerly submitted to her delightful inquisitiveness, but tonight, he took command and took his time exploring every last inch of her body, driving them both to the edge even before joining their bodies. She squirmed beneath him, pleading for more until he finally entered her, groaning with a shudder of exquisite pleasure. The orgasm crashed through him with such force that he trembled.

"Sweet heaven above," he breathed. It took a few minutes before he could ask, "Have I told you yet today that you are amazing?"

"Mmmm. I don't think so."

"Well, you are."

Aaron half-expected the long-familiar guilt to wash over him once the fervor of their lovemaking faded, but all he felt of it was a fleeting thought of his wife. Instead of guilt, however, he was grateful for their time together and the understanding that if she were there right then, she'd tell him exactly what Skye had said, that she wanted him to be happy. As he curled around his sleeping lover, he realized he was. At last, he had found a new joy—different than what he'd shared with Erica, but as pervasive—and he was certain now that he loved Skye.

* * *

Of the next seven nights, Aaron was able to convince

Skye—with Jessie's enthusiastic assistance—to stay over six. The one night she hadn't stayed, he'd traded a shift with another deputy, who'd had a family emergency, and Skye had volunteered to let Jessie spend the night in the cabin. The newly turned five-year-old had been thrilled. Though he'd had the early shifts again, they had spent a lot of time together. Skye fixed Jessie breakfast each morning before taking her to her grandparents and had ended up spending most of the mornings either playing with Jessie or out on the ranch taking pictures. In the afternoons, Aaron helped on the ranch as it was time to start moving cows down from the summer pastures and allotments. Skye tagged along to take pictures.

Now the autumn peak had arrived, and Aaron was saddling two horses so Skye could get a real feel of fall on the ranch. Aaron hadn't told her where they were going, but he had a plan. The aptly named Aspen Creek Gulch was a narrow ravine that dove north and east into the Northstar Mountains, and situated at the edge of a large stand of quaking aspen was the original Hammond homestead, a smallish log cabin dating back to the late 1860s. His family had done a decent job of keeping the place intact over the years, and even the log-rail corrals still stood in defiance of the elements.

"Are we ready?" he asked.

Jessie bounded over to him, and he hoisted her into his saddle. Skye, who had never been on a horse, eyed the buckskin mare he'd saddled for her.

"I promise, Coyote is as gentle and steadfast as they come. She'll take good care of you."

"Coyote? Strange name for a horse, isn't it?" Skye

inquired.

"She had a run-in with one when she was just a wee skosh of a filly, and since she had about as much patience for that poor beast as Remington had for the mountain lion, it seemed a fitting name."

"Do all of your horses have such interesting stories to tell?"

"A few do. We had a gelding named Dog when I was Jessie's age, so named because he liked to follow everyone around like Chance does. He was one of the friendliest—and best—horses I've ever known. I learned how to rope and cut on him."

"Cut? As in cutting certain cows out of the herd?"

"Yep. This gentleman," he said, patting his bay gelding's neck, "is Rocket. A cousin of mine, who was eight at the time, named him that because he thought the white stripe on his nose looked like a rocket."

"It kinda does."

"Anyhow, are we going to stand around chatting all day or are we going to ride?"

Laughing softly, Skye cautiously stepped into the stirrup and swung her leg over Coyote's back. Aaron gave her a few more pointers, then climbed up behind his daughter and backed his bay gelding from the corral fence.

"Are you sure I'll be okay? I've never ridden before."

"So you said. You'll be fine. One, because I wouldn't let anything happen to you, and two, because Coyote frequently doubles as a trail ride horse, so she'll follow Rocket. If you get nervous, hold on to the saddle horn or Coyote's mane."

"I guess I'm ready. Just… don't go too fast."

Aaron nudged Rocket into an easy, long-legged walk. After a while, Skye began to relax, and gained enough confidence to agree to a slow lope to the mouth of the gulch. When Aaron slowed Rocket to traverse the boulder-strewn ground where a rock promontory jutted out from the western ridge of the gulch, Skye beamed proudly at him.

"That was fun," she said breathlessly.

Right then, with her dark hair plaited in a thick braid and a borrowed cowboy hat shading her golden eyes from the sharp morning sun, it was incredibly easy to imagine folding her into his life. She had taken to Jessie with such effortless love and enjoyed each and every adventure on the ranch and beyond, and he would not, even for a moment, regret loving her. He wanted her to stay in his life, but he had the sinking feeling that it was too soon for her. Shuddering with what felt a bit like grief, Aaron forced his thoughts elsewhere.

It was a perfect autumn day, the kind that instilled in him a limitless gratitude for the life he'd been born into. The air had been washed clean by a light snowfall yesterday morning, and the light was crystalline, making everything look sharp and vibrant. Above them, a few cirrus clouds dusted the sky, providing a nice contrast to the deep blue. The beauty of it all made him wish he had a camera… not that he had any hope of capturing it in the way Skye undoubtedly could.

At that thought, he realized they hadn't stopped once yet, and since he hadn't yet told Skye of their destination, he doubted she was waiting for that. "Whenever you want to stop to take pictures, just say the word," he offered.

The look of surprise she gave him was puzzling, and

he wondered why his offer had caught her off guard.

"What?" he asked. "We're here so you can take pictures, right?"

"Yes…." She frowned, then said, "On the rare occasions Darren came with me, he was always so impatient. I guess I just got in the habit of rushing through it, and taking as few shots as I could scrape by with."

"Well, if you've missed anything, we'll get it on the way back. I'd turn around, but I have something I want you to see first. And it's just on the other side of that willow thicket there."

"Okay."

He led the way along the narrow path through the willows. Their leaves were a confusion of green, yellow, and orange, as if they couldn't decide to cling to summer or give in to the inevitable, biting frost of winter. On the other side of the thicket was an open field rimmed on the left with pines. To the right was a long, natural one-acre pond. It butted up against the eastern ridge, and pines crowded along its eastern shore. Straight ahead was the old homestead, sheltered by the large aspen grove behind it.

"Wow," Skye breathed, pulling up alongside him and Jessie.

"I thought you might like to see this. It's the original ranch house of the Lazy H, built by William Hammond. He came from back east, like so many, to make it rich in the gold fields, but when his mine—which is further up the gulch—didn't perform, he went back to what he knew best—cattle. He was young when he built this place, maybe twenty. He met a young woman by the name of Henrietta Richards in Bannack, and they built a bigger house and barns where the main house is now, but this remained their romantic rendezvous long after."

"I can see why."

"Jessie, did you want to go fishing in the pond while Skye takes pictures? I packed our telescoping pole."

"Yeah!" his daughter cheered.

They dismounted and let the horses into the corrals, not because Aaron worried they might wander off but because he thought Skye might like to get a few shots of them with the cabin. While she wandered around with her camera and tripod, he joined his daughter beside the pond and helped her get her pole ready. The water was so clear that it was easy to see the brook trout gliding lazily beneath the surface. After he'd baited her barbless hook and attached a bobber, he helped her cast and left her for a moment to ask Skye if there was anything he could do to help.

"This is such a beautiful spot," she said, taking a break for a moment.

"Isn't it? It's one of my favorite places on the ranch."

"Is this the same creek that runs under the road between your house and Nick's?"

"Mmm-hmm."

Standing behind her, he curled his arms around her and knitted his fingers together, resting his hands just beneath her breasts.

"I can't believe I have only four days left in Northstar," she murmured.

"Do you really have to go?"

"I'm afraid so. My lease on the cabin is almost up, and I really need to get back to work. I have a lot of projects and photo shoots in October."

He sighed. "I'm not ready for you to leave yet."

"We both knew I'd have to go back eventually."

"I know. I just didn't expect 'eventually' to happen so fast." He turned her to face him. "I think I'm falling in love with you, Skye."

She opened her mouth, though whether it was to object or to question him, he didn't know, and he didn't give her the chance to do, either. He kissed her firmly, trying to express every wonderful thing she made him feel in that one caress.

"No," he whispered. "I don't *think* I'm falling in love with you. I *know* I'm falling in love with you."

"Aaron… we're not—"

"Not ready? Skye, something wonderful is happening here, and I don't want to fight it anymore. I want to give in to it, to let it wash away the heartache and pain. I want to wrap it around me and embrace the happiness it brings."

"And what about Erica?"

"I'll always love her, but she's gone."

"Do you really believe that?"

"I always have. You were never competing with her, Skye, but you *were* competing with my guilt over what happened. That's what I finally realized when Jerry confronted me this last time. I believed that—illogical as it may seem—Erica's death was my fault. *That's* what I couldn't accept, and it's kept me from believing I deserve to be happy."

"And now?"

"I'm not going to lie and say I'm completely over it, but at least I'm dealing with it now, and I know I will be able to forgive myself and overcome it. Thanks to you."

She didn't respond for a long time, but searched his

gaze for any sign that he didn't mean or believe what he said. He knew she wouldn't find any, because for the first time since his wife's death, he was being completely honest with himself. When Skye smiled and kissed him lightly, relief poured through him.

"I'm falling in love with you, too."

Icy dread leeched through the soothing relief at her tone. "But…?"

"I've barely been divorced a month, and I don't trust myself or what I feel."

As much as he wanted to convince her that she *could* trust herself—and them—he refused to push her, unwilling to treat her even remotely as her ex-husband had. She was a special woman, and she deserved so much more than Darren Fitzhugh had ever given her. If she'd let him, Aaron fully planned to show her exactly how much more. If she couldn't, or wouldn't, he'd let her go, as painful as that would be, because he wanted her to be happy.

"Go take your pictures," he murmured, smiling.

Half a moment later, Jessie squealed excitedly, and Aaron shoved his thoughts and feelings for Skye to the back of his mind to help his daughter reel in her fish.

Ten

"YOU DON'T HAVE to give up your sleep for me, Aaron," Skye remarked as she pulled blissfully warm clothes out of the dryer and dropped them into the laundry basket.

He leaned in the bathroom doorway with his legs crossed at the ankles and his arms folded loosely across his chest. His brows dipped in a faint frown. "Yes, I do, because you're leaving tomorrow, and because of these damned night shifts, I haven't been able to see much of you in the last few days. Besides, as long as I'm in bed and asleep by two, I'll still be able to get eight hours."

She picked up the basket, but before she could ask him to move out of the way, he took it from her, carried it into the living room, and set it on the coffee table. A small part of her wished he'd been content to say goodbye last night, as his daughter had been, but the rest of her was glad to spend even a few more minutes with him. When he snatched one of her sweaters out of the basket and folded it neatly, she shifted her weight nervously. The memory of Darren's frequent digs about how she folded laundry and the amazement that Aaron had voluntarily stepped in to help her were enough to reaffirm her decision to take a step back. She just couldn't trust herself to know the difference between real love and the novelty of a supportive man, but she did know she cared enough for Aaron that she couldn't lead him on.

They hadn't spent more than a handful of hours together since their ride to the homesteader's cabin, and Skye had keenly missed both Aaron and his radiant daughter. Jessie was another reason why she should walk away from them right now, perhaps even more important. Skye's eyes stung as she recalled the little girl's tearful goodbye last night. Maybe she shouldn't have done it, because Jessie had latched on to the idea, but Skye had been unable to see any other way to soothe Aaron's daughter than to promise her she'd come back for a visit soon.

"You look rather deep in thought," Aaron observed, placing another folded garment on the table.

"To be honest, I don't want to leave."

"Then don't."

"It's not that simple, Aaron."

"Are you sure you couldn't stay for even a few more days?"

"I really can't," she replied, wincing at the plea that edged into his voice. "And besides, it'd only make matters worse if I stayed."

"You talk like you're going away and never coming

back. Like this is the end."

"I'm not saying that at all. I just…. I have to get back to work. I have several shoots lined up starting on Monday." She lifted her gaze from the laundry to see him watching her with such intensity in his blue eyes that she swore he could read her deepest thoughts. "It's for the best, Aaron. I'm just not ready for the kind of commitment you want and deserve, and I won't be until I finish straightening myself out. I knew it was too soon…."

"Don't cheapen what we have with regret. Please."

She looked away again, unable to stand the flash of pain in his eyes. She'd seen it in his gaze before, but then she hadn't been its cause. "We'll keep in touch, and I have a promise to your daughter to keep, so I'll be back out this way before you know it."

"Uh-huh."

"Besides, I'm relying on you to keep me posted on Luke's football career. Even if I have to call you when the game is on so you can give me the play by play over the phone."

Aaron smiled suddenly, but instead of making her feel better, it added another crack in her heart. He lifted a piece of clothing out of the basket and wiggled his eyebrows suggestively. It was the bra she'd been wearing the day they'd first made love. Her pulse quickened at the thought of that incredible day, and she snatched the bra away before their laundry-folding party turned into something else.

"What a pair we are," she remarked. "It's my last day in Northstar and what are we doing? We're folding laundry."

He chuckled, then glanced at his watch and sighed.

"I should probably get headed home. I still need to eat before I attempt to trick my brain into thinking it wants to sleep. As to us… I guess we'll see what happens."

His tone stated plainly that he hoped this wasn't a final goodbye, and a rather loud voice in the back of her mind begged him to talk her out of leaving, but he didn't. He only stacked the laundry he'd folded and stood, stuffing his now-empty hands into his pockets as if he wasn't sure what to do with them. Skye pushed to her feet, and together, they walked out to the front deck into the brisk autumn day.

"I don't care what time you get home tomorrow, call me when you get there, okay?" Aaron said as he pulled her into his arms.

He was so warm and strong, she thought, and in his embrace was everything Darren had never given her. Was she being a fool? Most likely. But she'd been so certain she'd loved Darren, too, once, and she refused to make the same mistake twice. *This isn't goodbye*, she vowed, thought it certainly felt like one. *I'll come back, and we'll give it another shot. I just need to know if it's real.*

When Aaron tipped her head back to kiss her, she expected it to be a quick peck on the lips to say goodbye-for-now, but instead, he claimed her mouth as if trying to memorize the feel and taste of her. Though it was not as visceral as some of their kisses had been, it was every bit as powerful, and Skye's could only lean into him.

"I'm really going to miss you," he whispered when he pulled away.

Then convince me to stay, she thought, wishing she could say it. Instead, she replied, "I'm going to miss you, too."

With reluctance in every line of his body, he turned

away and slowly descended the steps. Skye watched him climb into his truck and drive away before closing the door quietly. For a moment, she leaned against the door with her forearms braced on it and her forehead resting against it. Her eyes stung with unshed tears, but she refused to let them fall.

After gathering her neatly folded clothing and packing it in her bags, she headed downstairs to the bedroom to pack up her camera and computer equipment. The picture of Luke, Aaron, and Jessie at the Gold Rush game was still on the screen, and Skye found herself sitting down at the desk. She knew she'd captured the shots she wanted for the book, but she wanted to make sure she'd taken enough of everything else to supply her with an adequate Northstar fix when she was back in Washington.

As she browsed the folder in which she'd sorted her favorite images of the Northstar Valley and its inhabitants, she tried to analyze her opposing emotions, unsure which was real. Each image she looked at brought a flood of fondness—or was it truly love?—and the thought that she was making a mistake by pushing Aaron away.

A knock on the front door yanked her from her ponderings. Confused at why Evie was so early, she glanced at the clock on her laptop and saw that almost two-thirds of an hour had passed. Her friend wasn't *that* early for their lunch date. Sighing, she closed her laptop.

"I'll be right out, Evie!" she called as she strode out of the room and grabbed her jacket off the back of the couch where she'd left it.

* * *

Aaron drove away from the rental cabin with a white-knuckled grip on the steering wheel and his jaw clenched tightly. He needed to eat something before he attempted to go to bed—not that he'd be getting any sleep today—but he had no motivation to cook, so instead of turning left at the intersection with the main road, he glanced up to the Bedspread Inn. When he spotted June's truck parked in front of the restaurant, he drove straight. A beer and a burger sounded wonderful, though he doubted one beer would be enough to take the edge off his thoughts.

After he parked beside June's truck, he sat for a moment. He should be bitter about Skye's apparent rejection, but he understood all too well exactly how she felt. With a deep breath, he climbed out of his truck and ascended the steps to the broad deck of the Bedspread Inn. The bell on the door jingled as he entered, and June and Aelissm, sitting on opposite sides of the bar at the back of the room, turned to see who'd come in.

"Hi, Aaron," Aelissm greeted. "What can I get you?"

"A cheese burger and a Trout Slayer," he replied.

"A little early to start drinking, isn't it?" Aeli inquired. "You never drink before five."

"Technically, it's my… eight at night. And the day calls for a beer."

"That's right," June said, "You have the night shift this week. And Skye's heading back to Washington tomorrow."

"Yep."

Aelissm popped the cap off the bottle and set it gently in front of him before ducking into the kitchen to get his burger on the grill. Aaron took a long swig of his beer, ignoring June's keen gaze. Sensing his mood in her almost uncanny way, she didn't voice the questions that were undoubtedly spinning in her mind.

"You two looked rather deep in discussion when I walked in. Anything exciting?" he asked.

"Actually, yes. We have a big wedding coming up the first weekend in November. They've booked all the cabins and rooms at the Ramshorn and all the rooms here, and we were discussing arrangements. I hate to bring it up, because the look on your face tells me it's a tender subject, but they're looking for a photographer. The one they hired backed out, and they'd be okay with Luke taking the pictures—I showed them some of the ones he took for Skye— but he has an away game that weekend, and anyhow, he isn't comfortable shooting a wedding by himself. Do you think Skye would mind coming back to shoot it for us?"

"I honestly don't know, June."

June jerked her head back. "What happened?"

Aaron was afraid to tell her because he didn't want to think about Skye's fear that their relationship wouldn't last, but the sympathy in June's kind eyes had the story tumbling out. "Nothing happened, really, but she told me she doesn't trust what she feels for me, that she isn't ready for the kind of commitment I want and deserve, and she won't be until she finishes straightening herself out. As much as it kills me, I understand that confusion. I'm not confused about her, but I've been exactly where she is."

"What do you mean, *not about her*?"

Aaron didn't reply immediately. Though it was tempered with concern, a knowing smile danced in June's eyes, and he suspected she knew exactly how much he loved Skye and only wanted him to say it out loud. So he did.

"I love her, and since you already know that, don't even try to play innocent."

"Nice to hear you confirm it. The question is, does *she* know it?"

Aaron thought back over their last couple weeks together and realized he hadn't ever said it, only that he was falling in love with her. Somehow, that just didn't seem to carry the same weight, sounding more like he was only on his way to being in love with her, not already head-over-heels in love and certainly not spend-the-rest-of-his-life-with-her in love. And that's exactly what it was—the exact same heart-pounding, invasive, wonderful love he had felt for Erica.

"I don't think I was too clear on the matter." He took another drink of his beer before adding, "I refuse to be like her ex-husband, and I will *not* push her into something she's not ready for."

"And I respect you for that, Aaron, but not pushing her and letting her know you love her are two different things. If you let her leave without making damned sure she knows how you feel, you're opening the door for doubt, and she'll end up questioning your relationship until she talks herself into believing it was just a fling."

Aaron nodded because he knew she was right. But knowing and doing were two different animals. What could he say to convince Skye that he loved her without making her feel like she was being backed into a corner? What if he was wrong and she truly didn't—and wouldn't, no matter what he said or did—feel what he did?

Aelissm returned from the kitchen, and June let the matter drop as the two longtime friends returned to the matter at hand. Aaron listened passively to their conversation, nursing his beer, and contemplated his options regarding Skye. He knew one thing for certain. He could not ask her to give up her career. She had far too much talent and far too great a love for her craft, and asking her to give it up for him was the surest way of making her resent him.

"Do you think she could make a living here as a photographer?" Aaron asked.

"Who? Skye?" Aeli inquired.

"Yeah."

"Whoa, whoa, whoa. You're asking if Skye… like she might actually be coming back for good, as in you two at the altar and the whole nine yards?"

"I really don't know yet, Aelissm, but it's something *I* am definitely thinking about."

"And you think she might not be thinking the same thing?"

"Again, I don't know. I'm not a mind-reader like June."

June nudged him playfully with her elbow.

"But you… finally… are thinking it."

"Yes, Aelissm."

"Interesting."

"In answer to your question, Aaron, I'm sure Skye could find enough work here. It might take a little more legwork to get started…." June glanced at Aelissm and the pile of papers spread out on the bar in front of her and laughed softly. "Then again, maybe not. There isn't much competition around here. In fact, considering our current plight with this wedding, I'd say there's actually a shortage of professional photographers in the area. You know, Marvin and

Mary have really jumped on board with my wedding package idea, and it's starting to take off. We have another wedding party coming in late December. If we could offer the photography as part of the deal…."

"Hmm." He glanced at his watch.

"Should I just put your burger in a box?" Aelissm asked.

"Yeah, you probably should. Thanks, Aeli."

Five minutes later, he strode out of the Bedspread Inn with the Styrofoam box containing his lunch in hand and his half-full beer sitting on the bar. June's heartfelt wish for good luck followed him out to his truck. *Good luck. Right,* he thought. *I could use some of that so I say the right words.*

In sharp contrast to his slow and unwilling departure, he bounded up the steps to the deck of the rental cabin and wasted no time before knocking. Skye's SUV was still parked out front, but that didn't mean she and her friend hadn't taken Evie's car, and he hoped he hadn't missed her. He breathed a sigh of relief when he heard her voice call out from inside, though he couldn't make out what she said. He lifted his hand to knock again when the door swung open.

Skye stopped abruptly with one arm in the sleeve of her jacket and her amber eyes wide with surprise.

"I can't let you leave without making sure you know how I feel," he said before she could question why he was standing there.

"Aaron…."

He kissed her fiercely but briefly. She didn't resist, and instead gave in to him in the most distracting way, sliding her hands up his chest and curling her fingers around the back of his neck. He touched his forehead to hers.

"I know what this is, Skye. I've felt it before, and yes, it's frightening and amazing and consuming, and you think it'll burn out. But it won't." He brushed his lips across her brow, then murmured, "You said the other day that you couldn't trust your heart. So trust mine."

Moving lower, he kissed her cheeks tenderly, then the tip of her nose. Lastly, he pressed a soft kiss to her lips. "I love you."

Again, he kissed her, neither letting her say it back in obligation nor argue against it.

"I don't expect you to say you love me, too, and I don't want you to say it until you believe it. I know you need to go back to Washington, and I know you need time, but I want you to come back."

"I don't know how long it'll—"

"Then I'll wait for you. However long it takes. Because I love you."

She threaded her arms around him and hugged him tightly. The sound of a car approaching intruded upon the moment, and Aaron glanced over his shoulder to see Evie pulling up in her vibrant yellow sedan. Nearly groaning at the interruption, he prayed he'd said enough to convince Skye of his love for her. If he had, that would have to be enough for now. They turned to face Skye's best friend, but Aaron kept an arm around her shoulders, and was pleased when she left hers draped around his waist.

"Having any luck talking her into staying?" Evie asked as she climbed out of her car.

"I think I have her talked in to coming back again in the not too distant future."

"Well, that is lovely, but if you really want to impress

me, Aaron, you'll convince her to stay here the next time she comes home to Northstar."

"I'm working on it, Evie." He tightened his arm around Skye's waist, and when she beamed up at him, lowered his head to kiss her gently. "Here's something that might help."

"Oh?" Skye asked. "You mean there's something more profound than you confessing your love for me?"

"Maybe not profound, but more... strategic. June and Aelissm need a photographer for a wedding they have booked the first weekend in November."

"When did you hear about this?" Skye asked.

The excitement in her voice thrilled him. "Just now, while I was ordering my lunch from the Bedspread. I should add that June told me the Ramshorn will have at least one more wedding to host before the end of the year. Sounds like a professional photographer might be in rather high demand around these parts."

"She said that, did she?"

"Mmm-hmm."

"Well, then, I guess I might need to have a chat with her this afternoon, because it looks like I might be back as early as the first week of November." She tipped her head up and gazed adoringly at him with the most beautiful, heart-melting smile. "And by the way, I'm pretty sure I love—"

He pressed a finger against her lips, then followed it with his lips. "I don't want you to say it until you believe it. *Really* believe it."

Though he'd stopped her from saying she loved him, he knew she did. It shone as brilliantly in her gorgeous honey-colored eyes as the autumn sun, and for now, that was enough. He tucked her into his arms and held her tightly, soaking up every precious moment with her to carry him through the long weeks until she came back to Northstar.

* * *

"The wedding's on November ninth?" Skye asked June. She sat on a stool at the log-slab bar at the Ramshorn, perusing the information June had laid out, with a steaming cup of coffee sitting ignored beside her.

"Yes."

"Damn. I have that costume party for the Agate Bluff Inn to shoot on Halloween, and Faye wants me to shoot that ninetieth birthday party on the second. It'll take me at least a couple days—each—to process all the shots from those, plus a day for driving from Washington to Northstar…. That wouldn't really give me much time to meet with your wedding party beforehand. When did you say they were coming in?"

"November fourth."

"And the rehearsal dinner is on the eighth, correct? You said they wanted shots of that, too, right?"

"Yes and yes."

Skye frowned at the calendar hanging on the wall behind the bar. If she left early on the sixth and arrived in Northstar in the evening, that would give her only a day before the rehearsal to go over what the clients wanted. Some of the conversation could be conducted over the phone, but Skye much preferred being able to show wedding clients her work to gather ideas, and walking through a rehearsal of the shoot always helped the actual shoot go more smoothly.

Emotions and stress usually ran high enough at weddings without adding photography issues to the mix. This wedding in particular promised to be challenging. It was a large party but a small venue, so the more time she had to prepare the better.

"You know what?" Skye said, straightening. "Joel can do the bulk of the processing for the costume party and he can shoot and process the birthday party. Faye needs to realize that he's more than capable of running that studio."

"Joel is your assistant?"

Skye nodded, smiling. "I think you'd like him. He and Luke are a lot alike in disposition."

"I probably would. But why does it matter if your client knows that he can run the studio?" June inquired lightly. "Are you planning more extended absences?"

It struck Skye that she really was… and had been. Maybe not fully consciously, but plans for handing her studio over to Joel had been percolating in the back of her mind since she'd first asked him what he'd do if she decided to stay in Northstar. "I guess I am," she replied.

"I can't say as I'm the least bit disappointed to hear that. And I get the feeling Aaron and Jessie will be very happy about it."

"Do you really think I could find enough work here to keep busy?"

"Since the December wedding I told Aaron about was just confirmed not five minutes before you arrived, I would say so."

Skye couldn't stop the broad smile that spread across her face. That wedding was set for the twentieth, so it was likely she would be spending Christmas with Aaron and

Jessie. The idea was very appealing. "Book me for it," she said without hesitation. "That is, if they need a photographer."

"They do indeed. I already passed along your website, and they seemed quite enthusiastic about enlisting your talents."

"Wonderful." She glanced at the clock. It was a little after two. "Do you think Aaron will be asleep yet?"

"Considering how worked up he was when he was at the Bedspread, I doubt it."

"All right. I'm going to pop down to his house for a bit, then. Thank you again, June."

"You're welcome, but honestly, shouldn't I be thanking you?"

Skye shook her head. "Maybe, but that's business."

She didn't bother to elaborate, certain the insightful woman would figure out exactly what Skye was grateful for. It certainly wasn't the money the two weddings would bring in, because she didn't need it. Her Washington clients kept her bank account at a comfortable level. No, it was the reasons to return to Northstar and, more importantly, to Aaron for which she was thankful.

After bidding June goodbye, she left the Ramshorn and drove south toward Aaron's house, amused that the main road through the valley had become as familiar to her as any of the roads back home in Kitsap County. She knocked quietly on his front door so as not to disturb him if he *was* asleep, but Chance loudly announced her presence. Moments later, Aaron opened the door still wide awake and dressed only in a pair of navy and evergreen plaid pajama pants. The words she'd planned to say abandoned her at the sight of his naked upper body, so she threaded her arms around him and kissed him fervently. Finally, she pulled away and breathlessly said, "I hope I didn't wake you."

"No, you didn't," he replied. Grinning with that sexy, lopsided quirk of his lips she so loved, he added, "This is quite a nice surprise."

"I just talked to June about those two weddings. Looks like I will be back in Northstar around the first of November and also over Christmas. Do you think I could rent your parents' cabin again?"

"I have a better idea," he said. His tone was a distracting mixture of a boyish giddiness and sexy huskiness. "Why don't you stay here with me and Jessie?"

She started to object out of habit, then stubbornly snapped her mouth closed. A moment later, she replied, "I like that idea."

"I can set up a bed in the spare room if you don't want to sleep with me."

"If I'm staying here," she said slowly, trailing her fingers down his neck, "I'm *definitely* sleeping with you."

He pulled her inside, kicking the door closed before devouring her mouth. They stumbled across the living area and down the hallway to his bedroom, wasting no time in discarding their clothing. Though Aaron needed to sleep, they took their time exploring each other's bodies, committing to memory every beloved detail. As Aaron drove into her and brought her to the edge of oblivion, something as shattering and wonderful as the orgasm broke over her.

She was free.

When the quivers of ecstasy had subsided and Aaron had drifted into slumber, Skye propped herself up on her elbow and gazed at his handsome and cherished face as she marveled at the serenity that filled her.

She carefully and quietly slipped back into her clothes. She didn't want to leave. Not now and certainly not tomorrow morning, when she would begin the long drive back to Washington. Maybe not ever.

When she'd dressed, she leaned down to lightly kiss her sleeping lover, planning only to leave a note for him, but his eyes fluttered open.

"Where are you going?" he mumbled groggily.

"I have to finish packing." She sat on the bed beside him and curled her arms around him one more time. "But I'll be home again before you know it. November's not that far away."

"Yes, it is."

"Go back to sleep."

"Okay."

She glanced back at him as she tiptoed out of his room and smiled.

Home…. I'm not going home tomorrow—I'm leaving it.

Eleven

SKYE COULDN'T HELP the smug grin that spread across her face as Eloise Philips showed off the proof of the book to Faye of the Agate Bluff Inn. Both women positively gushed over the images printed in stunning, glossy clarity. She leaned back in her chair and knitted her fingers behind her head, positively delighted by how the book had come together. The way Eloise had arranged the text around the images and the colors she'd chosen really brought out the beauty of the shots, but it was the shots themselves that gave Skye the greatest sense of accomplishment. They were easily some of her finest, if not the best she'd ever captured. Maybe she was biased by her love of the people, places, animals, and objects in the pictures, but she was certain she had reached a new level of dedication to her art. Or maybe it was that she'd been free—no, not just free but *encouraged*—to truly delve into it for the first time. Whatever the reason, the shots were stunning.

"I think these may be the best shots you've ever taken," Faye remarked, echoing Skye's thoughts. "And that's saying a lot. There's something… something really incredible here. I can feel *you* in these shots. You always do such an amazing job of capturing *me* in the shots you take at my inn, but I don't think I've ever really gotten such a sense of you in them. Not like these."

"I wonder why that is," Joel remarked. His tone was casual, but the intensity in his gaze was anything but.

"Thank you, Faye," Skye said, ignoring her assistant. "I'm quite pleased with them and with the book."

The phone rang, and glancing at the caller ID, Skye excused herself from the conversation to answer the call. "Hi," she said shyly.

"Hi to you, too," Aaron replied. "I'm sure you're busy, so I'll keep this short. We're having a family dinner tomorrow night at Mom and Dad's, so Mom needs a general idea of what time you'll be here."

"I thought I'd leave around four in the morning, which'd put me there about, what, four. No, five. I forgot about the time zones."

"Sounds great. If you beat me home, the door will be open." He paused, then added, "I miss you."

"I miss you, too. I can't wait to see you tomorrow."

"Do you have a minute? Jessie wants to talk to you."

"Sure."

Shuffling sounds drifted over the line, followed by Jessie's young voice. "Hi, Skye!" she greeted.

"Hi, pumpkin. How are you?"

"Good. I miss you, but you're coming home

tomorrow, right? So Daddy says I can't miss you too much."

"That's right," she said with a laugh. "Hey, you take care of your daddy until I get there tomorrow night, okay?"

"I will. Are you gonna eat dinner with us and Grandma and Grandpa Hammond?"

"I think that's the plan."

"Okay, Daddy wants the phone back. I love you, Skye."

"I love you, too, sweetheart, and I'll be there before you know it."

A moment later, Aaron was back on the phone. "Drive safe tomorrow. The roads are pretty crappy right now. The weathermen say it's supposed to melt off tomorrow before the coldest air comes in, but it's still snowing."

"I'll be very careful," she said. "I can't wait to see you."

After she ended the call, she stared at the phone for almost a minute. She was tempted to leave for Northstar tonight, but she was already leaving too closely on the tail of the snowstorm that had brought almost a foot of snow to the Cascades.

Turning back to her companions, she expected to find them still deep in conversation about the book. Instead, Joel, Eloise, and Faye regarded her with varying expressions of amusement and curiosity. Silence stretched.

"So, you're leaving for Montana tomorrow?" Faye finally asked.

"Yes. I have a wedding to shoot on the ninth."

"When will you be back?"

"I'm driving back on the twelfth."

Faye glanced sideways at Joel. "I'm still not entirely

comfortable having Joel shoot the birthday party next week."

"Whyever not?" Eloise asked, surprised. "You said you loved the shots he took of the costume ball."

"Well, yes, I did, but it's not the same thing."

"Faye, if I didn't *know* he could do the job, I never would have hired him," Skye said, irritated and defensive.

The inn owner opened her mouth, but before she could retort, Joel interrupted.

"Would you prefer to use a different studio?" he asked quietly with no outward reaction whatsoever to Faye's continuing lack of faith.

"Excuse me?"

"She has another wedding to shoot in Montana in December, and beyond that…." He shrugged as if to say *who knows*, but the intensity hadn't left his gaze. "I'm certain Skye will be coming back from one of these trips with a ring on her finger, which means a one-way trip to Northstar, and I'm betting sooner rather than later."

"What does that mean for Hathaway Photography?" Eloise asked.

"*If* Joel's prediction comes true, I'll start the process of handing everything over to him. I won't just drop him into it because I want him to succeed. He has the talent and the heart and the motivation, but he doesn't yet have the support." Skye looked pointedly at Faye. "So, if you'd rather use a different studio, please say so now."

"No. No, of course not. I've always been happy with your work, and if you say he's good enough, I'll trust you."

"Thank you. Eloise, I'll call you as soon as Hammonds have seen the proof. I know they signed the releases, but I want their approval before we publish."

"I completely agree," the publisher replied. "I'll be looking forward to your call."

Eloise excused herself, and Faye followed her out into the dismal, rainy afternoon. Skye stared at the door long after the women had left. She really hoped Faye kept her word about sticking with the studio even if Skye was no longer a part of it.

She turned on her assistant. He met her gaze and smiled. And refused to be drawn into conversation about his statement. After a dozen failed attempts to get him to explain himself, she finally had no choice but to shrug it off.

She gathered up her gear and the proof of the book, which she had convinced Eloise to call *Ranching by Tradition: the Lazy H*. Joel helped her pack the equipment in her SUV, jogging through the pouring rain to bring out the various cases while she secured everything in place. When that work was done, she headed back inside for a moment to make sure she hadn't forgotten anything.

Tingling excitement grew, and she wondered if she'd be able to sleep at all tonight.

"I guess that'll about do it," she remarked. "I just have a couple more emails to send, and then I'll be out of here. You certainly don't have to stay, though, Joel. Go on home, and I'll—"

Unexpectedly, Joel hugged her. "I better get an invitation to the wedding."

"Why are you so certain Aaron and I will get married?"

Maybe he'd answer her this time.

"I just am."

Nope.

"Well, if we do, I fully expect you to be my photographer."

"You don't want to have that football player friend of yours do it?"

"He can help, but you're my leading man, Joel."

"That means a lot, Skye. Truly."

"I'll see you in a week," she said and hugged him again.

"Uh-huh. Can't wait to see the rock."

"Don't get your hopes up."

"I'm not hopeful. I'm confident."

Laughing, Skye stepped back and watched him gather his things. He hugged her one last time and told her to drive safe before stepping back out into the rain.

Joel's words permeated her thoughts long after he'd left. She and Aaron had been dating a little over two months, and half of that had been spent apart, but she was comfortable with their relationship. The conversation she'd had with him the day before she'd left Northstar—or rather, Aaron's unreserved and heartfelt declarations—certainly gave the impression that he was thinking along the lines of marriage and happily ever after. But Joel hadn't been there to hear it, and Skye had kept it close to her heart. She hadn't told anyone what Aaron had said—not Evie, not Lindsay, not her parents. So how did Joel know? Maybe it was all the phone calls he'd overheard.

Her lips curved. She might not be as confident as Joel about the direction her relationship with Aaron was heading, but she was hopeful. Aaron had told her not to say she loved him until she believed it, and she was more sure with each passing day that she did, but she was waiting for something… and she had no idea what yet.

The door of the studio opened, interrupting her musings. She lifted her gaze from her computer screen with a smile to ask her assistant what he'd forgotten, but it wasn't Joel who stood just inside the studio.

It was Darren.

And the moment her eyes met his, she knew without a doubt that something had changed since the last time she'd seen him. She felt no flutter of nerves, no inkling of anxiety, only the anticipation of returning to Northstar and reuniting with Aaron and Jessie. There was a mild jolt of recognition, but it was no more than she might experience seeing an old friend she had long since lost touch with. At some point over the last few weeks, she had relegated him to the past. They hadn't really ever been just friends, so it wasn't exactly friendship she felt, but she didn't hate him. Truthfully, she didn't feel anything for him.

"Hello, Darren," she said softly.

"Hi, babe," he replied in his usual sugary tone. "I'm glad I caught you."

"What can I do for you?"

If the politeness in her voice—and the absolute lack of hostility—surprised her, it stunned him. He stared at her for what seemed like minutes, testing her newfound peace. Skye prodded it herself, marveling at the serenity that wafted through her and not quite believing it. She studied her ex-husband's astounded expression with a critical eye, no longer blinded by foolish, maltreated love. He was a good-looking man, more proud and bluntly masculine in the face than Aaron, who was handsome in a charming, almost boyish way. Where Aaron's blue eyes exuded compassion and kindness, Darren's brown ones emanated haughtiness and confidence. Though both men had great bodies, Darren had a heavier build with a barrel-like chest that reminded her a bit of a strutting bull or a puffed-up pigeon. She much preferred Aaron's strong shoulders and chest, narrow hips, long legs, and easy grace, but then again, there was much about him she preferred.

"What, no snappy remarks today?" Darren finally asked.

"No."

"Pity. I rather liked that cattiness."

"It doesn't really matter what you like anymore," Skye remarked with the same, unwavering civility. "Because I am no longer yours to judge. If you don't mind, I need to get out of here. I have to leave for Northstar early in the morning, and I still have some packing to finish up."

"You're going back to Montana? To Aaron or whatever his name was?"

"Yes, I am. I also have a wedding to shoot. So what was it you needed?"

Darren's dark brows knitted together in a frown of consternation. "Leslie and I are engaged."

Skye studied him for a moment. He'd said the words in a rush, and she wondered if he was nervous to tell her or lying in an attempt to sabotage her self-esteem one last time. The smug glint in his eyes led her to believe it was the latter, and the pity she felt for Leslie shocked her. She hoped he hadn't actually asked the woman to marry him if it was simply out of revenge.

"Be honest with me, Darren, for once in your life.

Did you actually propose to her, or are you just telling me that because you think it might hurt me or make me come running back to you?"

He opened his mouth, then closed it and stared at her.

"I am not coming back to you." A tiny voice in the back of her mind gleefully begged her to rub his nose in the fact that she had found a man who loved, respected, and valued her and to tell him that she wouldn't spend the rest of her life alone, but she ignored it. She had moved beyond pettiness; Aaron had helped her move beyond it. Since Darren was apparently incapable of speech, she said, "Never mind. It doesn't matter. I wish you and Leslie the best. Truly."

She quickly finished sending her emails, gathered the few things she hadn't yet taken out to her car, slipped into her jacket and stood. Darren was still staring at her, so she strode across the studio, and ushered him out the door, locking it behind them. Gently pressing her lips to his cheek, she murmured, "Goodbye, Darren."

As she walked by Darren's car, she spotted Leslie in the passenger seat. Skye lifted her hand in acknowledgement, and the woman warily returned the greeting. She momentarily considered warning her ex-husband's mistress about him, an urge prompted by an inexplicable gratitude to Leslie for giving her the reason to leave him, but decided it was none of her business. She had other, better things to think about, so she continued around to the driver side of her SUV and climbed in.

Curling her fingers around the wheel, she closed her eyes and inhaled deeply. The tranquility deepened, sweet and healing. *That* was what she'd been waiting for—her sign that she was ready to open heart fully and without reservation to Aaron. Darren's destructive influence over her was fully shattered and swept away.

When she got home, she immediately called him. He picked up on the third ring, and the sound of his voice sent a gale of warmth through the cool serenity, wrapping her in love.

"This is a pleasant surprise," he said by way of greeting.

"I love you," she said immediately. "I believe it now."

"I love you, too," he replied slowly. Even through the phone line, she heard the smile in his voice. "What happened?"

"Darren stopped by the studio just as I was getting ready to walk out the door."

"Are you all right?"

"I'm great," she replied honestly. "It was like I barely knew him. All the anger and hate and sadness.... It was gone. I just felt relieved. Even when he told me he and Leslie are engaged."

"I'm proud of you. It takes a very strong woman to be able to truly forgive so quickly, and I think you'd give June a run for her money in that department."

To some, comparing her to an ex-girlfriend might seem like an odd compliment, but to Skye, he couldn't have said anything more profound or reassuring. "Anyhow, I just wanted to call you to tell you I love you and I appreciate everything you've given me."

"The feeling is mutual, and that's exactly why we'll make it." He paused. "Tomorrow can't come soon enough."

"No, it can't." Her lips curled, and she laughed. "Give Jessie my love."

"You bet I will. Drive safe."

* * *

For once, the weathermen had correctly predicted the weather. Much of the snow that had fallen over the past couple of days—six inches or so, Aaron figured—had melted during the warmer morning hours, leaving the landscape a patchwork of white and brown. Now, with the coldest air firmly in place, the lingering snow had refrozen and crunched loudly beneath his boots as he strode out to his truck from the post office. The frigid air bit the exposed skin of his face and the thermometer on his truck read fifteen degrees. He'd wanted Skye to see the valley in all its white, winter glory, but she would only be home for a week, and the forecasters weren't calling for any more snow in that timeframe.

It was just after five, and he hoped he'd have time to change out of his uniform and make a quick phone call before she arrived so they could head immediately to the main ranch house. Her SUV wasn't at his house when he pulled up, but as soon as he stepped inside, he saw the message light flashing on his machine. Hitting play, he listened to her voice with a grin. She'd called from Devyn nearly an hour ago to let him know she'd taken the interstate instead of attempting the back way through the Bitterroot Valley. With the knowledge that she'd be there any minute, he grabbed the cordless phone from the kitchen counter and ducked into his bedroom—*their* bedroom for at least the next week—to change.

As he unbuttoned his brown and tan work shirt, he dialed Skye's parents' number, which he'd procured weeks ago from a very enthusiastic Evie. Mrs. Hathaway answered the phone, and at once, he was glad he'd had the forethought to call Skye's parents several times to get to know them a little. It would make his invitation less out-of-the-blue.

"Mrs. Hathaway, it's Aaron."

"Oh, Aaron, honey! How are you?"

"I'm good. You?"

"Can't complain. Is Skye there yet?"

"Not yet, but she should be here any minute. Listen, I have a proposition for you. Skye's been swamped with work, and with that wedding shoot for the Ramshorn so close to the holidays, it's going to be a struggle for her to get back to spend Christmas with you. I'd like to bring you and your husband out here so she can have some time off… and so we can all spend Christmas together. I'm hoping this isn't too short notice, and I hope I'm not being presumptuous."

"It's not at all presumptuous. In fact, it's incredibly thoughtful. A trip to Montana sounds like a lot more fun than the quiet dinner at home we were planning. When Tom gets home, I'll ask him, but I'm sure he'll be delighted. Skye's talked about you and Northstar so much that he's been thinking about finding a way to get out there to meet you and see your home. So Christmas would be perfect."

"Great. Call me back and let me know so I can make arrangements for you."

"I will. Thank you, honey."

He ended the call, traded his slacks for a pair of jeans,

and tugged a blue sweater on, then headed into the living room with his socks over his shoulder. He had just sat down in his recliner to tug them on his feet when Chance raced to the front window. With his tail wagging, the black Lab let out a happy yip and bounded toward the door. It was all Aaron could do not to race to the door with his dog and throw his arms around Skye the minute the door opened. Instead, he hastily finished pulling on his socks.

In a swirl of icy air, with cold-reddened cheeks and the broadest and most beautiful smile he'd yet seen on her face, Skye Hathaway stepped back into his life. Abandoning pride, he stood and folded her tightly into his arms, pushing his dog out of the way and breathing deeply to take in the scent of her.

"Welcome home," he murmured, then kissed her long and hard.

"It's good to be back," she replied. "I missed you so much."

The black Lab finally nudged his way between them with his tail wagging his whole body. Skye laughed.

"Yes, Chance, I missed you, too."

The dog bounced circles around them, whining and wiggling, until she finally gave in and reached down to give him a vigorous belly rub. Aaron took a moment to stuff his feet into his boots while she lavished his dog with attention and headed outside to start unloading her car. He'd already cleared out the spare bedroom for her office and shoved his rarely used computer to one side of the large desk to make room for her laptop. With Chance at her side, she came out to help Aaron unload, and between the two of them, the task was accomplished in short order.

"If you're ready, we should probably get headed," he said.

"As long as you think I don't look too road-weary, I'm ready."

"You look amazing, as always. I just need to put another log on the fire, grab something, and let Chance out real quick—because I'm pretty sure he was too happy to see you to actually do his business while we were unloading. My truck's still warm and running, so hop in, and I'll be out in a minute."

With a nod, she headed out to the truck. Aaron ducked back into his bedroom and slipped a tiny box from its hiding place in his nightstand drawer. So much for waiting until Christmas, but he couldn't wait that long. He tucked it into the pocket of his Carhartt coat, then let Chance out while he stuffed a couple logs in the woodstove. After he let the dog in—more amused than miffed when the black Lab promptly curled up on the couch—he darted outside and hopped in behind the wheel of his truck. Skye had a slim, plain satchel sitting on her lap that Aaron hadn't yet seen.

"What's that?" he asked.

"You'll see soon enough."

"Fine. Be that way," he teased, eliciting an adorably sly grin from her.

Anticipation built on the drive from his house to his parents', and by the time they arrived, he thought he might not be able to wait until after dinner. They stepped out of the warmth of his truck into the frosty November evening and paused for a moment to appreciate the beauty that surrounded them. The sun had sunk below the western peaks, plunging the valley into cool blue shadow, though the sky still glowed brightly above. The clouds, thin and scattered, were brushed with soft pinks, peach, and lavender.

Aaron gently pulled Skye into his arms and kissed her lightly. His heart hammered so hard against his ribs he was certain she'd be able to hear the knocking.

"I have everything I want in life, right here, right now," he said quietly. "My daughter and my family gathered in that house just behind us, the magical beauty of my home all around me, and the woman I love in my arms."

"Even a month ago, I wasn't completely sure of it, but now…." Skye smiled up at him before letting her gaze sweep over the valley and the mountains and the sky. "This is heaven."

"Then marry me."

She jerked her attention back to him. "Wh-what?"

"I love you, and I want to spend the rest of my life with you," Aaron said. He pulled the ring box out of his coat pocket, but before he opened it, he asked, "Will you marry me, Skye?"

Without a moment of hesitation, she whispered, "Yes."

The answer seemed to surprise her, because she pulled away a few inches and stared at him. Then, a slow, breathtaking smile spread over her face, and firmly, she repeated, "Yes."

Almost disbelieving that she had answered so quickly, he asked, "You don't want to think about it first?"

She shook her head. "I don't need to think anymore. I trust you to be faithful, to keep me safe, and to love me in the same way."

Words didn't seem necessary, so he only kissed her again and showed her the ring he'd picked out. It was a simple, half-carat, square-cut diamond solitaire in a low, unobtrusive setting on a slender platinum band.

"It's beautiful," she said, then frowned and asked, "It's not Erica's, is it?"

"No. I'm saving her ring for—God help me—the day a man worthy of my daughter asks me for permission to marry her," he replied. "Speaking of asking permission, I'd like to hold off telling everyone until Christmas."

"Why?"

"A couple reasons. First, I want to give you time to see how the photography thing will work here. I want you to be absolutely certain this is the move you want to make. Second… I invited your parents out, and I'd like to ask for their blessing. I wasn't planning to propose until Christmas, anyhow, after I'd had a chance to ask them, but when you walked through my door…." He clasped her face and brushed his thumbs over her rosy cheeks.

"You invited my parents out for Christmas?"

The way her eyes lit up with gratitude and love was breathtaking, and he barely managed a nod. "I hope that's okay."

"It's more than okay. It's…." She choked on the words as tears threatened. "Are you always going to be so considerate?"

"It's the only way I know how to be."

"Does that mean I can't wear my ring?"

"I'm afraid so." He tilted his head and glanced at the ring. "It's nothing fancy."

"Shuddup," she said. She pressed a kiss to his lips.

"Because I love it. It's simple and beautiful, like us. Can I try it one, just for a minute, to see how it looks?"

He slipped the ring on her finger, and she stared at it with that wide-eyed gaze of a woman looking beyond the object in front of her eyes. "I love you."

"I love you, too. I'll get you a necklace to put it on so you can still wear it. If you want."

"I think I have one. And you bet your sweet, sexy ass I want to wear it. However I can."

Beaming, she hugged him tightly. Then she laughed softly. "Well, I guess Joel's getting the studio."

"What do you mean, my love?"

"I told Joel I'd give him Hathaway Photography if you and I got married."

"That's generous."

"He's earned it." She smiled. "And telling him will feel almost as good as this."

"Speaking of your photography, I have another client lined up for you."

"Really? You actually found more work for me?"

"Don't sound so surprised."

"Well, keep in mind the jackass I married the first time."

"Fair enough."

"Who's the client?"

"Jim and Jessie Robinson. They've seen the shots you took of Vince and Evie's wedding, and I told them about your book deal, so they'd like you to take some photographs of their place for advertising purposes."

"Wow. I'm flattered."

When she shivered, Aaron was suddenly reminded of

the chilly evening air that coaxed the color from Skye's cheeks and nose in the most adorable and sexy way.

"Cold?"

She nodded.

"We can head in in just a minute, but there is *one* person I need to tell before we do. And she's going to make keeping our secret even more difficult than it already is. Wait here just a few minutes more, and then I promise we can go in and get warm."

He jogged to the house and popped his head in. "Jessie!" he called. "Come out here for a minute. Skye's home!"

The little girl raced around the corner from the kitchen, skidding on the linoleum floor of the entryway in her haste. She started to dart past him without her coat, but he stopped her.

"Ah-ah-ah. It's freezing out. It'll take you two seconds to put your jacket on."

With his daughter shielded from the frigid breeze and her tiny hand gripped tightly in his, he led her out to where Skye waited admiring her ring.

"You're back!" Jessie squealed.

She nearly threw herself at her soon-to-be stepmother, and Skye hoisted the little girl off the ground to give her a bear hug.

"Hi, sweetheart! I promised you I'd be back, didn't I?"

After a moment, Skye set Jessie down and turned her gaze on Aaron, waiting for him to break the news. Jessie glanced between them, frowning and trying to figure out what weighty thing was afoot. Finally, she looked at him and asked, "Did you ask her to be my new mommy?"

"I did," Aaron confirmed. "Are you still all right with that?"

"Will I call her mommy?"

"Only if you want to," Skye replied. "I certainly don't want to replace your mother because she was a wonderful woman, and you should always remember how much of your beauty and wonderfulness comes from her."

"You can't replace her."

Aaron's heart dropped into his stomach like a lead ball. She had been so enthusiastic when he'd asked her—not once but several times over the last two weeks—if she wanted Skye to join their family. What had changed?

"She was my first mommy," Jessie said with a solemnity far greater than her five years. "You'll be my second."

Relief washed over him, dizzying in its intensity, and Aaron embraced his daughter and the woman who would soon be his wife. "I love you both. So much. Now, Jessie, we have to keep this a secret for a while, okay? Until Christmas."

"But why?"

"Because Skye's parents are probably going to be coming out, and this will be our Christmas present to them. We don't want to ruin the surprise for them, do we?"

She shook her head solemnly, and he hoped the sanctity of Christmas gifts would keep her honest little lips sealed. "I promise I won't tell. Can we go in now? It's cold."

"See? Aren't you glad I made you put on your coat?"

She nodded, and he set her down. She raced back to the house.

Aaron held his arm out for Skye, and she slipped her hand around his elbow, and together, they followed his daughter to the house.

Aaron held the door open for his girls and joined them in the blissful warmth of his parents' home. They kicked off their boots in the entryway and headed in to the open kitchen and dining room, where everyone was either sitting lazily in the chairs at the table or leaning against the counters. His mother and father, both brothers, sister-in-law, and nephew were all accounted for. In an overlapping chorus, they all welcomed Skye back to Northstar. He hadn't doubted that she was glad to be back or that her family adored her and vice versa, but the teary-eyed grin drove it all home.

"Well, hell," she muttered, wiping tears away with her thumb. "Guess I might as well bring out the book, huh?"

She pulled a book with a glossy dust jacket out of the satchel still hanging from her shoulder. Everyone gathered around the table as she set it down. On the front cover was a stunning image of the homesteader's cabin up Aspen Creek Gulch with the aspen glowing brilliantly gold and Rocket and Coyote in the corral beside it. He thought it was a perfect introduction to the subject of the book. His mother paged slowly through, and a wide, smug grin claimed Aaron's face as his family complimented both Skye's incredible eye and her written descriptions and explanations. Aaron had always been appreciative of his family's ranch and way of life, but to see it through her eyes gave him a whole new level of gratitude.

His mother leaned back and smiled at Skye. "This is beautiful. Thank you."

"You like it?"

"Like it? We *love* it. It shows so much of what we love

about our home." Tracie's eyes swam with tears. "Truly."

"There aren't any changes you'd like me to make, any information that needs to be corrected? This is just the proof, so changes can still be made."

"No. No changes necessary. It's perfect."

When Skye stepped back to let the Hammond family browse at their leisure, Aaron folded his arms around her.

Henry rose from his seat at the table and pulled him aside. Leaning in so only Aaron could hear, he said, "Well? Did you ask her?"

Aaron lifted a brow. "Ask her what?"

"You haven't, you dumbass."

He sighed, but said nothing. It was going to be unbelievably difficult to keep the secret. If they made it all the way to Christmas without someone finding out, it would be a miracle.

"But you *are* planning to ask her."

"That's the plan. Probably Christmas."

"If not before," Henry added with a wink. He gripped Aaron's shoulder. "Guess I was right about thinking with your dick."

"Maybe so, but I'll go you one better." He met his brother's gaze head on. "You've got something special going on with Lindsay Miller—and don't try to tell me she was just a fling. I know you've talked with her on the phone a couple times a week since she left Northstar. Thinking with your dick got you into that mess with Melanie, so try thinking with your heart this time." To punctuate his statement, he prodded his twin in the chest.

Henry's brows dipped in a thoughtful frown, and Aaron returned to Skye, leaving his his brother to ponder what he'd said.

His gaze found its way to the picture of him and Erica at their wedding that hung with the other family photos on the walls around the dining room. Out of nowhere came a peculiar sensation, and he strangely felt closer to his late wife than he had since her death, as if she stood on his other side, surveying the family gathering. At once, he knew Skye was right. Erica had loved him, and she would not have wanted to suffer as he had, nor spent so many years blaming himself for her death. What had started that day in Papa T's, when he'd at last forgiven himself, now eradicated every last bit of guilt that had cast a shadow over his memories of Erica. As he'd told Skye that day at the homesteader cabin, he'd always love his first wife. But he knew he loved Skye just as much. He swore he could hear Erica say, *You're happy again. Finally.*

Epilogue

"HONEY, COME ON!" came Aaron's voice from the hall. "We're going to be late for the appointment. And we still have to pick Jessie up from school."

Skye leaned back in her chair, finally happy with the design for her new logo. The studio formerly known as Hathaway Photography was, as of two weeks ago, Joel's. She had spent the ten months between Aaron's proposal and their wedding and the first four of the six months since helping Joel get situated and assuring herself that she was handing him a solid client list that appreciated and wanted his talents. She'd also built a rapport with an entirely new set of clients here in Montana—including the Royal R Ranch, the Ramshorn Hot Springs and Lodge, and the Bedspread Inn, as well as several other small businesses in Devyn and the surrounding areas—still under Hathaway

Photography. She had signed over the physical studio and her Washington clients, but Joel had started his own business from it. Technically, she could have just moved Hathaway Photography to Northstar—she'd already started the process—but that hadn't felt right. She wanted something new, something that wasn't connected to her old life. So she'd spent the last two weeks on hiatus, trying to come up with something that represented what she had now.

"Come in here for a minute, would you?" she called back. She minimized the window with her logo. The picture she'd taken of Luke, Jessie, and Aaron at their first Gold Rush game was still on her desktop, and she smiled fondly at the memory. They'd gone again this past year, and it had been every bit as much fun, but of all the pictures she'd taken at both games—and the many others they'd attended—this shot was still her favorite. It reminded her of how precious each and every day with Aaron and Jessie and their friends and family here in Northstar were.

Aaron appeared in the doorway, momentarily leaning in with both hands braced on the doorframe before coming to stand beside her. "What do you need?"

"I want to show you something. My new logo."

She brought the window back up and heard him inhale sharply.

"It's the homesteader cabin," he said.

She was pleased that he was able to recognize it immediately. "Yep."

The logo was a simplified version of the image on the cover of her first book, *Ranching by Tradition*, with the homesteader cabin and horses backed by the aspen stand.

"Hammond Photography," Aaron remarked. "You

didn't use your maiden name like you did for your Washington business."

"No, I didn't. Then I was married to a man I didn't trust, who didn't support me or my career, and I didn't want him to have any part of my business. This time, I want my husband to be a part of it because he's the reason I have it."

He knelt beside her and studied the screen a moment longer before rising up just enough to kiss her.

"There's a lot I didn't trust Darren with that I trust you with," she remarked, placing a hand on her belly. "Speaking of which, we'd better get going. I know Jessie's excited to see if she's going to get that brother she wants. I just hope she won't be too disappointed if this little one is a girl."

"I doubt it. She's just thrilled she'll be a big sister."

Skye double-checked to make sure she'd save the most recent tweaks she'd made to the logo, closed the program, and shut her computer down. Aaron helped her into her coat before stuffing his arms into his well-worn Carhartt coat. When they stepped outside with Chance bounding ahead of them, excited to be going for a ride, Skye couldn't believe it was almost April. The landscape was draped in pillowy white, courtesy of a late-season snowstorm that had dumped nearly a foot in the Northstar Valley over the past twenty-four hours. Not that she was complaining. She loved the snow, and despite the assurances from her parents and her Washington friends, she still wasn't tired of winter. She sincerely doubted she'd ever get tired of anything here.

Aaron let Chance into the back of Skye's SUV and climbed in behind the wheel. Skye slid into the passenger seat, content to let her Montana-native husband navigate the snowy roads. Before she knew it, he was parking in front of the tiny Northstar School to get Jessie. Skye went in with him and helped Jessie pull on her snow boots and slip into her coat and backpack while Aaron chatted briefly with her teacher.

"Come *on*, Daddy! Let's *go!*" Jessie said impatiently.

Laughing, he followed his girls out to the car. All the way to Devyn, Jessie chattered on about everything from school to the weather to her dog and her cat, and asked question after question about the baby.

"I *really* hope he's a boy."

"What are you going to do if you get a sister?" Aaron asked.

"I'll love her, too, but I'd rather have a brother."

"Well, we're about to find out, because we're here," Skye said.

There was something to be said for small towns, Skye thought, as they were checked in and led immediately to an examination room. Short waits. The nurse came in and was still checking Skye's blood pressure when their obstetrician arrived. She asked a few questions and answered a few, then squirted the gel onto Skye's bared belly and brought the sonogram wand over. After checking the baby's development, she smiled.

"This is it. I know Mom and Dad don't have a preference, but what are you hoping for, Jessie? Boy or girl?"

"A little brother. Because I don't like dolls."

The doctor laughed. "Well, my dear, you're in luck."

"He's a boy?" Jessie asked excitedly.

"Yep. He's a boy."

Jessie launched herself into her father's arms. "I'm

getting a little brother!"

Aaron laughed. He reached for Skye's hand and squeezed it, then pressed his lips to her cheek. "Are you happy?" he asked.

"My love, I've been happy since your beautiful daughter introduced us, even if I didn't know it then." She pulled him closer and kissed him firmly on the mouth. "I'd like this little guy's middle name—if not his first name—to be Eric, if that's all right with you and Jessie. And with Jim and Jessie, of course."

"They would be honored. I love it. What do you think, pumpkin?"

"I like it, too. Little Eric."

* * * * *

Once Burned

Lindsay Miller and Henry Hammond aren't looking for love, but a one-night stand may turn into something a lot bigger… and last a lot longer than her vacation.

Lindsay has sworn off men until her son is old enough not to be hurt by them, but on a kid-free vacation to see her best friend married off, a casual fling with a willing cowboy reminds her that she's more than a tired, struggling single mother.

Devastated after learning that his son isn't his, Henry is in no mood to entertain ideas about starting a new relationship, but when Lindsay boldly introduces herself, he's intrigued. She's fiercely independent but also vulnerable after dating the wrong men. Even after Lindsay returns home, Henry can't stop thinking about her. This could be the real deal, but how can he prove that she and her son are more than a rebound family for him when they're seven hundred miles away?

AVAILABLE NOW

Visit www.suzieoconnell.com for more information.

About the Author

Suzie O'Connell is the *USA Today* bestselling author of the Northstar romances. The series is the product of a love affair with Southwestern Montana that began with a two-week adventure at her stepsister's rustic cabin in her teens. That love affair shows no sign of abating.

She has been writing stories for as long as she can remember, and her love of writing and of Montana pushed her to earn a Bachelor of Arts in Literature and Writing from the University of Montana-Western. What else would you expect from a self-professed mountain-loving nerd?

When she isn't writing, you'll probably find Suzie in the mountains with a camera in hand and enjoying the beauty of Montana with her husband Mark, their daughter Maddie, and their golden retrievers Reilly and Angus.

Find Suzie online at www.suzieoconnell.com

www.ingramcontent.com/pod-product-compliance
Lightning Source LLC
Chambersburg PA
CBHW010345170726
48284CB00009B/2795